NO SHOW
OF REMORSE

Also by David J. Walker

NO SHOW
OF
REMORSE

═══

DAVID J. WALKER

ST. MARTIN'S MINOTAUR
NEW YORK

To Hugh Holton, an inspiration
. . . and I should have told him

ACKNOWLEDGMENTS

This book is a work of fiction, and the persons and places it depicts are imaginary or used fictitiously.

One thing that's real, though, is my gratitude to those who helped with the book. These include Sergeant David Case, for police and weapons information; Michele Mellett, M.D., for medical and trauma details; my agent, Jane Jordan Browne, and her staff, for encouragement and advice; and my editor, Kelley Ragland, and her assistant, Ben Sevier, for—what else?—inspired editing.

The fact is, in my opinion, that we often buy money very much too dear.

—W. M. THACKERAY: BARRY LYNDON XIII

The wages of sin is death.

—ROMANS 6:23

NO SHOW
OF REMORSE

INTERVIEW OF MARLON SHADES
TAPE 1: SIDE A (EXCERPT)

Marlon, how Mr. Foley here s'posed to help you, you won't tell him where you was?

I can't, Mama. I be sittin' up in the shithouse fifty years or somethin' . . . they don't kill me first. I can't tell him that part.

Dammit, boy, you like to drive me—

Sally Rose, please. Let me talk to him, all right? . . . LENGTHY SILENCE *. . . Marlon, I believe you when you say you had nothing to do with killing anyone. But you have to tell me what happened.*

How I know you ain't gonna jus' tell everyone what I say? Shit. You another one of them—

Hush up, boy. This here's your lawyer. He can't tell nobody, 'cause o' that . . . whatchacallit . . . priv'lege. Ain't that right, Mr. Foley?

Yes, and—

I ain't tellin' where I was. Y'all don't . . . INAUDIBLE *. . .*

You have to speak up, Marlon. My . . . uh . . . my hearing's bad. I didn't hear that last part.

Nothin'. I said I ain't tellin' you where I was.

It's up to you, but what your mother says is true. Anything you say here is privileged. The rules say I can't tell. I could lose my license if I did.

Fuck the rules! Rules don't mean shit when—

Marlon! You watch your mouth, boy.

1

Sorry, Mama, but . . . but how I know . . . INAUDIBLE *. . . Plus, how I know they ain't gonna change the rules, man? Then they make you tell.*

Goddammit, Marlon, I don't care if they erase all the rules, or what they say, or do, or . . . whatever. I won't tell anyone, that's all. I just won't. Not ever. You have my word on that.

CHAPTER

==

1

"So then, Mr. Foley, your law license was suspended because you deliberately ignored a direct order of the Illinois Supreme Court."

I didn't respond.

"Well?" she said.

"Oh," I said. "Was that a question? It sounded like a state—"

"Very well." A deep, pseudo-patient sigh. "Isn't it true, sir, that five years ago you deliberately ignored the order of the Illinois Supreme Court requiring you to reveal what Marlon Shades told you?"

"No." Obviously, I should have said yes and let her get on to her next question, but Stefanie Randle, young and cute and righteous as hell, was getting on my nerves. "No," I repeated, "that's not true."

"Well, sir"—another sigh—"let me show you—for the third time *today*, I might add—Foley Deposition Exhibit Seven, and ask you whether—"

"I've seen that order a thousand times, Ms. Randle," I said, "and it's not true that I ignored it. The fact is, I flat out disobeyed the damn thing."

"Stop it, Mal!" Renata Carroway sounded as disgusted as Stefanie, and Renata was my own lawyer. "Would you mind—"

"Sorry, Renata." I stood up. "Let's take a break, huh?"

"No," Ms. Randle said. "The rules don't permit conferences between the deponent and his lawyer during the course of interrogation." She never even looked up as she spoke, just kept paging through the papers on the table in front of her.

"He didn't ask for a conference," Renata said. "He asked for a break. But that's moot. Let the record reflect that I'm not feeling well; that it's two-forty-two P.M. and I'm terminating this session of Mr. Foley's deposition; and that I'll call Ms. Randle tomorrow to schedule a mutually convenient time to resume. Thank you."

By the time she got to "Thank you," Renata had her own papers stuffed back in her briefcase and was shoving me out the door of the conference room. She kept on pushing, down the hallway to the reception area and through the glass doors that said: *Illinois Attorney Registration and Disciplinary Commission.* I'm sure she'd have pushed me all the way out to Randolph Street—and then maybe three blocks east, which would have had me treading water in Lake Michigan— except we were on the fifteenth floor and we had to wait for an elevator.

The ride down was about as congenial as I deserved. "I'm sorry you're not feeling well," I said, and didn't get so much as a dirty look in response.

It wasn't until we were out on the street and I was waving for a cab that Renata spoke. "Forget that. We'll walk to my office."

"Whatever you say." We went west on Randolph, toward Michigan Avenue. With the temperature in the seventies, and brilliant sunshine in place of the gray April clouds that had shrouded the city for two days, Renata's scowl looked out of place. I decided to try again. "I'm sorry you're not feeling—"

"Oh shut up, Mal. The only thing making me sick is you. It's just a deposition and Stefanie is just doing her job, for chrissake. But you . . . you have to start out uncooperative, and move from there to sullen, and then rude."

Even though she had no way to know what was really bothering me, she was right and I was a pain in the ass. So, naturally, I didn't admit it. " 'Stefanie,' is it?" I said. "You're on a first-name basis with the enemy?"

"Listen to me," she said. She stopped walking, planted her briefcase on the sidewalk, and peered up at me through her round, thick lenses. "I represent people charged with armed robbery, rape, and murder, people nobody else wants to be on the same planet with. And I do a damn good job of it." Renata understated her genius by a mile. "I fight like hell when I have to, but I don't treat opposing counsel like scum. They're human beings. They have names. Stefanie Randle is one of them. Their office was closed this afternoon, for God's sake. She only scheduled your dep for today to accommodate my schedule."

"Hell," I said, "she was happy to do it. Kept her away from some damn training seminar. Anyway, I'm just trying to get back my law license, and she acts like she's Saint Peter and I'm some sleazeball trying to con my way through the gate."

"She's young . . . and nervous around you. You *do* have a reputation for—"

"Even the way she spells her name irritates me. There oughta be a 'ph' in it." I recognized how stupid that was, though, even with everything else on my mind. I picked up Renata's briefcase. "I need to think. Let's walk this way." The light changed and we crossed Randolph, staying on the east side of Michigan. "I apologize, Renata. I really do."

"Thank you." She obviously took the apology as genuine and I was glad, because it was. "I'm partly to blame," she said. "I should have talked you out of petitioning for reinstatement to the bar. It wasn't a good idea."

The east side of Michigan Avenue, from Randolph all the way down to the Art Institute three blocks to the south, had been torn up for years while they rebuilt the underground parking garage. But now it was park again. They say Chicago has fewer acres of park per person than most other major cities, but for those who can haul themselves across town and get close to the lakefront, you can't beat it. In this particular oasis there were people pushing baby strollers, sitting on benches and along the edges of low retaining walls, even some lying on blankets. A hundred yards away a blue and white squad car sat parked in the grass, the only reminder that we weren't in paradise just yet.

To our left a woman with long auburn hair, who should have been staring into her computer monitor over on the business side of Michigan Avenue, was flat on her back working on her tan. Her eyes were closed against the sun, her tailored blouse stretched open at the throat down to bra level, and her skirt hiked at least a foot above her bare knees.

I switched Renata's briefcase to my other hand and twisted my head to keep the sunbather in sight as we passed. "God, this is still a great city."

"Did you hear what I said?" Renata asked.

"Sure. That you should have talked me out of filing the petition, and that it's not a good idea."

"No. I mean after that. While you were gawking at that girl."

"You mean woman," I said. "And I bet you were just as turned on as—" I stopped. Renata was gay, and in a relationship more rigorously monogamous than most people I knew. "Sorry."

"What I said was that you ought to move to dismiss your petition. You're not really interested in practicing law. You can just as easily tilt at windmills with your private detective's license . . . if you can hold on to that."

"We really need to talk," I said. "Let's sit down a minute."

To our left a wiry little ebony-skinned man, wearing

dreadlocks down to his shoulders and nothing else but snow white pants cut off mid-calf, was standing on a park bench. But not on the seat. He was balanced motionless on one bare foot like a yogi, up on the back of the bolted-down bench. Arms spread wide, he smiled serenely toward the sky and seemed oblivious of us. As soon as we sat down on his bench, though, he dropped lightly to the ground and ran away.

"You're right, Renata. I said all along that if they were going to keep on insisting that I 'express remorse' for the conduct that got my license pulled in the first place—I'd dump the petition." I paused and watched the yogi stop at another bench, where he chatted with an old black man wearing at least three ragged overcoats and a cap with the ear flaps tied down with a string under his chin. "But it's different now," I added.

"What are you talking about?"

I took an envelope from my jacket pocket. "Read this." I handed her a sheet of paper from the envelope. "It was with yesterday's mail."

She unfolded the paper. " 'Forget your law license, asshole,' " she read, " 'or you'll come apart just as easy.' " She stared for a long time at the paper, then handed it back to me. "That's some sort of bug, right?" She pointed to a chunky black blob near the bottom of the page, held there under a piece of transparent tape.

"A spider, I think, from the number of legs." Lined up in a row beside the blob, under a separate piece of tape, were what looked like eight crooked spider's legs.

Renata stood up, but I just sat there. She wasn't much over five feet tall and standing put her eyes about level with mine. "I'll file a motion to withdraw the petition," she said, "first thing in the morning."

"No. I told you . . . this note changes everything. Now, whether I want my license or not, I have to stay with it. Otherwise, I'll look like I'm backing down."

She grabbed her briefcase and glared at me. "That's the most foolish goddamn thing I've ever heard," she said, "even from you. Whoever mailed that note is probably psychotic. Dangerously unbalanced, for sure."

When I couldn't think of any response, she turned and stalked away. I watched her cross Michigan Avenue, and kept staring long after she was swept away in a river of pedestrians.

So . . . do we all back down? Just because the bullies are unbalanced?

CHAPTER

====

2

BESIDES, WHO'S TO SAY WHO'S UNBALANCED? People who
looked perfectly normal were just then lopping the tops off
whole mountains in West Virginia and dumping them into
the valleys and rivers below, to get the coal that made them
millions and able to buy wilderness homes in the Cascades,
where others were clear-cutting every last forest in sight.
Other people—like Renata herself, for example—worked
sixty, seventy hours a week, thinking that's how they'd give
the loved ones they seldom saw the best life had to offer.
Well-balanced?

Speaking of which, the little yogi with the dreadlocks had
reappeared, perched one-legged on the back of a bench
again, this one just ten yards to the south of where I sat. He
was still smiling, but not looking at the sky now. Looking
straight at me.

I couldn't help nodding to him, and when I did he leaped
to the ground and danced my way. "Hey, mon," he said, "got
a little change for a square?"

I stood up to dig into my pocket, but found only fourteen
cents in change, and nothing below a twenty in bills. "Here,"
I said.

He took the twenty without noticeable surprise. "T'ank
you, mon." He turned and started away, then swung back.
"They be watchin' you, big mon, y'know?"

"What?"

"They be watchin' you. I see 'em right now. The fuzzies,
y'know?"

"Fuzzies?" I looked over and the squad car was still parked where it had been. "Cops?"

"For sure. But not those gumballs, no. You look slow you might see the real ones. Takin' pictures, hey?" Not turning his head, he kept shifting his eyes to his left, toward Michigan Avenue, and back to me again. "Maybe they wanna make friends, hey, big mon?" He grinned and skipped off across the grass.

I shook my head and tried to look as though he'd said something that made me laugh, then casually turned toward Michigan Avenue. A car sat illegally at the curb, about fifty yards away. A dark green four-door Crown Victoria. An un-marked squad car. I'd have bet on it. I couldn't see the driver, but the man in the passenger seat had a camera in front of his face, pointed off to the north somewhere . . . for now.

I turned my back and, hoisting one foot up onto the bench seat, untied and retied my shoe. When I stood up again and looked around, the Crown Vic was driving away.

IT WAS THREE-THIRTY. I had a gig that weekend, at Miz Becky's Tap. I wanted to go home, open a cold one, and sit down at the Steinway upright to work on a couple of Cole Porter tunes. Instead, I retrieved my well-worn Chevy Cavalier from the Grant Park underground garage and headed south to-ward Hyde Park and the University of Chicago.

I could have taken the note with the dismembered spider to the police, but how could they help me? Even assuming they'd want to, which was always a questionable assumption for me. Funny. I'm a basically law-abiding citizen—within certain personal guidelines—and I know that the majority of police officers must be decent individuals.

So why do I constantly bump up against the minority?

No sense going to the postal inspectors, either, because—

contrary to Renata's assumption—the note hadn't been sent through the mail. It was *with* my mail, though, which meant someone had come right up to my door and put it through the mail slot. And not just some innocent delivery person, because the envelope the note came in was blank. There was no name or address on it.

I took Lake Shore Drive, and by the time I got to McCormick Place, was back to wondering how whoever left me the threat even knew I'd filed for reinstatement. The petition was a matter of public record, of course, but that meant only that it was in among the stacks of documents filed every week in the Supreme Court. It hadn't made the papers as far as I knew. Maybe someone just happened to notice it; or maybe someone had been watching for this, for years.

The notepaper and envelope were the sort available at any drugstore or copy shop, the words printed out by an inkjet printer. I'd looked for fingerprints myself. Nothing. The lab I was headed for now probably wouldn't turn up anything helpful, either, but—professional investigator that I am—I'd leave no stone unturned. Especially when I was the client.

It took just twenty minutes to get to Hyde Park, but another half hour to find a parking place within a half mile of where I was headed, which turned out to be a gray stone building that had to be one of the oldest on the U. of C. campus. The late afternoon sun threw a fittingly creepy shadow across the brass plaque beside the door that said: *Center for Entomological Studies.* Inside the lobby I pushed the button beside a card with the handwritten words: *Arachnid Research.*

The spider expert was exactly as helpful as I'd expected.

"Nothing exotic here," he said, looking up from his microscope. "A bit squashed, of course, but I'm sure it's one of a dozen types of common spiders. They're all over the place. Probably a few creeping around your bedroom right now.

11

Wonderful, beneficial animals, actually. Without them, we'd—"

"Thanks," I said, and took my once beneficial, now a bit squashed, animal with me on my way out.

No stone unturned.

CHAPTER

3

I DROVE HOME and checked my refrigerator. Plenty of beer, a few eggs, some bacon, and half a pizza with just a little fuzzy white stuff on one edge. I started a fresh pot of coffee, grabbed a bottle of Sam Adams, and tried to talk myself into going to the Steinway and working on some chord progressions for "Night and Day."

I didn't succeed.

It was only Tuesday and, although the deposition hadn't been much fun, it was far from the low point of my week so far. Even the note, with its mutilated spider and its sophomoric threat, wasn't the worst thing. That prize went to another letter I'd found in the same pile under my mail slot, this one in an envelope with a postmark and a return address. A letter from Lynnette Daniels, D.V.M.

I'd never owned an animal and might never have met a veterinarian if I hadn't been handed the stiff, mutilated body of a dog a while back, and wanted to find out what killed it. I should have guessed that a relationship that began with an autopsy might not end on any happier note. Lynnette and I had cared for each other, though, and even when it all started to break apart we never got into any raging, angry shouting matches. Instead, we each tried to adjust, doing what we thought would please the other—like her cutting back on her yoga and fitness classes, and me filing for reinstatement to the bar. There were those who said we'd be better off to scream at each other . . . but I doubt it would have helped in the long run.

The letter said Lynnette was moving to northern New Mexico, where she had—or did I read this part in?—another romantic interest. Not entirely unexpected. But you can study a dark wall of clouds from the time it first takes shape on the horizon and starts to roll in, and still be surprised at how hard the storm hits.

But that was yesterday, right?

I felt suddenly light-headed, and remembered I hadn't eaten since before I'd torn Lynnette's letter into snowflake-sized pieces and flushed it down the toilet—twenty-four hours ago. I popped the cap off another Sam Adams, and fried up some bacon. It was Canadian bacon because Lynnette said it had less fat. Less flavor too. But with her off to Santa Fe or wherever, I put my fat-conscious lifestyle on hold and whipped up some butter and half-and-half in a bowl with three eggs and, when the bacon was done, slid the frothy mixture into the frying pan.

While the eggs cooked, I finished my beer and blamed myself for the break-up. I ought to be less independent and more understanding; less stubborn and more considerate. Less of a lot of this and more of a lot of that.

Two pieces of wheat toast popped up. I loaded them up with butter and homemade strawberry jam, dropped the empty beer bottles in the recycling bin, and poured coffee into a mug that had a quote on its side from someone who liked dogs better than people—thinking I'd have kept my mouth shut about it if I felt that way. I sat down at the kitchen table and ate, and thought about how I *would* change, dammit.

The food was gone before I tasted it. So I made two more pieces of toast and ate them, this time very slowly, with lots more strawberry jam. It tasted so good I decided to call the Lady—she's the one who made the jam—and tell her so, as soon as I finished the dishes.

My "coach house" was an apartment over a six-bay garage beside a crushed stone drive leading to the Lady's mansion by the lake in Evanston, not far from the Northwestern campus. The Lady had come to Chicago from England, planning to stay a few months while her husband, Sir Richard Bower, crisscrossed the country, lecturing neurovascular surgeons about some procedure he'd pioneered. Then, one dark November day, Sir Richard's chartered jet fell out of the sky at O'Hare.

I'd just started practicing law then, and was working with my friend Barney Green for Barney's dad, a very successful personal injury lawyer who made his money the old-fashioned way—chasing cases. One of those cases was the Lady's wrongful-death suit and Barney and I took it over when his dad suddenly dropped dead. We worked the case hard and finally settled it and I dumped my half of a pretty big fee into a trust which was set up so the principal couldn't be invaded, either by me or by anyone I might owe money to. The trust started kicking out regular income and eventually I left Barney and went on my own, mostly criminal defense work—until I lost my law license. These days the trust income was still coming in, but wasn't enough to live on. I had my private detective's license, though, and an occasional paying client; plus the gig at Miz Becky's, which about kept me in beer and paid the piano tuner.

Meanwhile, the Lady—with her inheritance, life insurance proceeds, and the lawsuit settlement—had found herself with more money than she thought she needed. She decided there was nothing for her back home, and plenty she wanted to do right here. She bought the Evanston mansion, leased the coach house to me, and got busy. Now she owned two other big old homes, both in the city, and ran them as shelters for battered women—most of them prostitutes trying to get out of the life. She'd never had children of her own and I

15

sometimes wondered whether she thought of me as a surrogate son, or as simply one more beat-up Chicagoan in need.

When the dishes were stowed away I sat down at the table again and tapped out her number. She wasn't in and the woman who answered the phone said I could either leave a message or be transferred to her voice mail.

"Voice mail," I said.

"This is Helene . . ." That's her name, Helene Bower, although most people call her "the Lady," which she doesn't care for, and the message was the usual one about being out or on another line, and sounded like a BBC announcer reading the news.

"It's Mal," I said, after the beep. "Just wanted to tell you again how good that strawberry jam is. Everything's fine. Oh, Lynnette's moving to New Mexico. Anyway, let's get together, when you have time."

I hung up the phone and sat there for a while, then went out to the living room and lay on my side on the sofa and stared into the empty fireplace in the dark.

TWO HOURS LATER the phone woke me up. It had to be the Lady. She's very alert—sometimes to a fault—and she'd have known right off that my "everything's fine" was a lie. When I got to the kitchen phone, though, my caller I.D. said "anonymous" and I knew it couldn't be the Lady.

"Hello," I said.

"Mr. Foley?" A woman's voice. "Is this Malachy Foley?" She pronounced my first name correctly—rhyming the last syllable of mine with the last syllable of hers—but that's not what surprised me. "Well," she finally said, "are you going to answer or not?"

"It's past ten o'clock. Besides, the rules say you can't talk to me except through my lawyer."

16

"I'm sorry," Stefanie Randle said. "But this is different. This is . . . personal."

"Oh? And here I thought I wasn't at my charming best this—"

"Don't be absurd. I don't mean . . ." She sounded worried. "What I mean is, I need your help with something."

"You haven't been drinking, have you?"

"Please. Something wrong is going on and I'm not certain what it is."

"What are you talking about?"

"Not on the phone. It's . . . I just don't know what to do." More than worried, now. Frightened. "We need to talk, but I'm not sure how to arrange a meeting."

"Simple enough," I said. "You suggest a restaurant and a time, like noon tomorrow, and—"

"No! I know it sounds crazy, but I think maybe I'm being . . . *watched*." Frightened, for sure; with crazy seeming more possible every minute. But then, being *watched* is a scary, crazy-making experience. Ask me about it.

Hanging up was the obviously sensible choice, but I had nothing to do except look for Lynnette Daniels in my fireplace and mess around with a petition I'd have gladly abandoned if it weren't for some goof who thought a dose of pureed spider would send me away in tears. So, if not hanging up was a dumb mistake it wouldn't be the first—

"Mr. Foley? Are you still there?"

"We'll meet tomorrow, right at your office. Renata will come with me and it'll look official and no one will think anything of it. What time?"

"I guess . . . ten o'clock. But I don't want Ms. Carroway to hear what I say."

"We'll be there," I said. "And Renata's okay. She likes you. She told me you were a human being, with a name. Which reminds me. Was it your parents who spelled it with an 'f'?

17

Or did you change it yourself, like . . . maybe in seventh—"

"I'm not happy about calling you like this, Mr. Foley." She paused, and this time I did hear a sigh. "So could you just put away the goddamn sarcasm?"

CHAPTER

═══

4

I SET THE TIMER for the morning coffee and went down the backstairs to make sure the outer door was locked. Then I had to run back up, because the phone was ringing again. This time it *was* the Lady.

"Your assurance that 'everything's fine' is clearly untrue." Her vocabulary always fit perfectly with her British accent.

"I read somewhere," I said, "that it's not a lie if you know your listener will know it's—"

"Perhaps you'd like to come over now, Malachy." With her it was never *Mal*, always *Malachy*. "We'll have a sip of brandy," she added.

A "SIP" is about all you get of the Lady's brandy, unless you have nerve enough to keep pouring your own, which I did. She stocks only the best—not that I'd know without reading the label—and it would last her forever if I didn't give her a hand with it. We sat face-to-face in two wingback chairs in front of the fireplace in her front parlor. She had two "parlors" on the first floor, but no "living room," of course. God knows how many other women were living in the house just then . . . maybe two, maybe three or four. I seldom saw any of them coming or going.

People who've heard of the Lady are usually surprised to find her so unremarkable in appearance, with her short gray hair and her plain, pleasant features. "Tell me about you and Lynnette," she said, and lifted her glass to her lips.

So I told her, going on longer than I should have. She was

19

interested and concerned, and absolutely nonjudgmental—about both me *and* Lynette. She'd been the same a couple of years earlier, when my marriage disintegrated. That had hit her hard because she'd been close to Cass. And here I was, having messed up another relationship, but again she never uttered a word of blame. Someone once remarked you could tell the Lady you'd had an affair with a Burmese yak, and she'd nod and say something like, "Really, dear, and however did you happen across a yak?" She does sound a little too good to be true . . . but there you are.

Eventually I finished my sad saga and we both sat silently for a while.

"So that's the end of that," I finally said.

"Yes." She sipped some brandy. "What about that request to get your law license back? Since it was Lynette who wanted you to do that, will you drop it now?"

"No," I shook my head, "I can't."

"Can't?" She likes accuracy in speech, and that's a word she loves to pounce on.

"Won't, then." I went on to tell her about the threatening note. And about Stefanie Randle's phone call.

"So then," she said, "you don't actually *want* your law license, but feel compelled to prove you're unafraid of whoever is opposed to your getting it back."

"Something like that," I said. "Except I don't have to prove that I'm not afraid. I have to show them that—afraid or not—they can't push me around."

"Ah." That's all she said.

" 'Ah' what?"

"Since we're being precise, Malachy, it's clear you feel a need to demonstrate something to *someone*. But is it really to them?" She smiled.

I understood where she was going, but kept still.

"At any rate"—she stood up—"you'll do whatever you be-

20

lieve the circumstances require." She walked me to the front door, then turned. "The universe is so amazing, isn't it?"

"Amazing?"

"The manner in which everything gets . . . oh . . . put together or something." She paused. "Consider this. A woman you've become quite fond of is about to go away and leave a void; but first, knowingly or not, she herself causes a circumstance which ensures that after she's gone—when you might otherwise be inclined to *wallow* a bit—you're left with a project to keep you occupied." She opened the door. "Rather amazing."

I stepped outside and stared back at her. "I suppose so."

"Always something to be thankful for, isn't there? Good night, Malachy." She smiled and closed the door.

"Rather amazing," I said, and stared at the door. It was solid oak, several inches thick.

I turned and walked back down the drive to the coach house. The night air was warm and heavy with fog, and maybe I caught a glimpse of the back of someone farther down the drive, disappearing beyond the Lady's wide-open iron gate. I know I heard a car drive off.

"Always something to be thankful for," I said, staring at my own front door now. This one was thick plate glass, beveled around the edges . . . and smeared all over with fresh-smelling excrement.

CHAPTER

5

WE HAD TO CHANGE THE TIME of the meeting to fit Renata's schedule. Even so, it was past noon before she got to the disciplinary commission, and I'd been waiting a half hour. The receptionist directed us to the same conference room where my deposition had begun less than twenty-four hours earlier.

Stefanie Randle was already there. "I know you're pressed for time, Renata," she said.

"That's right, and so far no one's told me what's going on."

"Well," Stefanie said, "I'm not sure just how to ex—"

"It's simple," I said. "There's a reason why I need to talk to Ms. Randle, privately. But since you're my lawyer she won't do it without your permission."

"Your talking to her privately is absurd," Renata said. "And besides, I could have given my okay on the phone, or by fax. Except . . ." Her eyes narrowed a bit behind her glasses. "Except if I wasn't here it might appear strange to someone, might be noticed." She was as quick a study as anyone I'd ever known, and she'd figured out why I dragged her here.

"There's no phone in here," I said, "so why don't you go down the hall and make some important calls? Ms. Randle and I will wait here for you."

Renata didn't much like being manipulated—and I'd hear about that. "Fifteen minutes," she said, and closed the door remarkably quietly as she left.

Stefanie sat down across the polished wood table from me and studied her left palm. "Maybe I should start by—"

"Just a minute," I said. "Stand up." She did, and I checked the table and the six chairs—the only furniture in the room—and found nothing. That didn't mean there wasn't a little microphone somewhere, inside a wall, up in a ceiling light fixture—maybe even hidden on Stefanie, for that matter. "Keep your voice low, and get to the point."

We both sat down again. "I've only been at the commission six months," she said, "but my caseload is already so heavy I wasn't able to get really familiar with your case. I just knew the supreme court ordered you to reveal what a client told you, and when you refused they jailed you and suspended your license indefinitely. Yesterday, when you broke off the deposition, I had extra time, and went through our old file on your case more carefully. There's a huge stack of police reports and transcripts."

"I know. I had access to your whole file, long ago, and I read everything. I can't believe there's anything there that made you call me."

"No, but it was fascinating, and I couldn't stop reading. It finally hit me that when you disobeyed the court's order it was really a matter of principle. I'd thought you were simply an arrogant, stubborn person. But, I mean, sitting there in jail month after month, when you could have gotten out in a minute."

"The court said the attorney-client privilege didn't apply, which made no sense to me. It was that simple. But privilege or not, I'd promised Marlon that whatever he said wouldn't get beyond me, ever. Which doesn't mean," I added, "that I'm not an arrogant, stubborn person. Just ask Renata." I looked at my watch. "Why did you call me?"

"I called because . . ." She took a deep breath, then started over. "You knew I agreed to take your deposition yesterday, even though our office closed at noon."

"Right. Renata reminded me how cooperative you were

23

being, and what a jackass I was. I said you were probably avoiding a boring meeting somewhere."

She smiled and I knew I was right. "A training seminar; at the bar association. Anyway, our phones were all switched to voice mail and there was hardly anyone here. Reading your file, I lost track of time. I had a vague sense that a few people went by my office, saying good night. But I just kept reading. Before I knew it, it was past seven o'clock."

"No one expecting you for supper?"

"No. I have a young daughter, but she's with her father for a few days. Actually, with his mother. He . . . Anyway, when I saw how late it was I grabbed my coat and purse and switched off the light. Then I heard voices. Two people, I thought, a man and a woman. Coming closer, probably on their way out to the elevators. Even before I could make out their words I knew they were arguing about something, and . . . well . . . I didn't want them to see me."

"Why not?"

"I know it sounds strange, but for some reason I felt embarrassed being there so late, when the office was closed. Plus, I guess I didn't want them to think I was listening in on their argument. So I decided to stay where I was and let them go by. My office is a small room, with no window; and it was very dark. As they came closer I could tell one of the voices was Clark Woolford's. I guess you know who he is."

"The administrator of the commission. Your boss. And the woman?"

"I didn't recognize her voice. But I stayed where I was and . . . and . . ."

"You eavesdropped."

"Yes. I mean not really, but . . ." She was blushing.

"Hey, don't look for *me* to blame you. I'd put eavesdropping in paragraph one on my résumé . . . if I had a résumé."

24

That was supposed to make her smile again—but it didn't work. "So, what were they arguing about?"

"The first words I made out were Mr. Woolford saying, 'I can't do that.' The woman said, 'Yes, you *can* do it, and you will.' By this time they were getting close to my office and I stepped off to the side, sort of behind the door, so they wouldn't see me if they looked in. But they stopped walking, and stood right by my door." Stefanie looked down at her hands.

"Well," I said, "go on. What else did they say?"

"She said again that Mr. Woolford would have to do what she wanted. 'Otherwise,' she said, 'you can forget about that judgeship we talked about.'"

"'Judgeship'?"

"That's what she said."

"Did she say what it was she wanted?" I asked. "I mean, not that you were eavesdropping."

"Yes. That is, Mr. Woolford did. He said the commission couldn't just lie down, because the court back then had been very angry. 'Their order was very clear,' he said, 'and if they don't get an apology, or some show of remorse from him, they won't stand for us not objecting.' But the woman interrupted. 'If that man goes forward with his petition,' she said, 'remorse or not, there's to be no objection raised by your office.' That's what she said, and by then I had a bad feeling I knew what they were talking about."

"Funny thing," I said. "I have the same bad feeling."

"Then Mr. Woolford said, 'I've already told the lawyer assigned to the case that the man has no choice but to knuckle under to the court. Now do I tell her we're reversing our position on *your* directions? In fact,' he said, 'this is her office.' Then he actually flicked on my ceiling light. I thought I'd scream, but I just stayed put behind the door. 'See?' Mr.

25

Woolford said. 'That's probably his file spread out all over her desk. She took his deposition today.' "

"My bad feeling just got worse," I said.

"But what she said next really scared me. 'I know which lawyer has the case. A woman named Stefanie Randle.' That's what she said. How could she know that?"

"It's a public file. You're listed as counsel and—"

"Well, I suppose so." Stefanie looked like she hadn't thought of that. "But that's not the worst part. The woman went on to say, 'I don't care *what* you tell her. But don't you dare mention my name. There are some people,' she said, 'with a great interest in this case. People who . . . who are not above violence. If this Randle person learns I've so much as mentioned the matter to you, it would be dangerous for her.' "

"She said all that?" I asked.

"In almost those exact words. They're like burned into my mind. Then Mr. Woolford said, 'Why not just have this Foley person locked up if he's so dangerous?' and she told him he didn't understand. 'I'm not talking about Foley,' she said. 'That idiot knows nothing about me or what I'm telling you.' Then she told Mr. Woolford someone was trying to get you to drop your petition. 'If he doesn't listen,' she said, 'God help him. He might not live long enough for there to be any reinstatement hearing.' "

"Jesus Christ."

"She said she couldn't control whoever it was. 'But this Foley has a reputation as a survivor,' she said, 'which is why I insist that the commission not file any objections. Period.' Then my office light went off and they started to walk away."

"And that's it?"

"Not quite. I was shaking so bad by then I could hardly walk, but I went to my doorway and peeked out. They were going the other way and the only lights were the emergency lights that stay on all night, so I couldn't see who she was." Stefanie looked down at the table, then up at me again. "But I heard something else she said."

"Which was what?"

"Mr. Woolford said again that the court would be furious, but she said, 'You just worry about what I tell you to do. Leave the other six to me.'"

"The 'other six'? That's what she said?"

"I'm positive. Then Mr. Woolford said something I couldn't hear, and she said, 'I can make you a judge, and I can handle my colleagues.' And then they went out the door."

"You heard her say 'colleagues'?"

"Yes. And I was afraid I knew what that meant. I waited a while. Then I went home and called you."

"But why? I mean, why call *me*?"

"I was panicked," she said. "I thought if I didn't tell someone right away, I might get so scared I'd never tell anyone. I don't know, as I sit here today, whether you were the right one to call."

"That makes two of us."

"The thing is, she wasn't kidding when she said that if I were to find out about her, and what she was saying, I'd be in danger. So who could I go to who wouldn't just . . . tell me to go to the police or something?" She leaned toward me across the table. "But I can't do that. I'm frightened," she said, "really frightened."

"Who wouldn't be?"

"Not just for myself. I mean, if something happened to me, who'd watch out for my little girl?" She shook her head. "I called you because I believe what she said about you being in danger, too, and that you weren't a part of whatever's going on. And I'd just read your file, and saw that you're not easily pushed around and . . . and can keep a secret."

"There's no attorney-client privilege here."

"I know."

I stood up and went to the windows. They faced south, toward the Art Institute, and there were lots of people in the park again. I looked for the little yogi, but if he was down there I couldn't pick him out from that distance. I turned back to Stefanie. "So now what?"

"So," she said, "now I need you to tell me what to do."

CHAPTER

═══

6

ILLINOIS SUPREME COURT justices are elected by the people, and serve ten-year terms. They have to be licensed attorneys: three from Cook County—metropolitan Chicago—and one from each of four other districts.

So there were seven justices, and a few were even said to be quite bright, although legal scholarship has never been the primary qualification. What counts is the ability to get elected, which means outspending and outmaneuvering the other candidates, and getting the backing of the majority party in your district.

Assuming the woman talking to Clark Woolford was actually a supreme court justice—and Stefanie sure hadn't made the whole thing up—it had to be one of only two women on the court, both from Cook County. One was Dolores Aguilar. She had a distinctive Hispanic accent and Stefanie was certain it wasn't Aguilar she'd heard.

So it had to be Maura Flanagan, who, at maybe forty-five years old, was the youngest member on the court. Flanagan came from a long-time political family, and after law school worked for various county and city agencies. Her last lawyer job was with the Chicago Park District, where she handled labor issues and was said to have an abrasive, often belligerent, style. It was there that she first captured the public eye when the *Sun-Times*, in a story about unions and public employees, quoted an exhausted, frustrated union lawyer who, after a long and unsuccessful negotiating session, unwisely opined in the presence of a reporter that Flanagan was "one tough broad," and he hoped she wouldn't "fall off her broomstick on the way home."

Left alone, the flap over those remarks would have died quickly. Maura Flanagan, though, knew a good thing when she saw it. Shouting her outrage that women who stand up for principle must still endure that sort of demeaning sexist insult, she managed to keep the story alive week after week in the media.

Within months of that she'd been tapped by the supreme court to serve out the term of an appellate court justice who resigned amid charges by his two women law clerks that he considered regular spankings a reasonable condition of their employment. Then, after hardly a year on the appellate court, the Democrats ran her for the supreme court. The people loved her. Billboards sprang up everywhere with her name and the words: "One tough broad . . . and just right for the Illinois Supreme Court."

Once on the court, Flanagan's personality and connections made her a power to be reckoned with. She came out consistently "tough on crime" and a "moderate" when it came to big business and the insurance and medical lobbies. In other words, she was a Democrat, yes, but she never forgot where the money was. That's about all I knew about Maura Flanagan as I sat in that conference room with Stefanie Randle. That, and the new information that Flanagan considered me an idiot, thought I might not live much longer if I didn't cave in and drop my petition, and didn't want the commission filing objections to my reinstatement. All in all, it made no sense. And here sat Stefanie, who yesterday seemed ready—even anxious—to file those objections, asking me what she should do.

Fortunately, Renata returned just then, and insisted on leaving at once. "I'll think about it," I told Stefanie, "and get back to you."

I RODE WITH RENATA in a cab to the federal courthouse. "Well?" she finally asked, after two blocks of silence.

"Ms. Randle's not in any hurry to reschedule my dep."

"Fine. Nor am I. You should dismiss your petition and get on with your life."

"Uh-huh." I stared out the window. "So, what are you rushing to now?"

"At one-thirty," she said, "I have a client being sentenced for his part in a heroin conspiracy. His name is Johnnie Lee Bedlow and he's twenty-one years old. His older brother's a major drug dealer, but Johnnie Lee himself kept pretty clean, at least for a kid from the projects on the west side. This was his third bust, though. He's got two prior drug convictions, both guilty pleas to dealing coke, small amounts. While he was on probation for the last one he saw the light. He went back and got a high school diploma. Wants to go to college, be a social worker, work with gang kids."

"Great," I said. "Now he just has to wait until he gets out of the slammer to be a good guy." It was a flippant, stupid remark, out before I could stop it.

She turned toward me. "I'm so glad you think it's great," she said. "And guess how old he'll be then." The anger rose in her voice, directed at me, but only because I was handy. "Sixty-one. That's how old, dammit. One night his big brother's short a lookout, so he strongarms Johnnie Lee into standing on the corner and lifting his cap if he sees anyone driving by who looks like an undercover cop. Well, the kid missed one, so now he's going away for forty years." Her voice was trembling. "The goddamn sentencing guidelines make it mandatory. The judge knows how wrong it is, but he can't do a thing about it. Even if the prosecutors were to ask for leniency—which God knows they won't—his hands are tied." The cab stopped at the federal building and Renata got out, then leaned down beside the open door. "So forgive me if I'm not overly excited about a case like yours, where you don't even want what you're asking for, but insist on going forward . . . so you can prove your so-called manhood."

She slammed the door and I told the cabbie to take me to the Art Institute.

I KNEW RENATA about as well as I knew anyone. Even though she had a right to be angry, she'd already be feeling bad about yelling at me. She might even call and apologize . . . or maybe not. But either way it wouldn't be long before she put the incident—and Johnnie Lee's sentence, too—behind her, as part of a past she couldn't change. She had a place to go home to, and a woman there who loved her—not to mention a baby girl they'd adopted, and an application in for another. She had a life, and that helped her through the absurdity.

All I had was my own sense of right and wrong, and the sense that it was right to follow through on something you started, and wrong to let the bad guys scare you off, even if the bad guys were—in Maura Flanagan's words—"not above violence." Of course, maybe I'd have felt differently if I'd had a woman at home who loved me.

IN FRONT OF THE ART INSTITUTE I paid the fare while two people waited to replace me in the cab. Even on a sunny day like that, there were always lots of tourists unwilling to take a chance on how long a walk it was to the next red star on their maps. I strolled north on Michigan Avenue and went into the park to sit on a bench and figure out what the hell to tell Stefanie.

"Hey, big mon!"

"Hey," I answered, and twisted around. It was the little

yogi with the dreadlocks and the bare feet. Today, though, he wore ragged blue jeans and a bright yellow T-shirt. On the front of the shirt was the news that *Bob Marley lives!* along with an illustration that was beyond my comprehension, but may have included snakes and palm trees. His left eye was swollen shut.

He grinned. "How you doin', big mon?"

"I'm all right, but what did *you* run into?"

"That bread you gave me? 'Member that?"

"I do."

"Gone, mon," he said. "Some dopey traded me for it. Gave me this here." He pointed to his eye and grinned again. "Say, mon, I don't guess—"

"No problem," I said, and gave him another twenty.

"This be good karma for you, hey?" He slid the bill into his jeans. "Plus maybe I do somethin' for you sometime. For the bread, hey?"

I stared at him. "You see anyone watching us now?"

"No, mon. Sure no."

"You have a name?"

"Lotsa names. You gimme 'nother one. That be best, I tink."

"Okay," I said. "Yogi. Like in Yogi Bear. How'd that be?"

"Be fine. So what you want?" He patted his pocket, where he'd put the twenty.

"You busy at five o'clock?"

"Never busy." He winked his one good eye. "Almost never."

"I need you over at the Prudential Building." I pointed. "Five o'clock. And you got any shoes?" He nodded, and I told him what I had in mind. "There's another twenty in it for you," I said.

His smile grew even wider. His skin was very dark and his

33

teeth were very white. "I be there, mon. Reeboks an' all."

I couldn't have explained why, but watching him scamper off across the grass I had the sense he was honest and reliable. He'd show up. And if he didn't, I'd have to come up with another idea.

CHAPTER

===

7

I CALLED THE DISCIPLINARY COMMISSION and got through to Stefanie Randle. "We need to talk," I said. "Did you drive to work?"

"No, I usually take the el."

"Good. And you'll be available today, say about five-fifteen, down in the lobby?"

"Yes, but . . . I mean, what if somebody sees us?"

"I won't be there to be seen. There'll be a small, dark-skinned man, with dreadlocks, near the foot of the escalator by the Beaubien Street exit. Know where I mean?"

"The west end of the lobby," she said. "But it's Beaubien *Court*."

"Uh-huh. Anyway, ask him what time it is. He'll say something like he doesn't have a watch. Then, when he leaves, follow him until I meet up with you. Okay?"

"I guess so, but it sounds so . . . so *something*."

"Melodramatic? I know. But it beats meeting me in the lobby."

"I guess so," she said. "But what if I don't see any little man with dreadlocks?"

"If he's there, you'll see him. If he's not . . . just go on home. Not a big deal. We'll meet some other way. Okay?"

She agreed, and I hung up.

Still not convinced cell phones were secure, I was using a pay phone at the Art Institute. It took half a dozen more calls, but I had lots of change and finally found someone able to

35

put me in touch with Jimmy Coletta. I wasn't sure he'd agree to see me.

He did, though.

UNTIL THAT CALL, Jimmy Coletta and I had never once spoken to each other, but our fates had gotten intertwined five years earlier through an incident that changed both our lives forever. Jimmy, with his brother Sal and two other cops named Richard Kilgallon and Arthur Frankel, got caught up in a deadly shootout on the West Side. It happened about two in the morning at a squalid two-flat on a mostly deserted block near Garfield Park. A drug dealer and his woman inside the second-floor apartment were shot dead on the scene. According to the cops, a third man in the apartment escaped. Arthur Frankel was carried out with a through-and-through to the thigh. Sal Coletta had multiple chest wounds and was DOA at the trauma center. Jimmy Coletta took just one slug, but he took it low in the spine, and he lost the use of his legs forever.

All I lost was my law license, and that was because I'd told my client, Marlon Shades, that he could talk freely to me about the shootout even though his mother was with us in my office. Marlon was twenty years old, a low-life gangbanger and a street tough, but so scared that day that he wouldn't see me without his mother being there, and had to run to the men's room before we could talk. My bladder and bowel control would have been shaky, too, if I'd been in his shoes, with three cops shot and about three thousand others looking for me with blood in their eyes.

That was after I'd given up handling personal injury clients with Barney Green and gone off on my own. I had only a few clients, criminal cases, and I'd agreed to see Marlon Shades as a favor to his mother, Sally Rose Shades. She was thirty-six and a pretty good person, all things considered. She

36

was a waitress at a diner in Union Station who may or may not have supplemented her income by turning tricks. She was a former client, not well-educated, but pretty bright. I paid her to take statements from witnesses for me, to photograph crime scenes, or to bring people in to my law office. When she brought her son in, I figured she was my agent and her being present didn't affect the attorney-client privilege, and Marlon could talk freely with her in the room.

A month or so later, the supreme court justices—Maura Flanagan not yet among them—took a different view from mine. They said that my client Marlon, who'd disappeared after talking to me, was a material witness—and a possible suspect—in a cop killing; that Sally Rose was his mother and neither my client nor my agent; and that anything Marlon said in her presence wasn't privileged. Finally, the court proclaimed that my explanation for why I wouldn't reveal what Marlon told me was "a contrived obfuscation," and that I'd rot on my worthless ass in jail until I changed my mind. Or words to that effect.

I understood the court's position, even though it was obviously wrong. What I didn't like was the "contrived obfuscation" remark. I told them, in a response I filed from a Cook County Jail cell, that if anyone was deliberately confusing the issues it was the court, and that the justices could go screw themselves. Or words to that effect.

Shortly after that they suspended my law license "until further order," and transferred me to a downstate jail to rethink my ethics.

Months went by before they decided it was useless to keep paying my room and board, and let me out. Marlon Shades was already in jail on unrelated charges, had a public defender, and was taking the fifth amendment. Arthur Frankel was back on the job, and Jimmy Coletta was progressing in rehab. Sally Rose, who'd fled after Marlon disappeared, had turned up again. She was dead. Multiple blows to the head, by a person unknown, in a motel room rented in her name near Midway Airport on the southwest side. The police theory was that the perpetrator was a client of hers. As suspicious as I was, it never seemed worth pursuing. It certainly wouldn't have done Sally Rose much good.

Eventually, Marlon got himself murdered in prison. Jimmy Coletta, on the other hand, had turned himself into something of a local celebrity. Not because he'd gotten shot, but because after that he'd gotten religion. Jimmy had joined some charismatic, evangelical church I never heard of. He'd dedicated his life, he said, to "service of the Lord through service of others," and had started some sort of program for disadvantaged kids. He was touted as a real-life hero, even by some of the cynics of this world.

There were still a few holdouts, though, like me.

I HAD SOME RESEARCH I WANTED TO DO, about Stefanie, before meeting her that evening, but there'd be time for that. I dug out the Art Institute membership card the Lady had given me for Christmas and went through the turnstyle to spend some time with Whistler and Winslow and Hopper and the gang.

And to think about Jimmy Coletta. He'd agreed on a time and place to meet me the next day, without even asking what I wanted to talk about—which meant he had a pretty good idea already.

CHAPTER

8

AT THE WEST END of the Prudential Building lobby were three revolving doors out to Beaubien Court. But to the left of those doors was an escalator down to the "pedway," a below-street-level system of pedestrian tunnels. Yogi was to lead Stefanie that way, to the underground station for Metra southbound commuter trains.

Arriving at the station by a different route, I bought a *Rolling Stone* and stood where I could watch people stream in. At about five-thirty Yogi showed up, sporting an ancient pair of Reeboks and a jacket that looked like a Harris Tweed—threadbare, but a perfect fit over his Bob Marley T-shirt. His dreadlocks were tied back into a sort of pony tail, and in the bustling crowd he looked surprisingly ordinary.

A few yards behind him came Stefanie, dark-haired and trim, in a navy pants suit—also a perfect fit, and on a far more interesting frame. She was an attractive woman, for sure, but wore a look of chronic hostility and suspicion, as though she'd been dealt a long series of bad hands and had given up expecting anything better.

Rush hour was going strong, with the noise and confusion of hundreds of people in a hurry, some to board trains, others merely passing through on their way to more pedway tunnels, headed for the subway or somewhere else on the north end of the Loop. Not far to my left, eating frozen yogurt with a pink plastic spoon, a uniformed security guard leaned against a pillar and watched people try not to run into each other. Yogi was weaving and elbowing his way in a zigzag pattern through the crowd, headed toward the far end of the station area. He may have nodded just slightly once in my direction as he passed, or he may not have seen me at all.

As for Stefanie, she was focused on keeping up with Yogi and I was certain she hadn't seen me—and equally certain she was unaware of the man who stood off to my right and who'd spent the last few hours focused on keeping up with me. A thin, fiftyish, intense-looking guy in stylish wire-rimmed glasses, I'd first spotted him when I left the Art Institute. He wore a tan raincoat and held a cell phone pressed to his right ear.

I stepped into the crowd, moving toward the man and against the flow of commuters. When I reached the man, I flipped my wallet open and shut in front of his face, too quickly for him to read my Art Institute membership card. "Excuse me, sir," I said. "The use of cell phones is prohibited in the station area."

He stood there for an instant, eyes wide, then just stepped to his right to go around me and join the moving crowd. I sidestepped to stay in his way, smiling and shrugging my shoulders. "Sorry," I said. "Federal regulations."

By then we were doing a little side-to-side dance together, and blocking people in a hurry to get home. When some of them started to jostle us and complain, the man finally jammed the phone into his coat pocket and poked his finger at me. "Listen up, bud—"

"Thank you very much." I turned and saw the security guard staring at us, even as he scraped for the last trace of yogurt in the depths of his cup. "Officer!" I called. "Quick! Over here!" Instead of approaching, the guard dropped the cup in a trash receptacle and started talking into his radio. No dummy, that one.

I moved in close to my dancing partner. "Whatever it is

you're doing," I said, "I don't think you want to explain it if the security guy calls for assistance."

He opened his mouth, closed it, then turned and walked away, pretty much an admission that he couldn't afford to draw attention to himself. By the time he disappeared through the entrance to the tunnel to the Prudential Building he was on the phone again.

"Got a problem here?" The guard had finally thought it safe to come over.

"Yeah, I mean, the creep bumped into me, y'know?" I said. "And I swear he was going after my wallet. But like he says, I still got it, so . . ."

"Didn't look like our usual pickpocket," the guard said. "But hey, man, you oughta keep your wallet in your front pocket."

Oh sure, blame the victim.

I CAUGHT UP WITH YOGI and Stefanie in the lower level of Marshall Field's, in the cookware department. Yogi was planted amid a half-dozen women watching a silver-tongued, smiling young man demonstrate the joy and ease of greaseless, fat-free stir-frying in a pan as slick as he was. "Not plastic, not Teflon," he proclaimed, "but a space-age miracle destined to revolutionize cooking forever."

Stefanie stood off to the side, arms folded.

"Come here often?" I asked. She spun around and I slipped my arm through hers and walked her away from the cookware. "Has anyone ever mentioned," I said, "how often you have that hostile and suspicious look on your face?"

"Yes," she said. "My ex-husband."

"Ah, an observant man."

"Not at all. Just a self-centered, mean-tempered man, with the emotional maturity of a twelve-year-old." It slid out so easily, it had to be a line spoken many times before.

"Oh, another one of *those*," I said, steering her into a left turn. "Field's has a food court down here somewhere."

They were about ready to close, but we ordered from the Mexican counter and went to a table in a corner of the nearly deserted dining area. Not a very secluded spot, certainly, but staying out of sight is all a matter of percentages. I hadn't spotted anyone tailing Stefanie, and the chance of there being more than one person on me was pretty slim. Even Yogi had disappeared.

I peeled the foil wrappings from a ground beef taco and a vegetarian quesadilla, pulled the tops off two little containers of salsa, and slipped a straw through the plastic lid of a cup of root beer. Stefanie had an easier time of it. She added a tablet of sweetener and was ready to sip her supper—decaf coffee.

"I guess you'll eat when you get home, huh?" I said.

"Maybe some popcorn." She glanced around the room, then looked down at her cup. "I'm beginning to wish I hadn't called you last night."

"Uh-huh." I poured salsa over the taco filling. "I've been wishing the same thing." I bit into the taco. Not bad. Not very Mexican-tasting, but not bad. "What I'm wishing now is that you'd tell me some things you haven't told me yet."

She made a point of stirring her coffee—which she'd already done once, quite thoroughly—and arranged her paper napkin at just the right angle to the edge of the table. "What things?"

"For instance, you told me your daughter was staying with her father on the night you overheard Justice Flanagan talking to your boss. I checked with the court clerk's office. Why don't I find any divorce action involving a Stefanie Randle in the last ten years?"

"You don't even know whether I'm divorced or not."

"You just called him your 'ex-husband.' In my trade we call that a clue."

"Why would you check? Why would it make any difference?"

"Just fishing," I said. "It's what I do. And maybe it doesn't make any difference."

"Actually, it *does*, or it might, but I had no idea there was any connection. That is, I . . ."

"Just slow down and tell me."

"I was divorced two years ago. The divorce case was in our married name, which I no longer use." She rotated her cup on the table. "He was a Chicago police officer. I mean, he still is, but he's not my husband anymore. He . . ." She stared off over my shoulder for a moment. "In law school I got involved in a crime victims advocacy program and started meeting lots of police officers. They were so . . . I don't know . . . exciting or something. Richard was one of them and before I knew it we were married."

"And it didn't work."

"I tried, you know, but I couldn't adjust to . . . to the whole cop thing. The dark humor, the cynicism, the negativity, the—"

"There are lots and lots of good cops." I almost said *some of my best friends are cops,* but caught myself.

"I didn't say he wasn't a good cop."

"That's true. And what I meant was that if your husband's 'a self-centered, mean-tempered man, with the emotional maturity of a twelve-year-old,' it's not necessarily because he's a cop."

"He's my ex-husband."

"What's his name?" I'd finished the taco and was working on the quesadilla.

"Kilgallon." She sighed. "Richard Kilgallon."

"Jesus." I set down my plastic fork. "You said you'd read the police reports about my case."

"Yesterday, for the first time." She shook her head. "Look, before that it never occurred to me that there was the slightest connection between Richard and . . . between my ex-husband and you."

"He was Sal Coletta's partner, for God's sake. He was there the night Arthur Frankel and the Coletta brothers got shot."

"I know that now."

"How could you have let Woolford assign my case to you? You must have heard about the shooting, about the cops leaning on me to tell what my client had told me."

"Except that I didn't. I would have if Richard had been shot, sure. But he wasn't. At that time I had a small child and I was in law school. I didn't have time to read the papers or watch the news. Richard didn't like me being in school and was no help at all. Besides, by then he had a girl— He was away from home a lot and when he was there we hardly even spoke to each other. I didn't pay any attention to what he did—on the job or anywhere else. My marriage was dead." She looked at me. "Believe me, I didn't know there was any connection. Until yesterday, when I read the police reports."

"I believe you," I said. "But you know, a few things didn't get into the reports. Like how, after my client didn't show up to turn himself in, your husband sat and watched a couple of other cops slap me around on and off over the next twelve hours. How they had me in custody and wouldn't let me contact anyone. How one of them told me I was a dead man if I didn't cooperate."

"Richard's not my husband; he's my my ex-husband. And I'm surprised he only sat and watched. He enjoys hitting people, almost as much as he enjoys the track and the casinos. He sure didn't sit and watch in *my* case. He did the slapping

44

himself. But only twice; that's all. And I'm the one who told him he was a dead man if it ever happened again."

"Good for you. Me, I was cuffed to a wall ring and not really up to making any death threats. The time wasn't a total loss, though. I did manage to throw up on Richie's shoes."

CHAPTER

===

9

BY THE TIME WE SPLIT UP, Stefanie and I had agreed to stay in touch, and disagreed on most everything else. I told her to tell Clark Woolford she'd seen her ex-husband's name in the police reports and get him to take her off my case. She said no, that might make him suspicious, and he could find out from the security desk sign-out book that she hadn't left the office the night before until after he and Flanagan left.

She lived in East Rogers Park, a neighborhood along the lakefront at the north edge of the city. Maura Flanagan's warning that Stefanie would be in danger if she learned of Flanagan's interest in my case had frightened her, made her wonder if someone was watching her. I said I'd take her home. She refused. I suggested a cab, but she said she'd take the el. She didn't want anyone to see her acting unusually.

So she was scared—but tough. On the other hand, I didn't think she was under surveillance. After all, no one knew she'd heard a supreme court justice putting pressure on the head of the disciplinary commission, bribing him with a judgeship in exchange for *not* objecting to my reinstatement to the bar . . . if I survived long enough to make it matter.

So Stefanie left and I followed her myself for a while. No one else did.

Then, leaving Marshall Field's at street level on Randolph, I walked to Michigan Avenue and headed south. It was dark and the air was turning cool, with a light rain blowing in from the east—off the lake. There weren't many people on the sidewalks and most of them kept their heads down as they hurried along. The streets were slick and shining with re-flected automobile lights—distorted streaks of red and white—and tires hissed and spat out tiny sprays of water behind them. I crossed Michigan, went past the Art Institute, then cut diagonally through the grass and trees of Grant Park, toward Columbus Drive and the Cavalier.

And someone followed me. I was sure of it, even though he stayed way back and in the shadows. Not recognizable in the dark and the rain, yet somehow familiar. Thin, like the man in the underground train station.

I left the trees, crossed to the east side of Columbus, and continued south on the sidewalk. More grass and trees along my left; on my right a row of parked cars facing north. Mine was at the end of the line, parked just beyond the last legal space on the block. From thirty yards away I spotted a park-ing ticket stuck to the windshield.

My shadow stayed with me, apparently satisfied to be just that—only a shadow, not a danger; much too far back to reach me before I got to the car and was out of there. Even so, I picked up the pace a bit. It was raining harder now.

The ticket was stuck with its own adhesive to my wind-shield, low on the passenger side. I pulled it off. I'd have to squeeze it into the glove compartment with the rest of them and one of these days take them all to traffic court and try to settle up with—

A footstep then—or maybe just a breath—behind me. I turned, but too late. What felt like a sock full of sand slammed hard across my left ear. It lifted me up on my toes and spun my head, and for an instant I saw someone a block away, running toward us on the sidewalk. The shadow, the one who'd drawn my attention away from the man hiding by my car.

But the man sapped me again, and there was nothing then but pounding pain and bright, wild streaks of red, like taillights reflecting off wet pavement that heaved and tilted up around me. My knees turned to pudding and my body slumped and I was glad, because I couldn't wait to be on the ground.

The man caught me under the arms, though, and stood me up with my back against the side of the car. I gasped for breath and he stuffed a wadded ball of paper into my gaping mouth. I choked and gagged, and he went to work on my body. Hard punches—painful, professional blows, deep into the gut. I took two of them, shook my head, but still saw only the blurred shape of a man in a ski mask in front of me. With my hands too heavy to lift above my waist, fighting for breath through blocked nasal passages, I could only sag back against the car and wait for more.

But instead, another blurred shape came from my left and threw itself into the man in front of me. The two of them went to the sidewalk, thrashing and kicking. One of them was silent, but the other kept shouting, *"Bam! Bam! Bam!"* over and over. I suddenly realized the noisy one was Yogi. He seemed to be pretending he was hitting my attacker, but he wasn't hitting anyone. He had his arms and legs wrapped around the man, trying to roll him around on the concrete.

I backed off a little and managed to get the wad of paper out of my mouth, breathing hard and trying to figure out how to get them apart without Yogi getting hurt. Then, as though magically, Yogi broke free of the man and was on his feet, and then suddenly up on the roof of the Cavalier.

He kept right on shouting, but it was *"Run! Run! Run!"* now, and it was me he was yelling at.

I stayed put, though, as the man lunged toward the car, reaching up for Yogi. Then he must suddenly have remembered me because he started to turn—and I caught the side of his jaw with my right elbow.

I was still too dazed to make it a direct hit, but it shook

him, and he turned and ran. I took three steps after him and knew it was hopeless.

"You okay, big mon?" Yogi called.

"Yeah. I'm fine." I swung around to find him back on the sidewalk. "I was just about to take the bastard down, though, until you got in the way. Now he's gone."

His mouth gaped open for just an instant, then he broke into a grin. "You jokin', hey?"

"Right," I said. "So that was you? Following me all the way from Marshall Field's?"

"Sure." He smiled a wide happy smile and tapped his temple with his finger. "Good tinkin', huh?"

"Good for me, maybe," I said. "But for you? Guys like that don't like to be interfered with."

"I be okay. I run away . . . quick an' easy."

"Yeah," I said. "That's how you got busted in the eye yesterday."

"Shoot, mon. That be a surprise." He stared down at his feet, then looked up again and grinned. "Like tonight, mon. You forget you should be watchin' out and then . . . *wham!* . . . and you—"

"Anyway, thanks."

"Tink nothin'. Gotta go now."

"Hold on. We need to—"

"Gotta go, big mon." And he was gone . . . quick an' easy.

It was dark and still raining, but I crawled around on my hands and knees until I found the wadded ball of paper the man had jammed into my mouth. I got into the car and smoothed out the crumpled-up paper. It was one sheet.

It was a copy of page one of my petition for reinstatement.

CHAPTER
10

I TOOK LAKE SHORE DRIVE HOME. The rain had slowed up and traffic was light. I drove slowly, staying in the lane closest to the lake, and with too many ideas tumbling through my mind. I finally picked just one to concentrate on: Maura Flanagan's order to Clark Woolford that his office not object to my reinstatement. It made no sense.

To begin with, just about everyone who had any reason to care—and there couldn't be many—was *against* my getting my license back. I myself didn't even want the damn thing that bad, for God's sake, so why should Maura Flanagan take up my cause? And Woolford? According to Barney Green, the guy seemed like a straight arrow. He'd spent twenty-five years as a partner in a successful little downtown law firm, and had run once for judge, unsuccessfully. Six months ago the supreme court tapped him to head the disciplinary commission. It was to be a temporary assignment until a divided court could agree on someone permanent.

Now Flanagan was saying she'd make him a judge, and she probably could. Judges were elected officials, but when one of them died or retired, the supreme court appointed someone to finish up the term. These appointed judges could run for election at the end of the terms they'd served out, and were generally thought to have a head start on their opponents. So being appointed a judge was a good deal.

And if Woolford wanted that, so what? Lots of lawyers did. Of course, lots of lawyers weren't making strange deals to secretly influence legal proceedings in exchange for what they wanted. Not that the deal was a sure thing, but Stefanie had the impression Woolford was giving in to Flanagan, even though she hadn't heard him say yes.

I TURNED IN AT THE LADY'S DRIVE about eight-thirty. Happily, no more shit had been smeared on my front door. I circled around and went up the rear stairway. On the landing at the top, I peered through the window in the kitchen door. The door was locked and the light was on and everything looked just as I'd left it. Except I hadn't left the light on.

Gun in hand, I went inside and headed straight for the room where the old Steinway upright rules the space. Nothing unusual there, thank God. Then back into the kitchen, still holding the Beretta—with a .22 LR cartridge in the chamber—but down beside my leg now. It was unlikely I'd find anyone still there. I knew I'd find a message somewhere, though, and not on the answering machine.

What I noticed first was the water. It stood in large, shallow puddles on the hardwood floor in the hallway. Then more water, trapped by the marble threshold and forming a half-inch deep lake on the tile floor in the bathroom, along with thousands of pieces—large and small—of the porcelain that had once been the toilet bowl. And lying flat under the water, stuck to the floor and too soggy to be picked up in one piece, was another copy of page one of my petition.

I grabbed all the towels I owned and mopped up the wood floor in the hallway. The bathroom could wait till morning, when maybe some of the water in there would have dried up.

The coach house had only one bathroom, but there was a working sink and toilet downstairs in the garage, where forty or fifty years ago someone had turned one of the parking bays into a workshop. The inconvenience would be a pain in the ass, but what bothered me more was that the

51

shattered fixture had been an antique, a pre-1920s beauty of a toilet with the manufacturer's trademark and the model name—*Expulso*—embedded in blue Victorian script in the porcelain at the rear of the bowl. I'm not an antiques buff, but hell, that thing was probably irreplaceable.

HALF AN HOUR LATER I was at the Lady's house. I'd been clearing God knows how many years of dirt and debris out of my new bathroom in the garage, and had gone over just to borrow her vacuum cleaner. I ended up telling her what had happened since the night before, right up to how someone had gotten into the coach house.

"They left the kitchen light on," I said. "Deliberately, I'm sure. Wanted me to be nervous about going in. I checked the piano first, but it was fine."

"I'm glad of that," the Lady said.

"I'm glad, too," I said. "But dammit, I'll never find another Expulso."

"No, quite probably you won't." The Lady poured herself another cup of some tea I'd given her. It was a foul-tasting Japanese tea I'd gotten from Dr. Sato, a martial arts *sensei* who took my money every week so he could throw me around his *dojo* and teach me about pain and humility. "Tea?" she asked.

I took a cup, knowing I wouldn't drink it. "I don't like people coming right into my house, trying to intimidate me. I'm gonna find out what's going on."

"I'm sure you are." She seemed preoccupied, as though trying to figure something out, but all she said was, "I take it the facilities in the garage are adequate?"

"Fine," I said, "but that spider guy was right. I replaced the burned-out bulbs and found those things crawling all over the place in there. You have any bug spray?"

She sipped her tea. She seemed actually to like the stuff.

52

"Have you ever read *Pilgrim at Tinker Creek*, by Annie Dillard?" When I shook my head she went on. "Dillard used to hang a towel over the side of her bathtub so the spiders could get out, since they ·can't get a grip on the smooth surface. She said any predator who sits in a corner and waits for food to come along needs all the help it can get." She sipped more tea. "That struck me as so . . . compassionate."

I took that to mean she didn't have any bug spray. "Anyway, Helene, you need to be careful. These creeps might get the idea to do something to *your* place."

"I thought of that after we spoke last night, and this morning I called several of my graduates. One arrived an hour ago. The others will be here tomorrow. They'll watch the coach house, too. They . . . well, they're not easily frightened."

"I can imagine." The women the Lady took in were fresh off the street. Malnourished, strung out, many of them prostitutes and still terrified of the pimps they'd been hustling for. She had a group of "graduates" who'd take turns staying with them. "Not a pimp in the world who wouldn't back off from one of your graduates," I said. "Even a sewer rat values its own stinking skin."

"The pimps are victims, too, Malachy. Abused and beaten as children, they—"

"Fine, okay." She had a point, but sometimes I didn't want to hear it. I stood up. "Let's find that vacuum cleaner and I'll get out of here." She didn't move, though, so I sat back down.

"It is a bit puzzling, isn't it?" she said. "I mean, that conversation between Justice Flanagan and Mr. Woolford."

"Well, I sure don't know why she wants me to get my license back."

"She said there were 'others' involved, so perhaps it's not she who cares, but those others. What interests me, though, is why she—or whoever—should care whether someone *ob*-

jects or not. May not the court grant your request, even despite there being objections?"

"Sure, if I'm still alive. Anyway, maybe she thinks they won't, not if—"

"She claims she can control the other justices, so . . ." She sipped her tea. "Does whether there are objections make a difference in how they handle your petition?"

"Objections or not, there'll be a hearing—like a trial—and I'll have to prove that I've been . . . rehabilitated." I hadn't done anything wrong in the first place, so *rehabilitated* had a bad taste to it.

"And who'll testify at the trial?"

"If the commission doesn't file any objections it'll just be me, and some character witnesses to say that I'm a better person now than I used to be. If I can come up with anyone."

"And if there *are* objections?"

"Then, after me and my witnesses, the commission's lawyer—that's Stefanie—would put on some witnesses. Probably people who are angry that I won't tell what that kid told me, because the cops are still looking for a guy that got away." I swished the tea around in my cup. "You know, Helene, you've never once asked me what the kid said, or whether it would have helped catch anyone."

"You gave your word you'd tell no one. Why would I ask?"

"I might tell you anyway, someday." She didn't say anything, so I went on. "So, the commission's witnesses will say I shouldn't get my license back because I'm still standing in the way of justice being done."

"And they'll testify about the shooting? The effects on the police officers and their families?"

"Stefanie already said—back when she first talked to Renata about my petition—that she intended to call the three surviving cops to testify. Then everyone could compare those heroes to me—a guy who doesn't care about justice, who still refuses to help identify a cop killer."

"Ah, that's it." She smiled, finally, and drank some tea. "That's probably it."

"What's probably what?"

"Well, it seems Justice Flanagan, or whomever she's speaking for, doesn't care whether you get your license back or not. Don't you see?"

"Maybe I'm slow, because . . ." I stared at her. "You know," I said, "I oughta drink as much of that tea as you do. It's not about my license, is it? What they're worried about is a *hearing,* or one where the commission puts on witnesses, anyway."

"And why would that be?"

"It could only be because somebody doesn't want those cops testifying about what happened."

"Well then, that's solved." The Lady stood up. "The Hoover's in the hall closet." She always called vacuum cleaners Hoovers. Maybe it was a British thing.

"Solved?" I said. "But why is Maura Flanagan, a supreme court justice, involved in the first place? And those cops will say what they said before about that shooting, whether it's true or not, so what's the big deal about them testifying? When you think about it, Helene, nothing's actually been *solved.*"

"But it's a start, Malachy." She smiled. "And I have to leave *something* for you to do." That was the Lady's idea of a joke, so I smiled, too.

One of her "graduates" showed up to escort us to the front door. Her name was Layla, the Lady said, and she seemed to be some mix of Asian and African-American, with skin the color of dark gold, and long, straight hair dyed auburn. She was very pretty, despite the scars—two thin parallel tracks, a quarter-inch apart—that ran from her left ear to her chin. She didn't smile, though, and the look in her eyes said she didn't take shit from pimps or anyone else.

Careful not to make her mad, I went out the door and down the stone driveway, dragging the Lady's Hoover with me.

CHAPTER

==

11

I SPENT HALF THE NEXT MORNING suffering through a workout with Dr. Sato, the *sensei*. The other half I spent at the Steinway, working on *"Moon River,"* a tune I hate, but one the drinkers can't get enough of.

Just before two o'clock, I parked the Cavalier beside a *No Parking* sign outside the Ralph Ellison Community Center, a tired-looking brick building on the corner of an old, neglected block in Englewood, on the south side. Rain had been predicted all day, and now an ominous wind had risen up and thunder rumbled in the distance. Inside the center, just beyond a small lobby, was a gymnasium barely large enough for one basketball court. It was warm and damp in there, smelling like perspiration and mildew, and the white paint on the old metal backboards had long ago turned yellow.

The players racing up and down the floor looked to be in their teens and early twenties—all of them African-American, two of them females. They whirled this way and that—sometimes haphazardly, it seemed—yelling, waving their arms. They were drenched in sweat, most of them panting as though they'd been at it too long. I stood there for several minutes and didn't see the ball go through either hoop. Then a skinny kid wearing goggles lofted a desperate one-hander from the top of the key. The ball caught the rim, bounced high in the air, then dropped through with a swish of the net.

Everyone clapped and cheered. Everyone. Both teams.

"Way to go, Randy!" Jimmy Coletta was clapping too. "Okay, everyone, it's late. Go home and shower up. See you Tuesday!"

The players, all of them in wheelchairs, whooped and exchanged high fives, then propelled themselves toward the far end of the gym, where family members and friends were waiting. A smiling Randy was still pumping one fist high in the air. His other hand was strapped down, with the fingers spread over the buttons of his chair's control box.

Coletta spun his own wheelchair around, his eyes bright with tears. When he saw me he faked a sneeze and wiped his nose with the back of his hand. "Allergies," he said. He wore running shoes that had no laces, and dark blue shorts, and his legs were in pretty good shape, considering the muscles weren't able to function on their own. The slogan on his T-shirt said: *YES, I CAN! 'CAUSE I GOT JESUS IN MY CORNER!*

"Mal Foley," I said, stepping toward him.

"Right." He didn't stretch out his hand to me.

"Seems like a great group of kids."

"Yes." He frowned, more to himself than at me. "Sometimes I think I push them too hard. Mostly, though, people don't push them hard enough."

The gym echoed with laughter and raucous talk, as the players struggled to get into jackets and get their legs covered up—the ones who had legs—for the trip home. Then, without warning, all the lights went out and it was very dark and suddenly silent . . . and then came the deafening crash of nearby thunder. The lights flickered on, then off, and finally on to stay, and the rain came—in a million tiny pellets, blasted by the wind against the frosted glass of the high windows. The players clapped and cheered like patriots at a fireworks display.

"Looks to me like they love it," I said. The muscles in Coletta's upper body, even through the T-shirt, were well-defined. "Looks like you work yourself pretty hard, too, officer."

"I'm not a police officer," he said, "although sometimes I let the kids call me that, so they can think of me as a cop who's on their side. I'm on disability, not with the department anymore." He stared down at his thighs, massaging them with his hands. "I get a lot of physical therapy, and I work out six days a week." He looked up. "I'm gonna walk again, you know. It's matter of the Lord's help, progress in medical science, and . . . and determination."

"From what I hear," I said, "determination seems—"

"Fine, let's get to it." It was as though he'd suddenly remembered who I was. "I picked this place to meet because I wanted you to know that nobody'd be around to listen in. No wires, either." He grabbed the hem of his T-shirt. "See?" He yanked the shirt up and off over his head.

"Right," I said, and if pride in his physique was part of his motivation I could give him that. I sat on the bleachers—the lowest bench, so I'd have to look up a little to meet his eyes. "I've given up worrying about eavesdropping, anyway." For all I knew, he could have had a micro-mike poked up his left nostril. "So let's just go ahead and talk." When he nodded, I said, "I've filed a petition to get my law license back."

"I know. That was inevitable."

"Wrong." He looked surprised, but said nothing. "Not inevitable at all," I said. "In fact, it's never really been that important to me. I filed because it seemed to mean a lot to a woman, and the woman meant a lot to me."

He smiled. "That'll do it."

"Uh-huh." His smile went away in a hurry, but to my surprise I started to like him. Damn. This was a guy whose family helped organize a campaign to convince the supreme court to keep me locked up in hell until I'd go back on my word to my client. The last thing I wanted was to like him. I didn't want to find out, either, that he really was someone who'd used a terrible misfortune to turn himself into a true-life hero, or that his born-again-Christian reputation was based on more than talk, or that his dedication to helping kids with handicaps, mostly minorities, was the real thing. Damn. "Anyway," I said, "the woman's up and gone to Taos now . . . or somewhere."

"Really?" The voice was casual enough, but I was paying attention. *Because,* as Dr. Sato loves to repeat, *attention is quite most important secret weapon.* Sometimes I do better than others, and this time I saw the muscles in Coletta's face and neck relax a little. "So," he added, "are you dropping it?"

"I might have." The look of hope—and that's what it was—disappeared. "Except I keep being followed around. By cops, I think. Coming right into my home, leaving what they think are very scary messages, telling me I better drop it." A door slammed, and I noticed the gym was suddenly silent then, only the sound of the rain still slapping hard against the windows. "I'm like you, I guess. When something gets in my way it tends to increase my—what word did you use?—'*determination.*'" I left medical science and the Lord out of it.

"So," he said, "you're going ahead?" I nodded, and was surprised at how quickly the flush of anger flooded his face. "You don't even want that law license. But you wanna prove yourself. And you being a tough guy and all, you figure you'll start with the guy you think's a cripple, right?"

"'Cripple?' I hadn't really thought about it. And if I start . . . well, forget it." I knew his anger rose up out of fear—fear of the trouble I might unleash—and I should have backed off a little, but I was angry, too. "Someone's leaning on me, Coletta, and I intend to lean back, hard, on whoever it is. If you're there you'll get—" I finally caught myself, and

60

took a deep breath. "Right now, though, I'm here just to talk . . . about what really happened that night at Lonnie Bright's place."

"You don't need to talk to me. What happened is just what the police reports—" He stopped, and there was another shift in his expression. He looked down at his hand on the arm of the wheelchair.

"I'm listening," I said.

He looked up at me and seemed angry again. "If somebody's following you around, threatening you, that's between you and them. I don't want to talk to you."

"But I said I wanted to talk to you, and you said to come out."

"Yeah, well, I changed my mind. I don't like being pushed either," he added, "so get outta here."

"Damn," I said. "Why don't you give me a—"

"I don't really care if they give you back your bloodsucker's license, Foley. I just want you away from me." He leaned forward; he'd lost the battle to control his temper. "And legs or no legs, I can still whip your tail."

I stood up . . . and walked away. Jimmy Coletta couldn't whip my tail. With both legs and his dead brother back to help him, they couldn't have whipped my tail. So what should I do? Tell him that?

The gymnasium door fell closed behind me. There'd be other days. Besides, much of what I'd wanted from the man he'd told me.

I'd learned that, whatever he'd been before, Jimmy Coletta was a good man now, even if he had a temper he couldn't always keep under rein; and that he was worried—frightened, in fact—about my asking for my license back. He'd been relieved to think I might drop the idea, and then scared again to find out I wouldn't. I couldn't tell whether he knew who was putting the squeeze on me, but I was damn certain he wasn't involved. Most important of all, though, I'd learned Jimmy Coletta was a man who'd stop short when he caught himself about to tell a lie.

CHAPTER

━━

12

I LEFT THE COMMUNITY CENTER and drove up to Fifty-fifth Street, then east to the Dan Ryan. Rain poured down as though it were the sky's last chance to prove it couldn't be pushed around.

I didn't know the whole story about what happened the night Jimmy Coletta got shot, but what I did know was enough to hurt Jimmy if it came out. That's exactly what he was afraid of. But why would Jimmy—or some others who'd be hurt as bad, or worse—why would they think I'd break open now, after all these years? I'd said right in the petition I filed that I still didn't intend to reveal what my client Marlon Shades told me in confidence. Didn't they know me well enough to—

And then I understood.

Whether they knew me and thought I wouldn't tell wasn't the point. They knew Jimmy Coletta. He was the one they were worried about. He couldn't bring himself to lie to me even when he was angry. If the commission subpoenaed Jimmy and put him under oath he might not be able to get himself to lie, even if telling the truth meant dragging himself down, as well as the others.

I'd filed my petition thinking I'd see whether the supreme court would give my license back even though I still wouldn't tell what my client had told me. If I got the license, fine. If not, so be it. Now it seemed that if there was a hearing, even if I didn't tell what I knew to be the facts behind the shooting at Lonnie Bright's, Jimmy Coletta would.

63

Did I still want to go forward with the petition? Chances are I wouldn't get my license back. And if Jimmy brought himself and the others down, what purpose would be served? Would it bring "closure" to a bunch of innocent family members who thought they wanted the truth, but who'd only be hurt if they ever heard it? Would it achieve "justice"?

If it was justice I was after, maybe I should see what I could do to keep a hundred million children from going hungry that night while I fumbled around in my refrigerator for another Sam Adams and threw out that half-eaten pizza just because it had a little fuzzy stuff growing on it. "Justice" seemed to be mainly what people wanted it to be, to serve their purposes.

I probably wasn't going to eat that moldy pizza. I probably wasn't going to send a check to Ethiopia—or Englewood, either, for that matter. And I certainly wasn't going to tell myself that flushing Jimmy Coletta down the toilet would bring anyone "closure," or have a whole lot to do with "justice."

TRAFFIC WAS JAMMED up downtown. I parked illegally and ran inside and called Barney Green from the lobby of his building. I waited five minutes, then went up to his office and picked up a padded envelope he'd left for me at the reception desk. The envelope had my name on it and was stamped:*Attorney-Client-Privileged Material.* I left without seeing Barney or speaking with him or with anyone else.

Five years earlier I'd delivered that envelope to Barney. Inside the envelope was an audiocassette tape, a recording of a conversation I'd had with my client Marlon Shades and his mother. I hadn't told Barney that, but he'd known it was something big time and agreed to keep it safe and out of sight. That had been the day before I was to surrender Marlon, to be questioned as a witness in the cop killing. Marlon

64

was to keep his mouth shut and rely on the fifth amendment. He got scared, though, and skipped. I was taken into custody instead.

Marlon and his mother hadn't known I was recording our conversation. Did that make it illegal? Maybe yes and maybe no. The state eavesdropping statute, and how it was to be interpreted, was pretty unclear at that time. But I'd thought when I did it that, legal or not, the heat was on higher in that case than in anything else I'd ever been involved with, and I'd wanted to hold as many cards as possible.

EITHER EXPRESSWAY TRAFFIC MOVED more quickly than usual through the rain, or else I wasn't paying much attention. Before I knew it I was far north of downtown, near the junction where the Kennedy angles off to the left toward O'Hare and the Edens goes straight north. I stayed to the right, got off at the next exit, and drove to the parking lot of a picnic grove that was part of the Cook County Forest Preserve District.

It was a pretty dismal scene, just three other cars widely spaced along the row of parking slots. I took the end spot, as far from the others as possible, and made it four. Four men sitting alone in four cars and staring out at the rain, maybe some of them listening to the radio. I was probably the only one, though, with a cassette in his tape deck with information that could ruin a whole bunch of people's lives.

CHAPTER
===
13

I PUNCHED *Play* and heard my own voice, first with the date and time, then stating I was going out to get Marlon and his mother. Then silence, then the sounds of getting them into my office. I fast-forwarded through the beginning of the interview, to listen again to the part I still knew almost verbatim:

Marlon, how Mr. Foley here s'posed to help you, you won't tell him where you was?

I can't, Mama. I be sittin' up in the shithouse fifty years or somethin' . . . they don't kill me first. I can't tell him that part.

Dammit, boy, you like to drive me—

Sally Rose, please. Let me talk to him, all right? . . . LENGTHY SILENCE *. . . Marlon, I believe you when you say you had nothing to do with killing anyone. But you have to tell me what happened.*

How I know you ain't gonna jus' tell everyone what I say? Shit. You another one of them—

Hush up, boy. This here's your lawyer. He can't tell nobody, 'cause o' that . . . whatchacallit . . . priv'lege. Ain't that right, Mr. Foley?

Yes, and—

I ain't tellin' where I was. Y'all don't . . . INAUDIBLE *. . .*

You have to speak up, Marlon. My . . . uh . . . my hearing's bad. I didn't hear that last part.

Nothin'. I said I ain't tellin' you where I was.

It's up to you, but what your mother says is true. Anything you say here is privileged. The rules say I can't tell. I could lose my license if I did.

Fuck the rules! Rules don't mean shit when—

Marlon! You watch your mouth, boy.

Sorry, Mama, but . . . but how I know . . . INAUDIBLE *. . . Plus, how I know they ain't gonna change the rules, man? Then they make you tell.*

Goddammit, Marlon, I don't care if they erase all the rules, or what they say, or do, or . . . whatever. I won't tell anyone, that's all. I just won't. Not ever. You have my word on that.

Yeah, but . . . INAUDIBLE *. . .*

Well, that's fine. But I won't represent anyone who doesn't trust me. Sorry, Sally Rose, but—

It ain't I don't trust you, man. My mama trusts you, so I guess I do, too. Problem is . . . INAUDIBLE *. . . So I don't know. Maybe . . . I guess I tell you.*

Good. So when Lonnie Bright and Fay Rita and the police officers got shot, where were you? What were you doing?

OK. I'll tell y'all what I was doin'. . . . LENGTHY SILENCE *. . . Shit.*

Marlon?

Yeah. OK . . . I had been stayin' with my uncle—Lonnie, you know?—up at his crib since . . . I don't know . . .'bout January. But I wasn't up in there when it happened. The shootin', I mean. I didn't know nothin' about none o' that. When I heard them shots I was . . . INAUDIBLE *. . .*

What? You gotta speak up.

I was in the alley, behind Lonnie's place. I was—

Wait. Who was with you? Anyone who can back up your story?

It ain't no story, man. It's the truth. My uncle an' his lady know . . . but they dead. And . . . and the only other ones who could back me up ain't gonna do it.

67

Why are you so sure?

'Cause one of 'em dead, man.

Dead?

Yeah. And two be up in the hospital. And another one . . . well, I don't know who he is, but he ain't gonna help me any.

Why not?

'Cause he a cop, that's why. Jus' like the others.

You mean four police officers know where you were? Is that what you're saying?

Yeah. Well, it was four of 'em in on it, I think. But at least three I seen. 'Cept one of 'em dead.

Sal Coletta.

Right.

Damn. And his brother? James, is it?

It's Jimmy, far as I know. The one still up in the hospital.

Okay, and another one whose name you don't know?

Right. An' then there was one, like, out in front I think, but I don't—

Marlon, when the shooting happened, what were you doing in the alley?

It was a car there, an' I was . . . I was unloadin' some shit outta the trunk o' one car and into another.

Some shit? What kinda shit? Drugs, you mean? Heroin? Cocaine? What?

Coke, man. Bags and bags of it. My uncle had made this deal with the cops. It was a lotta shit, man. A whole lot.

And whose car were you taking it from?

It was a unmarked police car, man. One of the cops had pulled it up in the alley. The other one, he had opened—

What other one? Who?

The one they be callin' Jimmy, man . . . the dude still up in the hospital? . . . he had opened up the trunk, so Lonnie could check the shit out, man. Then him and two cops went up in the crib, and I was movin' the bags into Lonnie's car, with that Jimmy one watchin' me. I was almost done, man, an' then I heard some shots from upstairs.

And what did you do?

I didn't do nothin'. I didn't even close the trunk shut. I was, like, scared, man. Then this here Jimmy, he told me don't go nowhere and he run up the steps. I mean, I stood there like a second and then I tore ass down the alley and outta there. They bust me on this an' it be my third strike, man. I be up in the shithouse till I be dead, an'— Anyway, that's it, man. That's all of it.

Yeah. Well, that's . . . uh . . . that's a lot. But we need to go over it again, okay?

Yeah, awright man, but first I gotta go to the baffroom again.

CHAPTER

14

BY THE TIME I GOT HOME it was dark and the storm had spent itself. I'd rewound the tape and sat there in the Forest Preserve for a long time, then listened again and sat there some more. After that I ate a supper I didn't taste at a restaurant I hardly noticed, then rewound the tape again, but didn't play it. It wasn't going to get any better.

The iron gate to the Lady's drive was closed and chained, which it never was. A woman stepped out of the shadows, though, and unlocked the padlock and opened the gate. It was Layla, the Lady's graduate whom I'd met the night before. I drove through and parked the Cavalier half under the wide eaves of the coach house. Farther down the drive, at the Lady's house, the shade was up in one of the attic windows, where I'd never known the shade to be raised before. I stared up, and even though I couldn't see into the darkness beyond the glass, I could feel another graduate sitting up there, staring back down at me.

There was a message on my answering machine from Barney Green's secretary. She'd done a computer search and found an antiques dealer in San Francisco who might have a lead on an Expulso toilet bowl. In the meantime, she said, I better get a plumber to install a substitute. I took a few Polaroid shots of the tank and wrote down the measurements the dealer needed. I'd mail them in the morning.

I threw out the pizza, fretted and moped over a bag of pretzels and at least one beer too many, and went to bed. An hour later, I got up and trudged down to the bathroom in the garage for what I hoped was the last time that night. On my way back up the stairs, I finally came to a decision.

There was only one reason to go ahead with my petition. That was to prove that I couldn't be frightened into dropping it. If I stayed with it and there was a hearing, there'd be testimony about the shooting, its devastating effects on several families, and my continuing refusal to obey the supreme court and cooperate with the police investigation. I was thoroughly convinced now that a hearing would bring the cops' involvement in a drug deal out into the open. Put Jimmy Coletta under oath and he'd tell the truth.

That's why they were trying to bully me into dropping my petition. And Maura Flanagan had told Clark Woolford that if intimidation didn't work, I might not survive for there to be any hearing. Meanwhile, though, Flanagan was pressuring Woolford—bribing him, in fact—not to contest my reinstatement. But why?

With no contest, I'd still have to show I was rehabilitated, but there'd be no testimony from any cops. So there'd be no need to kill me. Maybe Flanagan was trying to do me a favor. Yeah, right. On the other hand, maybe she had her own reasons for not wanting testimony about the shootout at Lonnie Bright's.

There'd be statute of limitations and evidentiary problems, but three people had died—Sal Coletta, Lonnie Bright, and Lonnie's girlfriend, Fay Rita Jackson. So even if the cops hadn't started the shooting, the killings occurred in the commission of a felony, and they might all face felony murder charges. And there's no statute of limitations for murder.

Seeing a bunch of crooked cops get busted wouldn't be so bad, ordinarily, but Jimmy Coletta's being one of them made it a different story. At the very least, he might lose his police disability benefits. Now that I'd met the man, seen him in action with those kids in wheelchairs, I didn't want to take part in pulling him down, even if back then he'd been as guilty as the others.

That was reason enough to drop my petition.

So the hell with my goddamn ego and proving how tough I was. I'd call Renata the next day and tell her to withdraw my petition. That was the right decision, no doubt about it, and I fell asleep as soon as I hit the bed.

But then, eight hours later, I got the call about Yogi.

CHAPTER

15

THE CALL WAS FROM A DETECTIVE at Area Four, Violent Crimes. Lieutenant Theodosian. I didn't ask, but he spelled it for me. Then he invited me to come in for an interview.

"What about?"

"You know a skinny little dark-skinned fella with straggly braids?" he asked. "Hangs around the parks?"

"You got anything else?" It was a struggle to keep my voice level. "I mean, lots of people hang around lots of parks."

"This one does some sort of yoga or something . . . when he's not busy panhandling. Ring any bells?"

"Does he have a name?"

"I don't know."

"I . . . uh . . . I don't suppose you could ask him, huh?"

"No. I don't suppose we can."

"Damn." I didn't say anything more. I couldn't.

"I wanna talk to you. I'd like you to come down here."

"You mean Area Four? That's way out on the West Side."

"Kedzie and Harrison," he said. "But I'm not there. They got contractors in, tearing up and rebuilding the whole second floor, so I'm temporarily at Eleventh and State. Ninth floor. Makes it nice and convenient for you." He paused. "I wanna talk to you."

"I know," I said. "But that guy you mentioned, the 'little dark-skinned fella,' from the park. So, what happened to him?"

"It's an ongoing investigation. I'm inviting you. I don't

think you need a lawyer, really. But, you know, that's up to you."

"And what if I don't accept your invitation? Maybe I got a better offer or something."

"Ah, yes." There was an audible sigh, reminiscent of Stefanie Randle, in fact. "Well, I suppose then a couple of us would drive up there. In that case maybe you *would* need a lawyer. I don't know." He inhaled, maybe smoking a cigarette. "So, you comin' in?"

"It's six o'clock," I said. "You still be there in an hour?"

MAIN POLICE HEADQUARTERS at that time was still just a mile south of the Loop, at Eleventh and State. The rain had started in again, but just a drizzle, and it was too early for much traffic, so I made good time. I parked in a lot at Eighth and Wabash and locked my Beretta, along with the padded envelope with the tape of Marlon Shades's statement, in a steel box I'd had welded into the trunk of the Cavalier. It's always a worry, leaving a gun in the trunk of a car, but I sure couldn't take it into the police station and I wanted the goddamn thing handy. I walked to Eleventh Street, then a block west to State.

It was an old eleven- or twelve-story rectangle, and could have been designed by the same architect who did the equally ugly public housing highrises that ran along State Street three or four miles to the south. The First District police station clung like a barnacle to the north end of the building at ground level, and had its own separate entrance. Up in the main building, besides the offices full of department bureaucrats, there were still a few dingy misdemeanor courtrooms. The city was just finishing up a brand-new facility farther south, and with any luck this one would be torn down soon.

A uniformed cop stood guard beside a podium just inside the door and wanted to know where I was going. I told him. Clout must have gotten him this soft job. He was grossly overweight, and had a .357 Magnum in his holster and an unfriendly attitude that matched how I felt, perfectly, so I gave him a wink and a peace sign and went through the metal detector.

The elevator had to be fifty years old, and smelled like bleach mixed with cut-rate cologne. When I stepped off there were signs hand-printed on white cards taped to the faded gray wall in front of me. I followed the arrow on one of them to a closed door with a frosted glass window that had the words *Internal Affairs Division* painted on it. Taped to the wall beside the door was another white card that said *VIOLENT CRIMES* in very large letters, as though they were proud of it.

I thought maybe there'd be a big open area filled with desks and balding men in shirtsleeves hunched over their telephones or pecking at typewriters with index fingers. But there was just a small reception room with six wooden chairs and a russet-haired, Hispanic-looking woman, fortyish, behind the counter. She scowled at me as though she'd been working there all her life and I was the first person who'd ever dared come through that door.

"Hate to intrude," I said, "but I received an invitation."

"You one of the new guys?" She rhymed the last word with dice.

"Nope. I'm here to see one of the old guys." I rhymed it the same way.

"Ah." She picked up a ballpoint pen and held it poised over a sign-in sheet on the counter. "Name?"

"Theodosian."

She looked up at me. "No, honey. I mean *your* name."

"Oh. Well then, Malachy P. Foley. Here to see Lieutenant Theo—"

"Hey Lieutenant!" She leaned toward an open doorway to her left. "Someone to see you," she called. If anyone answered I didn't hear it, but she turned back to me. "Have a seat. He'll be out in a minute."

"Great," I said, and sat down on an uncomfortable wooden chair. Two or three minutes went by. "Um . . . got anything for customers to read?"

She smiled then, and looked very pretty all of a sudden when she did. "That's a joke, right?" she said.

"Yeah." I smiled back. I didn't feel like it, but you never know when you'll need a friend.

"Because most people come in here don't read much." She leaned down behind the counter, seemed surprised at what she found, and came up with a newspaper and a magazine. "Let's see. Yesterday's *Sun-Times*, and last month's *Playgirl*."

I took the *Sun-Times*. "Don't wanna get busted," I said.

She put the *Playgirl* back where it came from. A phone rang and she answered it while I paged through the paper.

There was nothing in it about anything I was interested in, because my interests had narrowed down to Yogi—what happened to him, who did it, and why.

"Malachai?" I recognized Theodosian's voice, but I didn't look up. "Malachai?" he repeated, rhyming the final syllable with "sigh," like it was a name he'd read in the Bible. He came out to my side of the counter.

I turned to the sports page.

"Hey you!" He was right in front of me now. Dark brown shoes stuck out from the cuffs of tan slacks, and were polished to a high gloss, but one of the shoestrings had broken and been tied back together with a clunky-looking knot. "Your name Foley?" he asked. "Or you just come in to check up on the White Sox?"

"Foley it is," I said, and finally looked up at him. "But it's not Mala-*kai*. It's Mala-*key*, as in *Key*-stone Cops." I put the paper on the chair beside me. "Which you would already know if we were on a first-name basis, Lieutenant Theodosian."

"Jesus." He shook his head, more resigned than angry, like someone who had to put up with bullshit of one sort or another on a daily basis. "C'mon this way."

He was six feet tall, medium build, with sharp, handsome features, deeply tanned skin and dark eyes. His jet-black hair was slicked back and he looked like a dealer in an upscale casino—except he looked smarter than that somehow. He wore a dark blue shirt and a bright yellow tie, no coat. I followed him through an opening at one end of the counter and then through the doorway. Still no big room full of desks and detectives in shirtsleeves, but a hallway with tiny offices on each side. We went into the third one on the right.

There was an old metal desk and a couple of chairs and a file cabinet, and a computer that looked sort of embarrassed to be there. One huge, sooty, double-hung window that probably didn't open anymore looked west across State Street. There was a housing development there, on what had been an abandoned railyard twenty years ago or so, until developers got cheap financing based on their solemn promise to include housing for poor people in the mix. If there were any poor people inside that walled community now, they left at sundown.

"Have a seat," he said, so I did, and he went around to the other side of the desk and sat down, too. "You're not a suspect. At least not so far. I just want to know what you know about this man." He took a black-and-white photo from a folder and slid it across the desk.

It was a head-and-shoulders shot of Yogi. He was lying on his back on what looked like a sidewalk and his dreadlocks were spread out around his bruised and swollen face like a halo. His eyes were closed, and his mouth was closed. He looked almost serene.

I pointed to a blotch on the concrete near his left ear. "Blood?"

"Yes." He took a fingernail file from his desk drawer, and went to work filing the nails of his left hand. They didn't look as though they needed it.

"He's dead, isn't he?"

"Do you know him?"

"Beaten to death?"

"Do you know him?" He stayed busy with his nails, and didn't look up at me.

"Not really. I've seen him in the park a couple of times. Downtown, near the Art Institute."

"What's his name?"

"I don't know. Where did you find him?"

"He know your name?" He started in on the nails of his right hand.

"How would I know whether he knew my name?"

"You'd know if you told him."

"I don't recall ever telling him my name."

He laid the fingernail file on the desk between us, then took a card out of his folder and slid it across, lining it up carefully beside Yogi's photo. "This your business card?"

I stared down at it. "It says 'Malachy P. Foley, Licensed Private Detective,' and that's my phone number, so it's a good bet it's one of my cards. Of course, anyone could have something like that printed up. Where'd you get it?"

"The victim would have—"

"The victim? He was beaten, then?"

"You thought he got those bruises from a heart attack, maybe?" When I didn't answer, he went on. "He'd have known your name if you gave him one of your cards, right?"

"That's a reasonable inference," I said. "Look, I don't think I ever saw the man before a couple of days ago. I've talked to him two or three times in the park. I gave him money when he said he was broke. That's about it." I paused for a second to think, then added. "Oh, and I think I saw him a couple nights ago walking through the Metra station—the Randolph Street underground station—but he was wearing a sport coat, and shoes, too." I tried to stay close to the truth, mostly because it might have been Theodosian's man I'd run into in the station.

"Did you give him one?"

"One what? Oh, one of my cards? No."

"I think you did. That card was found in his pocket. How do you suppose it got there, Mala—Mr. Foley?"

"I don't know how, Lieutenant." I stared at him. "I don't even know that it was in his pocket. All I know is you say it was. And with all due respect, I—"

"Shut up!" He swiveled around and looked out the window for a few seconds, then turned back to me. "Turn the fucking thing over." I reached for the fingernail file and used it to flip the card over. "That your printing?" he asked.

"No." I stared down at the card and read the words aloud: " 'Use your head, asshole. Or there's more to come.' " I looked up at Theodosian. "What does that mean?"

"I thought maybe you could tell me," he said.

I thought maybe I could, too. But I didn't.

I just stared down at Yogi's face and shook my head. Theodosian was talking, but I couldn't really hear what he was saying. Yogi probably couldn't really hear what I was saying, either, but I was telling him anyway, right then, that I'd changed my mind again. The message on that business card wasn't a message to Yogi; it was a message to me.

When I called Renata later that day, I wouldn't tell her I wanted to withdraw my petition. I'd tell her I wanted a motion to set the matter for a hearing at the earliest possible date . . . and I wanted a little publicity about it.

CHAPTER

===

16

THEODOSIAN HAD RUN OUT of questions. "For now, anyway," he said, "but keep yourself available."

"Find any prints on that card?" I asked.

He stared at me. "We'll talk again," was all he said, and five minutes later I was back at the Cavalier.

I sat for a few minutes to calm myself down, then headed over to the Kennedy and went north, just as I had the previous afternoon. But this time I veered left at the Edens Junction and didn't get off until an exit near O'Hare Airport. From there it was a short drive to Carl's Gun Shop. The sign in the window said: *Sales To Licensed Law Enforcement Officers Only.* I knew Carl, and if I'd wanted to buy a gun I could have. But I was headed for the pistol range in the rear.

I HATED IT. Hated the noise and the acrid smell, hated the weight of the ear cups, hated the pop-up targets with silhouettes of people on them. Hated the swagger and bravado of so much of the clientele, the talk about weapons and ammo and stopping power; and the talk about freedom and being willing to stand up—meaning to shoot people—to preserve it. Hated most that I was a regular there and everyone took it for granted I fit right in . . . and that maybe they were right and I fit in all too well.

But if I'd been sticking to things I really wanted to do I'd never have petitioned for reinstatement to the bar, and never have met Yogi in the first place. For that matter, if I'd gone with what appealed to me years ago I'd have given up Marlon Shades when the court ordered me to. He would have gone to jail for a long, long time—and taken a few bad cops along with him. That didn't happen.

So, like it or not, I fired my practice rounds until my arm was heavy and numb and my head ached. It's the price paid to make something difficult seem easy, effortless. Like the piano. It's a great kick to play, and every so often see someone nod and smile in remembrance of better times, but the cost is the hours sitting alone, going over and over the same old phrases. *"Long, hard practice make the difficult look easy,"* Dr. Sato preaches. *"So sure you must love practice."*

So sure I did. I loved it all—noise, smell, targets, ear cups, and even my fellow shooters—and I put in another forty-five minutes with my left hand, and then went for lunch with a couple of guys named Gene and Eddy who'd been beside me on the firing line. They were off-duty cops from the suburbs and had no idea who I was, at least not when they told me they knew this great place for lunch, right nearby.

I LOCKED THE BERETTA BACK IN THE TRUNK and we walked to a tavern a block from the gun shop. It was hot and dark inside, crowded and heavy with cigarette smoke. The bar ran from the front to the rear along the wall to our left and a row of booths along the wall to our right. In between, about a dozen round tables took up the center of the room, most of them occupied. It was a raucous crowd for that time of day, and it would have been way too loud in there even without the jukebox blaring.

I knew at once the place was full of cops and cop groupies—and not a great place for lunch at all, not for me. The booth nearest the door emptied out, though, just as we came in, so we grabbed it. If Gene and Eddy noticed I chose the bench seat on the side of the booth with a view of the entire room, and sat on the outside end, they didn't show it as they slid into the seat across the table.

A tired-looking middle-aged woman with an ample bosom and too much red dye in her hair showed up at once. She swiped halfheartedly at the table with a gray rag, and took our orders. We all picked burgers—the alternatives were Polish sausage and pizza by the slice—and Gene and Eddy ordered two bottles of Miller Lite each.

"You have any nonalcoholic beer?" I asked.

"O'Doul's," she said.

"Fine, but just one." The waitress left. "On the wagon," I explained, then added, "again," and tried to look like I knew it wouldn't last long this time, either.

The jukebox pounded out the Supremes, who explained why "You Can't Hurry Love," while the three of us traded opinions on various types of hollow-point rounds and how big a mess they made inside the human body.

"Don't know how you can drink that shit," Gene said, when the waitress set down my O'Doul's. A Miller Lite drinker, that Gene, and a real connoisseur.

"I tried it once," Eddy said. "Tastes like alligator piss." Then, as the waitress turned to leave, he said, "Say, Miss?"

She turned back.

"Would you wipe this spot . . . here?" Eddy held his two beers by the necks of the bottles in one hand and tapped his other index finger on the table in front of him. He was on the inside, near the wall, and the woman had to lean in deeply to wipe up a ring of liquid she'd missed before.

"Thanks." Eddy grinned as he watched her walk away. "Nice tits," he said.

"Jesus," Gene said. "She's twenty years older than you, man."

"Didn't say I wanna fuck her. Just she has nice tits." Eddy

82

sucked on his beer while the jukebox moved on to Tina Turner, wondering "What's Love Got to Do With It?" "Either o' you guys ever bang a redhead?" Eddy asked.

Must love practice, was Dr. Sato's advice. Not: *Must love fellow practicers.*

"Alligator piss reminds me," I said. "I got this cousin in Florida who wrestles alligators at a tourist place. He told me how one time he had his arms wrapped around this male alligator from behind. Standing up, you know? The spectators are clapping and cheering, and all the sudden the damn thing—" I stopped in the middle of my lie, because a man sitting at the bar had swiveled around . . . and we recognized each other simultaneously. "Shit," I said.

"Huh?" Eddy said. "You mean the alligator crapped on his—"

"No," I said. "I mean I shoulda got the hell outta here when I thought about it."

In the several years I'd been coming to Carl's I'd seen Richard Kilgallon on the firing range quite a few times—but always managed to avoid him. He still looked much as he had the day I'd showed up at the station to surrender Marlon Shades—but without Marlon. Curly black hair, even features, about six-one, and overweight. Not huge; just maybe thirty pounds too much, evenly distributed.

He was a good-looking guy—good enough six or eight years ago to snag Stefanie Randle—but he had a soft look, and my guess was he knew that. Maybe some part of him knew, too, that the effort to take off the extra weight wouldn't be worth it, because the softness started deeper than that. So he papered it over with meanness.

Too late now to slip out the door. He was already headed our way. The stubby glass he carried was filled with ice and a clear liquid. Water? The odds were a thousand to one against that; and equally high against its being his first of the

83

day, given the exaggerated care with which he maneuvered himself between tables on his way over.

"Well, well, well," he was saying, "now I know what stinks," and the volume and tone of his voice cut through the babble in the place. "I *thought* I smelled something rotten." The conversations around him died away, as though a carpet were unrolling out from him toward the corners of the room. "Like a dead possum or something."

By then even Tina, still questioning the relevance of love, went into a final fade and was gone. No new tune replaced her and I stared up at Kilgallon—right beside our booth now—and wondered if someone had pulled the plug on the box.

Kilgallon glanced around and seemed suddenly aware of how everyone's eyes were on him. Center stage, and I guess he decided to give it his best shot.

"Always thought you two were coppers," he said, looking at Gene and Eddy. He drank half his drink and set the glass down between Gene and me. Resting his palms on the table, he leaned low enough so I couldn't miss the automatic hanging in the breakaway holster under his jacket. "Musta been wrong, though," he added. It was vodka he was drinking. It *does* have an odor.

"You're not wrong, partner," Gene said. He smiled, but he was nervous. "Now why don't you just go back and—"

"Then what're you drinking with this piece o' shit for?" Kilgallon nodded my way.

Gene's eyes widened. "What're you—"

"Nice to see you, too, Richie," I interrupted. I'd called him that when he'd been watching his friends "interrogate" me about Marlon Shades, and had found out right away he didn't like it. "Your glass is half empty."

"Shut up," he said. "No one's talking to—"

"Or is it half *full*?" I lifted the O'Doul's and poured it out, poured it into Kilgallon's glass. "But hey, Richie, it's *completely* full now." I kept on pouring, and the liquid overflowed the glass onto the table and ran—it was my lucky day—right toward Kilgallon.

He just stared, didn't even move, until the running stream of cold liquid hit his hand. Then he straightened up. "What the fuck are you—"

"Just tryin' to help, Richie boy." By then the O'Doul's was gone and I'd grabbed one of Gene's Miller Lites—the full one—and poured it out, too. The stream was more of a river now, pouring over the edge of the table onto the floor, and would have splashed on his shoes except he instinctively stepped backward.

"They're right about you." Killgalon spoke quietly now, almost under his breath. "You really *are* out of your mind."

"People say that," I said. Conversations were resuming all around the room. Probably most people couldn't see what I'd done, but they saw Kilgallon step back from the table, and saw us talking more quietly.

He shook his head and started to turn away.

"Kilgallon," I said. He turned back. "I'm gonna find out who killed that little guy from the park." He stared, looking genuinely confused. "Just tell everyone," I said, "that I know most of what happened that night at Lonnie Bright's. And I'm gonna find out the rest of it."

"I don't know what your problem is," he said. "But you—"

"I *am* the problem," I said, "And there's only one way to stop me."

Kilgallon stared at me for a couple of heartbeats, then turned and wound his way back to the bar.

"Jesus," Gene said.

Eddy stared at me. "You *are* crazy, man."

"Maybe just a little," I said, and stood up. I fished out a twenty to give it to Gene. But just then the waitress showed up, carrying a tray with our burgers—in three little red plastic baskets lined with thin waxed paper—and cottage fries. I grabbed one of the baskets. "Gotta run," I told her, and put the twenty on the tray. "Take another beer for Gene out of here and keep whatever's left. Sorry about the mess."

I took my lunch, plastic basket and all, and left the tavern. That whole spilling thing was dumb, maybe. But when a small, innocent man gets beaten to death, just for helping you out, it *can* make you crazy. Besides, it impressed the hell out of Eddy and Gene.

So it was Friday afternoon and I was back in the Cavalier. I stopped at an Amoco station for a fill-up and a can of Pepsi and ate my lunch in the car, parked beside the self-service air machine. It was a surprisingly good burger, on dark rye bread with Cheddar, not too greasy. Actually, I'd ordered a plain bun . . . and no cheese. But it was tasty, nonetheless.

I left there and headed north on River Road, with no idea what to do until eight o'clock that night when I'd show up at Miz Becky's Tap and bang around on the piano for a few hours and drink lots of nothing but ginger ale and coffee, and keep a careful eye out for any strangers who seemed overly interested in me.

If any showed up, they'd probably be men, not unlike the two men in the dark blue Bonneville that had been behind me, usually two cars back, all day—ever since I left the coach house that morning for police headquarters. They'd picked me up again when I left the gun shop parking lot, and they'd driven by a couple of times—never looking my way, of course—while I was eating what must have been Eddy's cheeseburger and fries.

CHAPTER

═══

17

A CELL PHONE WOULD HAVE BEEN HANDY, because I knew just the person to call about the two goons following me. But so far I'd managed to avoid the damn things, and avoid one more monthly dribble out of my so-called budget.

I could have had a more expansive budget, of course, but I'd have had to abandon my game plan . . . and *work* for a living. As it was, I had enough money for whatever I wanted, as long as I stuck to what I *really* wanted, which didn't include a lot of stuff, and a house to store the stuff in, and a security system to keep the stuff from getting stolen. Most of it I'd never use, and most of what I did use would probably be to do things I didn't really want to do, anyway.

My system—Barney Green called it "complete liquidity"—might have had a lot to do with Lynette Daniels having gone off to Taos. The thing is, I owned just about nothing, not even a credit card. The Steinway upright was mine, but all the other furnishings and appliances came along with the coach house I leased from the Lady. I did own my clothes, such as they were; and the Beretta, a nifty little semiautomatic handling .22 LR cartridges in a seven-round magazine. But that was about it. I called the Chevy Cavalier mine, but really I leased it from Barney, or from some trust he owned or controlled or something.

Complete liquidity. Or call it *freedom*, maybe. I got by.

Anyway, not having a portable phone, I kept driving and watching for a public phone in just the right sort of place. Nothing was turning up, though, and with the traffic signals and all the starting and stopping, I was afraid the two guys in the Bonneville would get bored and drop off. So I changed course and headed back south, and finally found what I was looking for, just south of O'Hare airport. It was a pay phone at the far end of a huge, half-empty supermarket parking lot, with plenty of empty space surrounding me and the Cavalier. The Bonneville stayed down at the other end, where all the cars were parked, and that suited me fine. If I was wrong about who'd sent the two men, I'd want lots of room between me and them after I hung up.

I punched out the number I wanted and, halfway through the second ring, someone picked up.

"Yeah?" A man's voice, one I didn't recognize. "Who's this? Whaddaya want?"

"Good afternoon to you, too," I said. "My name is Mal Foley and I'd like to speak with Mr. Hanafan."

"Yeah? An' what makes you think Mr. Han—" There was a silence while the man's brain was probably shifting gears. "Ain't no Mr. Hanafan here, so—"

"Breaker wants to fuckin' talk to me, asshole." You have to speak the language. "You don't tell him it's me, he'll shove a pick handle up your—"

"Hold on." There was silence then, and finally he spoke again. "How does he know you're who you say you are?"

"Tell him it's about a blue Bonneville and a couple of friends of his that used to ride around in a Jaguar till all the windows got broken out. Tell him—"

"Foley?" A new voice.

"Hi, Breaker," I said. "How's the porn business?"

"How'd you get this number?"

"I'm a private detective. Sneaking around, invading people's privacy, that's what I do for a—"

"Fuck that shit. What do you want?"

"Uh-uh, it's what do *you* want? You send a couple smoothies like Mick and Fat Wilbur to tail me, you gotta know I'll spot 'em."

"They're not that bad. They do fine with the ordinary asshole," he said. I seldom knew, with Breaker, what to believe and what not to.

"I must be extrordinary," I said. "So, what is it you want?"

"A meeting."

"Why?"

"I got something to tell you," he said, "and you're gonna be glad I did."

This time I knew not to believe him.

Breaker called his boys in the Bonneville and they led the way, sticking to side streets once we got into the city. Fat Wilbur drove like the trip was a tryout for an action flick, with Mick slouched beside him—probably napping. I fell behind a few times because stoplights and school crossing guards slowed me down. They always waited, though, which they didn't have to do. I knew the way.

Breaker's place was still the warehouse on the near west side. But a new sign said his cover now was wholesale flowers, not the fruit and vegetable business he'd been hiding behind the last time we'd had dealings. In front of us a huge overhead door rose up, and I followed the Bonneville out of the midafternoon sunshine and into the building. The door rolled down on its tracks behind us. It was very dark, until I remembered to take off my sunglasses, and then it was only slightly better.

I stepped out of the car and into a huge cavern where the air was laced with the pleasant smell of flowers. Different kinds of flowers, that much I could tell, even if I couldn't pick one scent from another out of the mix. Lilies? Maybe roses? And something that smelled green, like pine branches. The effect of the mixture of fragrances was strangely relaxing, physically soothing.

Maybe it helped keep Breaker sane—if you could call him that. He'd carved his own little niche in the city's underbelly, and survived by keeping a comprehensive book on anyone who might help him or harm him, by watching his ass with a vengeance, and by having not a hint of a conscience to bother him.

I stood there beside my car. The cavern was an indoor trucking dock, over half a block long, with a concrete floor and brick walls. There were lots of windows, about twenty feet above ground level, but they were painted over and the only light came from the occasional bare bulb hanging from the ceiling, another ten feet above the windows. At the far end of the building, workers scurried around, unloading flowers from a truck—about the size of a UPS delivery van, but painted white.

Mick and Fat Wilbur got out of the Bonneville and we all stood and waited. Nobody said anything. Then, up on the wall to our right, a door opened. A man stepped out onto a small landing at the top of a set of iron steps, like a fire escape, maybe one and a half stories up. The stairway had no railing at all—not on the steps, not even around the landing by the door.

The man looked down at us. He was tall, broad, and very dark skinned, as dark as Yogi . . . or as Yogi had been. He turned and disappeared back through the door, leaving it open. I took that as an invitation and started toward the stairway.

"Stay right there." That was Mick. His voice was as mean and thin as he was, and when I turned around I saw a little revolver in his hand.

"Hi," I said.

Mick didn't move a muscle, but Fat Wilbur grinned at me. He was obese and had thick black hair so loaded with grease that it stuck together in clumps, one of which kept falling over his forehead so he had to push it back—about every thirty seconds—and try to stick it to the mess on top of his head. You had to love a guy like that. "I seen you trying to keep up with me," Fat Wilbur said. "You're sure one pussy of a driver."

The best I could think of was *Takes one to know one*, so I kept my mouth shut. Instead, I turned around and walked toward the iron stairway again.

"Hey!" Mick called. "I said don't move!"

"Actually, what you said was 'Stay right there.' " I kept walking. "I guess you could shoot me and then explain why to Breaker, since he's the one wants to see me." Mick was no genius; but he wasn't stupid enough to pull the trigger, either. Besides, I'd done him a little favor once, right on this very spot, and he wouldn't have forgotten.

Just then, though, the black man came out the high door again, and down the steps, wielding a hand-held metal detector as though it were a Star Wars wand. I stood still as he came up to me and ran the wand up my back from heels to head, down my front, up the inside of one leg and down the inside of the other, and finally once around the perimeter. He found my pen, my sunglasses, my belt buckle, my keys, and the change in my pocket. He even found a paper clip in my cuff.

I told him the clip was especially impressive and he seemed pleased.

"Thing can fuck up your credit cards, though," he said, waving the wand.

"Not to worry."

He followed me up the steps. I kept the back of my right hand in light contact with the brick wall beside me. The steps were wide enough, but the lack of a railing between myself and wide-open space was disorienting.

The door at the top was a metal door, with a peephole, no window. It opened from the inside with a panic bar, like a theater exit, and if you happened to be on the platform and someone inside pushed the door open hard enough, you'd be swept right off the platform and onto the concrete floor below. Just now, though, the door stood wide open.

Set into the wall to the right of the door was a picture window with one-way glass, so that Breaker could stand in his office, himself unseen, and look down over the entire space, from this end to the end where the white truck was being reloaded now, with boxes. I had no doubt Breaker was looking at me through the window. I paused on the last step before the metal-runged platform. "So," I said, talking over my shoulder to the man behind me, "do I go on up and in?"

"Why the hell else you think the door's open?"

"Maybe so Breaker can smell the flowers?" I said. "Or maybe—"

"Hey, Foley!" That was Breaker. "Get your ass in here!"

"I went up and into his office. The black man didn't follow me in. He just closed the door behind me. If he went back down the steps, I couldn't hear him.

I looked around. "My God, Breaker," I said, "you've re-decorated." He was off to my right, sitting behind a desk made of chrome and polished wood. He had a phone to his ear and was writing something on a legal pad on top of the otherwise empty desk. He didn't say anything into the phone, and he didn't answer me. "I mean, not just redeco-rated," I went on, "but remodeled, rebuilt. Or does the place just *look* bigger? Fresh flowers, matching sofa and chairs, in-direct lighting, wood paneling. Damn, even some windows. Must be fluorescent lights behind them, though, right?"

He still didn't answer, but gave me an irritated, why-don't-you-shut-up-a-minute glare and waved toward one of two leather chairs facing his desk.

"I mean, where are the metal chairs? The cement floor with the gray paint chipping off? What happened to all the crap piled everywhere?"

"Goddammit, Foley!" he said, holding one hand over the phone mouthpiece and pointing at the chair again. "Sid-down!"

"Oh," I said, "thanks." But instead of sitting down I took a few steps on the thick carpet. "Actually, I think I liked it better the old way. It was more . . . *you*, y'know?" At a wet bar in the corner, in a cabinet above the sink, I found rows of spotless glasses. I tried the cabinet below the sink and it turned out to be a refrigerator. "Aah," I said, taking out a bottle of beer, "Moretti. Some things haven't changed." I opened the bottle with the tail end of a corkscrew I found in a drawer and turned back to Breaker.

I hadn't heard him set the phone down, but when I turned around he was leaning back in his executive's chair, hands clasped behind his head, staring at me. Breaker himself seemed one of the things that hadn't changed. Still the same half-ring of thick white hair, from ear to ear around the back of his head, and the same bald dome. Still the same round, monklike face. Still the patch over the right eye. And still the same gray, mean, decidedly *un*-monklike left eye. He didn't look a day older than he had . . . what was it? . . . two years ago? Three? "You look good," I said.

"Yeah? Well, you look like shit."

"I must have an honest face," I said, staring down at the man on the Moretti label, "because I *feel* like shit."

He lowered his hands from his head and leaned forward across the desk. "That little prick from the park, he a friend of yours?"

"How do you know about that? What do you—"

93

He cut me off with a wave. "So, a friend of yours."

"I barely knew him."

"But still, a—"

"OK, OK. Sort of a friend. He was helping me. I liked him, goddammit, and I'm gonna find out who killed him."

"What?" For an instant he looked surprised, but then he asked, "Who'd you talk to at Eleventh and State?"

"Guy named Theodosian. Violent Crimes investigator. He's the one told me about Yogi."

"Theodosian's an asshole."

"You probably say that about all your cop friends. He seemed—"

"He's a goddamn prick." He slid his cup around on the desktop, then looked up at me with a solemn, sympathetic smile, like an undertaker. "So, anyway, you planning on goin' to your friend's funeral?"

"I . . . I hadn't thought about it." That was the truth.

"When people die, friends go to their funerals. Dress up in suits; pay their respects; pray at the graveside." He stared at me. "Shit," he added, "did you even ask about a funeral?"

I couldn't believe he was saying these things. "Jesus Christ, Breaker, you may *look* like Friar Tuck, y'know? But you're not my fucking spiritual guide, or whatever." I drank some beer, amazed at how pissed off I felt. "Like I said, I haven't thought about it. If someone has a funeral for him, maybe I'll go."

"I wouldn't plan on it," he said.

"Why?"

"Nobody's gonna arrange him a funeral."

"Why? Because he was homeless? No money to bury him?"

"You hadn't thought about it, huh?" He leaned toward me and smiled and there was no more monk now; just the mean bastard he was. "You never even thought of making sure your friend got a funeral."

94

I stood up. "I'm on my way."

"We been through this routine before, Foley." The mean smile disappeared. "The door's locked. You go when I say you can."

I dropped back into the chair. "Look," I said, "where we going with this? What do you care? And how do you know someone won't give him a funeral?"

"All I know is a funeral would be very unusual," he said, "because the little shit ain't *dead.*"

CHAPTER

18

To prove his point, Breaker called the morgue. There'd been no cadaver matching Yogi's description delivered there in the last forty-eight hours.

"Last I knew he was at County Hospital," Breaker said. "Critical but stable."

"Theodosian showed me a photograph."

He shrugged. "What? A picture of a guy who'd been beat up? Unconscious, maybe. Not dead." He leaned forward across the desk. "You said Theodosian met you at Eleventh and State. Why was that?"

"He said Area Four's got temporary space there, while they're remodeling Harrison and Kedzie."

"Uh-huh. See a lotta cops around while you were there? Suspects? Witnesses?"

"No." I shook my head. "But they're starting to empty the place out. Moving into the new central headquarters on the South—"

"I know. But I mean right there in that so-called temporary space. You see any suspects screamin' about their fuckin' rights? Any victims' relatives in hysterics?"

He was right. There should have been some activity. I thought about it and realized Theodosian let me assume Yogi was dead, but never really said so. After that, I didn't argue with Breaker anymore.

I asked how he knew about my connection with Yogi in the first place, and all he said was he'd been paying attention to me ever since he'd learned about my petition for reinstatement. "That was a couple weeks after it was filed," he said. "Seems like a horseshit idea." He paused, then added. "I don't figure you bein' happy as a lawyer."

"Not a world-beater of an idea, I agree." I spoke from across the room, where I was pulling a second Moretti from the refrigerator. "But I was a pretty good lawyer once."

"Good, bad, whatever. I said I don't figure you bein' *happy* as a lawyer. There's a difference. You're not . . . Hey, bring me a cup of coffee." He waved at a coffee maker on the counter by the sink. "It's decaf and it tastes like piss, but the doctors—"

"I don't serve coffee," I said, and returned to my chair with my beer. "And you told me all about your bad heart a long time ago."

His face reddened, but he heaved himself to his feet and went for his own coffee. He was maybe five-ten, thick-necked and stocky. Gray wool pants, white shirt open at the neck, suspenders; no belt, no tie. He looked like a guy who might run a wholesale flower business. "See what I mean?" he said, tearing open two packets each of fake sugar and fake cream. "How you gonna be happy as a lawyer? Too many rules. Too many people to suck up to."

"You probably won't be able to test your theory, anyway. Chances are good I won't get the license back."

"Chances are good you won't even survive, you keep on the way you are." He sat down behind his desk again.

"None of us survives, Breaker. Not in the long term."

"Don't give me that 'long-term' crap. I'm talkin' *short*-term."

"What do *you* care, anyway, whether I live or die?"

"Did somebody say I cared?" He shook his head. "But like I said, it's interesting . . . so I'm watching." He sipped his decaf and frowned in distaste.

"What do you want from me, Breaker?"

"You keep asking that," he said. "Why does it have to be

97

about me? Maybe I just don't like to see a guy chasin' his ass around in stupid directions."

"Uh-huh. And maybe Philip Morris doesn't want kids to smoke till they're twenty-one. And maybe the Muppets aren't about selling toys and cereal. And—"

"The Muppets? Jesus, how can anyone be a cynic about the goddamn Muppets?"

"Forget it," I said. "What were you gonna tell me that was gonna make me happy?"

"I told you already. The little guy from the park . . . he's still alive. That was it."

I didn't believe that was it. I'd seen his surprise when he found out I thought Yogi was dead. But I let it go. "Thanks for the news." I stood up. "And the beer."

"Sit down, asshole." He seemed more exasperated than angry.

"Ah," I said, and sat down. "So what is it you want from me?"

"I can help you get your license back."

"We already agreed that's a bad idea. What is it you want from me?"

"Your friend—Yogi or whatever—even if he doesn't die, somebody beat the shit outta him."

"What is it you—"

"Shut up, for chrissake, will you? I'm gettin' to it."

I stared at him and suddenly couldn't see the bastard I'd been talking to. I saw an old man, a tired old man who wanted something but couldn't ask for it without telling me first what he could do for me.

"I'm giving it up," he said, and I could barely hear him.
"What?"

"I said I'm giving it up." He sipped some of his decaf. "Retiring. Walking away."

"Why?"

98

He stood up and walked to the sink and emptied his cup into it. Then he reached into one of the cabinets and pulled out a bottle of Old Grand-Dad and refilled the cup. He took it back to his desk, sat down, and took a long drink of the bourbon. He looked at me. "You're a private investigator," he said. "That's a clue."

"Shit," I said.

He nodded.

As far as I knew, except for maybe a late-night beer once in a while, Breaker always stuck to the regimen his doctors imposed. Now, apparently, there was no need. "What is it?"

"Prostate," he said. "Malignant."

"Surgery?"

"The heart might not be up to it."

"Who knows?"

"My doctors." He shrugged. "Now . . . you."

"Damn." On the one hand, I didn't like Breaker. On the other hand . . . damn. "Why me?"

"I don't trust anybody else." The truth, I thought, was that he had nobody else to tell. "Plus, I got a job for you. A paying job. I want you to . . ." He hesitated, as though searching for words. "There's someone I want you to put away."

"Put away? That's your depart—"

"Not kill. That's too easy on him. I want him put away, in the fuckin' shithouse, for a long time."

"Good," I said. "Then call the police, tell them what crime he's committed. They'll—"

"Very funny. Even if I had hard evidence of his crimes, which I don't, I can't go to the cops. They'd laugh their asses off and you know it. Anyway, what's important to me is he's been fuckin' over someone I care about. I'm leavin' his crimes to you."

"So why should I be interested in his crimes?"

" 'Cause I think he fucked *you* over a few years ago, too.

He's a cop. That's why I want him locked up . . . so he'll get special treatment from the gangbangers and animals. His name's Kilgallon. Richard Kilgallon."

"Jesus! I just talked to him today."

"Really? Small world, ain't it. And guess what . . . it's gonna get even smaller."

"Who's Richie been— Who do you know he's mistreated?"

"Somebody you know, too." He stared at me. "A lawyer."

"A woman lawyer?" When he nodded I knew who she was. "So," I asked, "how do *you* know her?"

"She's my granddaughter."

"Stefanie Randle? She's your *grand*daughter?"

"My only granddaughter. She doesn't know me. That is, I'm sure she knows who I am, that I live in Chicago, the . . . uh . . . kinda work I do. But we've never met, never talked to each other."

"She must be twenty-five years old. How old are you?"

"I'm . . . over seventy."

"Damn, you look young for seventy."

"You think so, 'cause at your age you think even a guy who's only sixty is old. Seventy is beyond your fuckin' imagination." He sipped some bourbon. "So I look good, okay. Physically, I feel good, too. So far. But I'm a goddamn dying man."

"We're all dying, Breaker, soon as we land on the planet."

"You say that kinda shit pretty easy, y'know? But I don't think you really feel it." He swirled the liquid in his cup. "Me? I *feel* it. I wake up with it every day."

I looked at my watch. "So you want Richard Kilgallon sent down to Pontiac or Joliet or somewhere, and you want me to see it happens, right?" He nodded. "But why should I? I can't think of a goddamn thing I want from you in return."

"My time's runnin' out. Maybe a year. Maybe a little more. But I got money I'll never get to use. I'll pay fifty grand."

"Like I said, I can't think of a goddamn thing I want from—"

"Plus," he said, "I'll take care of your friend . . . Yogi."

"He's gonna live or die. You can't change that."

"I'll get him out of County Hospital, beyond the reach of whoever it was went after him. I'll see he's protected, gets the best medical care possible. And for you, fifty grand plus expenses. I want this fucker Kilgallon on his stomach over a bench in the shithouse." He took another sip of the bourbon. "And I want him to know why."

"I don't suppose Stefanie Randle knows anything about this?"

"Hell, no. And I don't want her to know. I got a will that'll take care of her and all my kids and grandkids. In the meantime, they keep away from me and I keep away from them. But this here's different. She's a good kid. She shouldn't have to suffer from a prick like him."

"If you don't have evidence of any crime he's committed, what makes you think someone else can find something? And why *me*, in particular?"

"Because by trying to get your license back you been poking a stick in an old pile of dog shit everyone thought was dried out for good. Now it's startin' to stink again, and Kilgallon stinks along with it. He was part of the deal that put Jimmy Coletta flat on his ass for life."

"Deal?" I asked, not believing for a minute that I could fool Breaker. "What deal was that?"

"Don't bullshit me. I don't know for sure what happened that night, but Lonnie Bright was a dealer, and anyone who actually believed things went down the way the cops said musta been smoking some bad shit. I think your boy Marlon Shades told you what happened. I think if you keep lookin', you'll turn up something that'll buy one of them orange jumpsuits for Richard Kilgallon. And if you don't find it by

101

the time I feel myself slidin' downhill . . . I'll just kill the bastard myself."

He went on to tell me how Kilgallon had mistreated Stefanie Randle. Most of it could have come out of the court file and transcripts from their divorce case—a continuing saga—but Breaker said he'd only recently found out how bad it had been.

The bottom line? Kilgallon was an asshole. Supporting another woman on the side for years. Terrorizing Stefanie with emotional and even physical abuse. And now he couldn't be bothered paying support for his little girl, or even showing up for visitation days, until recently, when he started fighting like hell to keep Stefanie from taking the child out of state and starting a new life.

Kilgallon was using the legal system to be mean, selfish, and cruel—like a thousand other ex-husbands whose files you could read at the courthouse. Not to mention ex-wives. Not all of them, though, had a grandfather-in-law who listed bone-breaking, and occasional homicide, on his *curriculum vitae.*

"What if I say okay," I finally said, "and you help Yogi and then I take a walk?"

"First, I know you, and you won't do that. Second, you wouldn't get your fifty grand." He drained the bourbon from his cup. "Make it a hundred."

I stood up. "I'll think it over, call you tomorrow."

"You don't have to call," he said. "And you don't have to think it over. I already made up your mind for you. We got a done deal here."

"Look," I said, "dying or not, you can't—"

"A done deal," he said. "Did I mention the third reason you won't take a walk?"

"A third reason?"

"Yeah. I'll be gettin' your little friend the best medical care money can buy." He pushed a button under his desk some-where, and I heard the door behind me unlock. "But I'll know right where he is. You walk on me, Foley, and the little sonovabitch will be as dead as you been thinkin' he was."

So I had a done deal. With Breaker Hanafan . . . the loving granddad.

CHAPTER

19

THEODOSIAN'S CALL had gotten me going that morning before six o'clock, and I was tired. Still, it was Friday night, so I showed up at Miz Becky's and gave it my best shot. But when the piano player can't keep even the piano player awake, he should call it a night. I left about eleven and drove home. I must have been asleep in five minutes.

Maybe I dreamed about a man who met a woman who sent him on a search for a treasure he didn't really want. The man started out, but the woman disappeared, so he was about to turn back when another guy came along and warned the man to give up and go home—or else—and the man got mad and kept going. There was a funeral then, and a magician came and said he could bring the dead person back to life. But first there was this task, you see, that the magician wanted the man to do.

I may have dreamed all that, or I may have dreamed only bits and pieces of it and then put them together when I woke up Saturday morning. Either way, the man in the dream looked like a fool. I got out of bed and had to go downstairs because I hadn't gotten a plumber to install a new toilet bowl, thinking I'd just wait for an authentic replacement for my antique Expulso.

Even outside the dream, the man didn't seem very smart.

AREA FOUR HEADQUARTERS was at Harrison and Kedzie, three miles straight west of the Loop—on what people call "I-290" if they're just passing through, "the Eisenhower" if they stick

104

around awhile, and just "the Ike" if they're one of those traffic reporters with the information—always far too late—that it's jammed up from downtown out to Iowa or someplace. Along the same route, but half the distance from downtown, was Cook County Hospital. I stopped there first. I wanted to talk to Yogi, and if he wasn't there I wanted to find out whether he'd really been a patient . . . and whether he was alive or dead when he left.

The trauma unit seemed awfully busy for nine o'clock on a Saturday morning, but what did I know? People lay on transport carts or sat hunched over in plastic chairs, friends and family hovering around them, alternately comforting them and hollering complaints about how long it was taking. Meanwhile, medical staff hustled around with an apparent calmness that surprised me. Getting right to the clerk, behind the swinging door from the waiting area, wasn't nearly as big a problem as hospital administration probably wanted it to be. Even my not knowing Yogi's real name wasn't as big a problem as it might have been if the hospital had had a real name for him, which they didn't.

I described him and the clerk remembered him. She was middle-aged, with close-cropped gray hair, and seemed both sympathetic and efficient. She entered something on her keyboard, then looked up at the monitor that sat facing her on the counter between us. "He was transferred early this morning," she said, "to . . . to another facility. I can't say where."

"I'm a close friend," I said. "I'd like to—"

A cart crashed through the swinging doors, with one uniformed paramedic pushing it and another one holding an IV pole steady and trying to keep the writhing, moaning body on the cart from falling off. A tall, dark-skinned man in a white lab coat trotted alongside, ripping bloody clothing away from the patient's chest and shouting orders that I probably couldn't have understood even without the accent he had.

Right behind them came a short, very round black woman in a shower cap and a worn bathrobe. "Why you takin' that man first?" she screamed, "when my chile been waitin' almos' a hour!"

The clerk in front of me stood up. "Mrs. Horton, you aren't supposed to come—"

"Y'all *know* that ain't right. My baby been—"

"Please, Mrs. Horton," the clerk said. By then she was on our side of the counter and had one arm wrapped gently around the woman's shoulders. "Your baby will be fine. We have to take the more urgent cases first."

"Well, I . . ." The woman started to cry. "I know that, but . . ."

A security guard had arrived by then and walked the woman back out into the waiting area, and the clerk hurried back to her station. She sat down and looked up at me as though she couldn't quite remember what I was there for.

"I was saying I'm a close friend of the patient." I nodded to the computer monitor to remind her who I was talking about. "I'd just like to find out how he's doing."

"Oh, yes," she said. She looked up at the monitor, frowned, then adjusted it and tilted the screen downward. "I'm very sorry," she said, "but at the request of the patient's next of kin, no information is available."

It was a wash. She didn't ask why a close friend didn't know the patient's name; and I didn't ask how his next of kin got him transferred out without giving his name.

"Can I talk to his doctor?"

"Of course you can, sir," she said, brightening a bit. "You'll just need a signed authorization from the patient . . . or a court order."

I was fresh out of both, so I moved on.

THE BUILDING AT HARRISON and Kedzie looked to be 1970s vintage, brown brick and tinted glass, with the Eleventh District police station on the first floor and Area Four Headquarters on the second. I went upstairs and found Area Four as friendly and hospitable as any other police station I've ever been in—which is to say I'd prefer a trauma center any day.

There were cops everywhere, dozens of them, coming in and going out. Mostly in plainclothes; joking, calling to each other in loud voices. A few were women, but even so a visitor—this visitor, anyway—felt as though he'd invaded the clubhouse of a close-knit, all-male fraternity. I had the feeling any moment a couple of wet, naked guys would dash through, whooping and whirling around, snapping towels at each other's asses.

I had to admit, though, that there was work going on. It was Saturday morning, and there seemed to have been some sort of gang "altercation" the night before. Bored-looking cops kept going past, bringing in handcuffed men—most of them young, all of them black—pulling or pushing them across the tile floor and disappearing down one hallway or another. Most of the prisoners had angry, sullen looks on their faces; a few screamed obscenities to which no one paid the slightest attention.

Lieutenant Theodosian wasn't in. "Medical leave," the desk man said. "Hasn't been here for months." He consulted first a list on a clipboard, and then a large calendar taped to the counter in front of him. "Doesn't say when he'll be back."

"But—"

The phone rang and he picked it up, listened a moment, and told whoever it was that they'd have to come in and talk to a detective in person. He hung up and turned away.

"Hey!" I said.

He turned back. "You still here? I thought I—"

"You did. But I just talked to Theodosian, about a case. Yesterday morning, about seven o'clock."

"Not yesterday morning. Not here."

"No, not here. At Eleventh and State. You know, because of the remodeling. I thought it was a homicide, but turns out it was a battery."

"Remodeling?" He leaned forward and peered at me. "What case? What's the victim's name?"

"I don't know. I just—"

"You got any ID, pal?"

"Driver's license." I dug it out and gave it to him. Cooperation's my middle name.

He took my license and studied it, then handed it back. "You oughta leave now, Mr. Foley," he said, "unless you got helpful information about a case . . . or proof someone here asked you to come in."

I was fresh out of both of those, too, so again I moved on.

ACCORDING TO THE ID TAG clipped to her shirt, the name of the receptionist who'd given me the choice of a *Sun-Times* or a *Playgirl* while I'd waited for Theodosian the previous morning had been Angelica Ruiz.

I drove back to Eleventh and State. The same fat cop with the same fat .357 Magnum was guarding the entrance. "Remember me, officer?" I asked. "Yesterday morning?"

He stared. "Yep."

"I was in a bad mood," I said. "Gave you a peace sign."

"I remember."

"Sorry about that."

"Didn't bother me. I don't give a shit people wanna be assholes." So it wasn't clout that got him this soft assignment after all, it was tolerance and people skills.

"I was on my way up, yesterday, to see an investigator named Theodosian."

"If you said that I don't remember it. Anyway, what's the deal? Who cares?"

"Just making talk," I said. "Gotta go up again and see Ms. Ruiz. See if I left my . . . my keys up there."

"Ruiz worked in Internal Affairs, but she ain't up there. That floor's empty as of today. They'll be hauling out the furniture today and tomorrow. Ruiz coulda gone with IAD, or she coulda been transferred anywhere. One of the districts. Who knows? You'd be damn lucky to find her . . . or your keys."

Luck was one more thing I was fresh out of, so I went home.

About noon I called Breaker Hanafan's number, but got an answering machine. "Call me," I said. "I want to visit the patient. Until then," I added, "no deal. Period."

I hung up and called Renata. It was Saturday, but she was in her office. I told her I was going ahead with the petition. "I want a hearing as soon as possible."

"No way," she said.

"Why not? All they have to do is complete my deposition. What else is there to do?"

"They've identified six or seven people they're going to call as witnesses—mostly cops and relatives of the one who was killed that night. They want to show the effect of your continuing refusal to help identify the guilty parties."

"So," I said, "let them call their witnesses."

"But we have to depose them first, see what they're going to say."

"We *know* what they're going to say. They'll say they're still suffering and it's my fault that they can't get 'closure.' I don't want deps, just a hearing."

"I can't even think about it right now. I have a huge drug conspiracy trial starting in a few days. I simply won't be able to get to your case for at least a month. Maybe longer."

"Fine. Then I'll represent myself."

"That would be consistent," she said. "All along you've been acting like a fool."

And Renata hadn't even been in last night's dream.

CHAPTER

═══

20

I spent Saturday afternoon trying to think up a plan of action, keeping busy while I thought, though, to make sure the day wasn't a total loss.

So I worked out for a couple of hours, reminded by the shots I'd taken to the side of the head Wednesday night to pay special attention to my neck and shoulder muscles. After that I set out for a run along Sheridan Road. My route took me through the Northwestern campus, where students by the thousands had fled their dorms for the warm sunshine. The crowded sidewalks and jogging paths irritated me; or maybe all those chattering young persons in shorts and T-shirts made me feel a little lonely, or at loose ends or something. Whatever. I cut the run short.

Back at the coach house, I called the Lady to invite myself over for supper that evening, but she wasn't in. So after a shower I settled down to work out the chords for some more Cole Parter tunes from a book the Lady had given me for Christmas. That carried me through until time to head back to the piano at Miz Becky's. It was a busy night there, mostly the usual neighborhood crowd.

All in all, things went fairly well. No one showed up to ambush me or threaten me. But no plan showed up, either.

It was past midnight when I got home. I wasn't happy to see the gate unlocked and standing open, but then I spotted someone pacing the crushed stone drive. Layla. She had a cell phone in her hand, and I was certain she had a partner watching out the attic window, where the shade was still up. By the time I'd parked up by the coach house, Layla had closed and locked the gate and was headed for the Lady's house. She was talking on the phone, and didn't even look my way as she went by. The Lady was taking this security stuff pretty seriously—and I was glad she was.

"Excuse me," I called. "Layla?"

She stopped and turned around. She wore a pants outfit like the coveralls the guys wear at Caesar Scallopino's body shop, except hers was sort of shiny purple in the darkness—and she filled it out differently. "Yes?" she said.

"Nice night, isn't it?" The first conversation I'd taken a stab at that day since Renata told me I wasn't very bright.

"Uh-huh." She slipped the phone into a little holster on her hip. "I guess so."

"I mean, just feel that breeze off the lake," I said.

She looked around as though the idea of feeling cool night breeze were new to her. "Yeah," she said. "It's cold." The conversation was really picking up.

"Hear that?" I pointed off to the east, beyond the Lady's house. "Those are waves on the lake, lapping up onto the shore."

"Right," she said. "I have to go now." She turned and started up the drive.

"Hold on a minute," I called. She stopped and faced me again. "Would you ask the Lady to call me? I mean, if she's still up."

"I'd ask her, but she ain't . . . I mean, she *isn't* home."

"Oh?" Surprising. The Lady's big on operas and concerts and the like, but was generally home by this time. "Well, whenever she gets home. I don't care how late it is. Tell her it's very important."

"Um, sure," she said. "Soon as I see her." She smiled and

112

walked away. Not much of a smile, but the best I'd seen in forty-eight hours or so. Things were looking up.

THERE WAS ONE MESSAGE on my answering machine. "About visiting your friend," Breaker said, "call me. And use your cell phone."

I punched out his number and he answered right away. "I don't have a cell phone," I said. "I'm calling from my kitchen."

"Shit. Don't you know your line might be—"

"So might yours," I said. "This one, at least, I've checked out as well as I can. Besides, I'm not doing anything illegal. Are you?"

"Fuck you. Maybe you don't care who knows where your friend's at."

"You said he'd be in a protected place." I paused. "All I need from you is assurance that I won't have trouble getting past the protection."

"That's taken care of. But you don't want me to tell you where he's at," he said, "not on the phone."

"You don't have to tell me," I said. "I already know." I explained how, with the trauma unit clerk busy with a tearful mother, I'd swiveled the monitor and read where Yogi was going. "It's right there in his chart. Anybody could get at it."

"Some strings I can pull, but I ain't no miracle worker. Fuckin' chart's confidential. Even the cops ain't supposed to see it, not without a subpoena or some goddamn thing, and I'd be notified." He paused, then exhaled loudly, as though blowing into the phone. He must have gone back to smoking as well as alcohol. "So you got to it," he said. "Congratulations. That's why I got you workin' for me."

"I'm not working for you."

"Whatever," he said. "Anyway, if they find him they ain't gonna get to him."

113

"But I will?"

"I said you'd be there tomorrow at . . . well, I guess it's today. Sunday, anyway, at ten. You can make your own arrangements if you go again. Now I gotta—"

"Listen up, Breaker. I got something to say."

"What?"

"Anything happens to Yogi—from you, I mean—and I'll be coming after you. You know that."

"Yeah? Well, I guess you forgot. I got worse than you coming." He hung up.

CHAPTER

21

By NINE O'CLOCK Sunday morning I'd eaten breakfast and was headed out to visit Yogi. First, though, I went over and twisted the old-fashioned key-turn doorbell in the center of the Lady's front door. I waited several minutes and finally the door opened. It was Layla, in a baggy sweatshirt and faded jeans. She had her hair wrapped up in a towel. She looked great.

"Well?" I said.

"Well what?"

"Is she home? She didn't call me."

"I guess you mean the Lady," she said.

"No, dammit, the Queen of—" I stopped, shaking my head at my own behavior. "I'm just . . . worried about her. She was to call me no matter how late it was. You said you'd tell her."

"I said I'd tell her as soon as I see her. And I will."

"What?"

"If you need her, she'll be home this afternoon, some time around three."

"I don't *need* her, for God's sake." I sounded angry, and didn't want to. "I just want to know she's okay."

"And now you know." She waggled her fingers at me. "Bye-bye, now." She closed the door.

I turned and went to the Cavalier, but before I got in I glanced up and saw movement at the attic window. One of Layla's partners, with a phone to her ear, was looking down at me. I waggled my fingers and mouthed "Bye-bye, now," then got into the car and slammed the door, hard.

' Why the hell would she think I *needed* the Lady, for chrissake?

THE VILLAGE OF LAKE BLUFF was right where its name said it should be, on a bluff overlooking Lake Michigan. At its north end it looked like a thousand other tired towns that have dug in and hung on for their lives to the flanks of military bases—in this case the Great Lakes Naval Training Center—but were now being weaned away, and gradually finding themselves the better for it.

Much of the rest of Lake Bluff, though, had the feel of Lake Forest, its woodsy and decidedly affluent neighbor to the south, and that's where I found Inverness Lane. The sign said it was private and had no outlet. It was the road to Inverness Clinic, once the estate of some clan who centuries ago owned half of Scotland or something, and it wound its way through what seemed to be—but wasn't, of course—a deep forest. I pulled over once and found tall chainlink fences, hidden from the road behind the trees and undergrowth, topped with barbed wire. There were paths behind them where guards, and maybe dogs, could patrol.

I drove on and pretty soon came to an ancient stone gatehouse. Twenty yards short of that the road split into two narrow lanes, one passing on each side of the little building. Low stone walls lined the pavement, to keep cars on the road. As I pulled up to the red-and-white-striped crossing gate in the right lane, two men in uniform stepped forward, one on either side of my car. They looked awfully official and not awfully friendly, although they'd obviously been trained to keep smiling. They were armed.

I lowered my window and looked up at the one staring down at me on my side of the car. The brass tag on his shirt said *B. Mackey.* He was young and cocky, and he irritated me without saying a word.

"Yo," I said, seeking the contemporary touch. "Nice fort. Expecting an attack?"

"No, sir." Still smiling, but a shift of mood in the eyes. "Identification?"

I held out my driver's license and Mackey took it with him into the gatehouse. He returned almost immediately and handed me a small square envelope, sealed. He didn't say anything, just waved me through with a sort of snappy, military-type gesture.

The gate went up as he did that, but I didn't drive forward. I put the shift lever in *Park* and carefully slid my finger under the flap of the envelope and opened it. Inside was a note-card, gray, to match the envelope. The writing on the card was in the same male script as my name on the front of the envelope. It said, "The patient is in Room 207. Please show this card." It was signed, "Robert Tyne, M.D."

A car pulled up behind me and sat there while I studied the card on both sides, then returned it to the envelope and put it in my shirt pocket. Then I took it out again and—

"Excuse me," Mackey said. "You goin' in, or not?"

I looked up. "Not until I get my license back."

His smile vanished. "You get that back on your way out."

"Oh," I said, "I don't think so."

By now there were two cars behind me. To get in, they'd have had to back up quite a distance and then use the exit lane, which had one of those spike things to puncture the tires of people who went the wrong way.

The other guard tapped on my passenger window, but I ignored him and he came around to my side. His tag said *G. Costigan* and his smile was still in place. "Except for our regular visitors, sir," he said, "that's the rule."

"Why not call Dr. Tyne," I said, "and verify that I'm the

117

exception?" I hit the door lock button, raised the window, and switched off the ignition.

The driver behind me tapped a short, polite *beep* on his horn. Mackey walked back to talk to him. Costigan smiled and glared at me at the same time, a nifty trick, but finally turned away and spoke into his cell phone. Then, saying nothing further to me, he walked into the gatehouse and came back with my license.

I passed through, with the cars behind me following, and we made a little parade: past more trees, around a bend, and then a straight shot toward a brick drive that circled a fountain in front of Inverness Clinic.

It was a large, castle-like building of gray stone, in some places three stories and in others four, with turrets and ells and wings seemingly stuck on here and there at whim. A bit overdone, in my opinion, but surrounded by well-tended lawns with curving walks and flowerbeds, shrubbery and scattered oak and maple trees. There were stone benches and lawn chairs and little round tables with umbrellas that hadn't yet been opened for the day.

It was the sort of place people with money, and a desire to shun publicity, could go to try to recuperate from . . . well . . . whatever. Booze, dope, women, men, depression, plastic surgery. Maybe all of the above. Maybe even old age, although that might be tough to recuperate from.

It was ten o'clock on a sunny, cool Sunday morning and there were no people in sight—other than the guy in a White Sox cap and a black windbreaker sitting at one of the round tables and turning the pages of a newspaper. Him I figured to be there on Breaker's nickel.

The members of my little parade all parked in a lot off the circular drive and I let the people from the other two cars go up the wide concrete steps and inside ahead of me.

I DON'T KNOW WHY I expected Robert Tyne, M.D., to be a pain in the ass, but I did—and he wasn't. He said he was glad he was there to meet me. He'd just completed his rounds and had been about to leave. Tall and thin, with wavy brown hair going gray, he was distinguished-looking rather than handsome, along the lines of Prince Charles.

We met in what looked like the living room of a large, comfortable home, complete with stone fireplace and stuffed furniture and large leaded windows letting in lots of morning light. I showed Tyne the card with his note, and he introduced himself as the medical director of Inverness Clinic. I wondered who owned the place, and what sort of connection the owners might have with someone like Breaker Hanafan.

"How's he doing?" I asked.

"You mean Johnathan Doherty," Tyne said. "That's the name we're using, since we don't know his given name."

"He can't tell you his name?"

"I think he could, frankly, but he hasn't. He came out of his coma late Friday night, before his transfer here, but hasn't done much talking at all. He did say he loves the name Johnathan Doherty. Recognized it at once as 'long for John Doe.' He calls me 'Doctor Bob.' "

"So he's thinking all right."

"I'd say so. Seems quite happy, too. He's in good condition for being beaten as badly as he was, but he's not out of the woods yet. We'll be running more tests tomorrow and . . ." He looked at his watch. "Why don't I just take you to him?"

We walked side-by-side up a wide curving stairway. "So," I said, "this place is what? Like a nursing home?"

"We're licensed as a hospital. Unique, really. Equipped to handle a maximum of thirty patients; but we've got, or can

119

quickly get hold of, most everything any metropolitan medical facility can offer."

On the second floor we turned right and went from the lushly carpeted landing into a hallway where our heels clicked on a floor that looked like oak, but was probably some synthetic.

We passed a couple of closed doors and I asked, "These are patient rooms?"

"Exactly. Six on this floor; three of them occupied right now. We keep the doors closed, whether the rooms are occupied or not. Our clients—we call them clients—value their privacy."

"Is there a nursing station somewhere?"

"In a sort of alcove at the far end of the hall." He pointed. "Actually, staff all come and go through an entrance at that end. Visitors generally come this way. Feel free to look around a bit, but right now . . . here's his room." He stopped at a closed door, then turned to face me. "I want you to feel assured that, whatever else happens, your friend is getting the finest medical care available."

"Thanks," I said, but not certain what he meant. "Let's go in."

Tyne knocked on the door and pushed it open a crack. "You have a visitor," he called. Then to me, "I have to go now. I'm sure you can find your own way out."

"Thanks." I went inside and Tyne pulled the door closed behind me.

It looked like another one of way too many hospital rooms I'd spent time in, with its highly polished floor and pastel painted walls. The TV set high up on the wall was turned off; soft sunlight filtered in through gauzy drapes drawn across the large window. The bed was surrounded by stainless-steel IV hangers and other poles, and a mile or so of plastic tubes and lines hooking Yogi up to various machines with little read-out screens and blinking lights.

There was just the one bed, but there were three visitors' chairs—and there were visitors sitting in two of them.

CHAPTER

22

BOTH VISITORS WERE MEN, and both rose from their chairs as I entered. I could have turned around right then and left in a hurry. I stayed, though, because Yogi was there. He was asleep in the bed, flat on his back and breathing in soft, peaceful snores, his mouth wide open. He didn't seem to be expecting anyone.

One of the men was Theodosian, the detective who'd made me think Yogi was dead, and he and his friend obviously *were* expecting someone—me. "Got delayed at the fortress gate," I said. "Have I inconvenienced anyone?"

It was Theodosian who answered. "Not today," he said, "at least not yet. We—"

"Forget it," the other man interrupted. He had the same intense look and the same wire-rimmed glasses he'd worn a few days ago, when I told him he couldn't use his cell phone in the underground train station. "No need to apologize."

"Good," I said, "because I didn't."

"Anyway," Theodosian said, "we need to talk." He nodded toward the man to his left. "This is Detective . . . uh . . . Smith. State of Illinois Corrupt Official Practices Task Force. Called ICOP."

"Delighted," I said, but neither of us made a move to shake hands. "Never heard the name 'Uh Smith' before. Is that Uh *hyphen* Smith? Or—"

"We're here on business," he said.

"Right. ICOP business. You dream that up yourself, Detective Uh-Smith?

122

He sat down and crossed one leg over the other, but he was red in the face and not as relaxed as he pretended. "*You* talk to this guy, will ya, Theo?" he said. "I don't have time to waste on assholes."

"Have a seat, Foley," Theodosian said.

I stayed standing. "I have the same time management problem as your partner here," I said. "Besides, you lied to me."

"You jumped to the conclusion that he was dead." He nodded in Yogi's direction. "I didn't correct you."

"Like I say, you lied to me."

"At the time I thought you might have stomped a guy half your size through the cracks in the concrete on Lower Wacker Drive. Now I don't think so." He shrugged. "I'm on temporary assignment to ICOP. Have a seat and see why we're here."

I sat. Theodosian angled his chair to face me, while Uh-Smith pulled a little black notebook out of his shirt pocket and studied the pages. Yogi snored on.

"So," Theodosian started, "we have a—"

"One more thing," I said. "Doctor Tyne. He knew you were in here?"

"He didn't like it, of course. Not at all. But . . . well, when we found out your friend Breaker Hanafan had—"

"He's not my friend."

"You've had dealings in the past."

"He's not my friend."

"Fine. Anyway, somehow Hanafan got the patient tranferred here, so we spoke to Doctor Tyne . . . about possible visitors."

"And he told you I'd be here today. So much for confidentiality."

"Inverness Clinic has an excellent reputation," Theodosian said. "Of course, it has to meet about a zillion state licensing requirements, you know, so . . ." He nodded toward Uh-Smith, who gave a little chuckle. "Anyway," Theodosian went on, "we thought a chat might be useful, for us and for you."

I was planning to stay until Yogi woke up on his own, anyway, so I sat there.

"First," Theodosian said, "this is off the record. None of it goes beyond this room. Okay?" He waited, but I didn't answer. "Do we have your word on that?"

"I'm listening."

"Jesus." Uh-Smith shook his head. "Do you *practice* being an—"

"I guess your partner forgot he doesn't have time to talk to me," I said, keeping my eyes on Theodosian. "Anyway, giving my word is what got me into this in the first place. I don't take it lightly."

"Put it this way, then," Theodosian said. "We'd like you to keep this to yourself."

"Fine. I understand your preference. Go ahead."

"I think you and I share a common interest." He said. "You want your law license back, and—"

"And you want to help," I said. "That's nice."

"I couldn't care less." He let my sarcasm go. "What I care about is what went down that night at Lonnie Bright's place."

"You were there," I said. "As I recall, there's even a report signed by you."

"Call like that comes in, 'Shots fired . . . police officer down,' *everyone* responds. I was a sergeant. My job turned out to be keeping cops out of there. Calm them down and send them on their way. Keep guys from fucking tripping all over each other and contaminating the scene." He seemed to be reliving the incident as he spoke. "Three or four cops shot; at least one dead. It was a goddamn nightmare. Guys running around, looking for someone to— Well, let's just say . . . emotions were running high."

"Tell me about it. I wasn't even in the picture for several days," I said, "and emotions were still, as you say, 'running high.' " I paused. "So you're saying it's still an open case, and you're working it with an undercover state dick. What is it you want from me?"

"What I really want is to know what your client Marlon Shades had to say."

"I just told you, when I give my word, I don't—"

"Right. I know." He leaned forward. "But . . . let's say your guy said something that could have gotten himself in trouble. Otherwise, you'd have advised him to talk. But maybe he didn't know anything helpful to the Lonnnie Bright case. You could at least reveal that. Besides, the client's dead, for chrissake."

"First," I said, "it's a lose-lose situation. If I say he didn't know anything helpful, everyone thinks I'm lying. If I refuse to say that, everyone thinks he *did* know something, and I get pushed even harder. Second, saying what my client *didn't* say is revealing the contents of the conversation—or close enough for me, anyway." I shrugged. "So there you have it."

"Actually," Theodosian said, "that's what I thought you'd say. So—"

"Wait a minute," Uh-Smith finally couldn't stand keeping his mouth shut. "Three people are fucking dead and we got a citizen here who can help sort things out. But no. This one's Mr. Tough Guy, and he's got his fucking *word* to live up to. Is that it?"

"Yeah," I said, "that's it. About all I *do* have in my trade is my word."

"Maybe." He stared at me. "Or maybe you're just one more faggoty freak who hates cops."

"I got no problem with most cops," I said, "homophobic or not. But my eyes have been open a long, long time. My dad was a cop and he was straight, right up to the end, and then a few bad cops fucked him over and took him down with them." I leaned in then, and poked a finger at his face. "So don't talk to me about—"

"Take it easy," Theodosian said, "both of you." He looked at his watch, and then at me. "Here's the deal. You aren't gonna tell us what your punk said. Fine. But you're stirring up a lotta shit right now. You got some people worried, and I wanna know who it is. What I want is for you to share with me anything you're learning—new stuff, not covered by the goddamn lawyer-client privilege—but anything that'll help me find out what really did happen, and close out this fucking case."

"And I get what? A certificate of good citizenship?"

"You get my testimony. I tell everyone how I understand your ethical position. I even say I respect your sticking to it—if I can say that without throwing up. I tell how you went out of your way to help the authorities this time. What I do is, I tell the supreme court that you oughta get your license back."

"And in the meantime," I said, "are you gonna tell me what *you* learn?"

"Why—" He stopped. "It's a police investigation. You know the drill."

"Of course," I said, remembering that my interest was supposed to be in my petition. "I just mean anything that'll help me get my license."

"I'll tell you anything I can."

"We got a deal," I said, thinking it wasn't much of one. "Someone sure doesn't want me to go ahead with my petition for reinstatement."

"Tell us about it."

"Well, I filed it and figured no one would pay much attention. Then one day I pick up my mail and there's a letter . . .

an anonymous letter. A threat. There was a spider taped to the paper, with its legs pulled off. The letter said that's what would happen to me if I didn't drop my petition."

Uh-Smith leaned forward. "You save this letter?"

"Why would I? It was a cowardly, chicken shit note, for chrissake. Or would it have scared *you?*"

"Jesus." His face was red again. "What kind of—"

"Forget it," Theodosian interrupted. "What else has happened?"

FIFTEEN MINUTES LATER I closed the door behind them. I'd moved on to tell them about the guy with the camera and the green Crown Vic. "Two white guys. Could have been you two."

"Could've been," Theodosian said, "but wasn't."

"After that it's Uh-Smith, here, tailing me in the train station."

Theodosian seemed surprised, but said nothing, and I went on to tell them about my broken toilet and the shit smeared on my front door; about the masked goon attacking me in the park and trying to make me eat my petition. I told them about pouring beer into Richie Kilgallon's drink. I told them Breaker Hanafan didn't know anything about any of it, but was helping Yogi as a payback to me for a debt long overdue.

There was more I didn't tell them—including about Stefanie Randle hearing Maura Flanagan tell Stefanie's boss not to file objections to the petition, and about my conversation with Jimmie Coletta. Stefanie and Jimmy were topics I wasn't ready to discuss with them yet.

Still, we were pretty close to even . . . because they left without telling *me* one damn thing.

CHAPTER

═══

23

I CLOSED THE DOOR behind them and hadn't even crossed back to Yogi's bed before a wide-bodied, no-nonsense nurse came backside first into the room, pulling a cart with a white cloth draped over whatever was on it, and asked—not unpleasantly—whether I didn't think my friends and I had spent enough time with the patient already.

"They're not my friends." My refrain for the day. "Besides, I haven't even talked to Yogi. He's been asleep the whole time."

"Yogi?"

"Mr. Doherty's nickname."

She asked me to wait in the corridor and I did. Fifteen minutes later she came out, smiling and shaking her head as though Yogi had said something funny, and warned me not to tire Mr. Doherty out, and I went back through the door.

"Hey, big mon." Yogi's voice was weak and hoarse, but not bad for a guy with a tube running into his nose and down his throat. The head of the bed was raised so that he was sitting up. "How you doin'?"

"I'm fine," I said. "But what about you? You in any pain?"

"Not so bad, uh-uh." He reached under the sheet and came out with a little push button device. "I get feelin' bad, mon, I just hit this here and the dope flow in an' the pain be gone."

"Who did this, Yogi?"

"Who gimme the button? Doctor Bob, mon, he—"

"No. Who beat you up?"

"Oh, I don' know, big mon. I don' be smokin' the shit so

much like before, mon, since I doin' the yoga thing. But, you know, sometimes I still hit the bong. Like last night . . . Thursday, Friday, whatever . . . I be floatin' along down there where they fixin' Lower Wacker an' *wham! wham! wham!* . . . an' I wake up in the County, missin' a kidney."

"What?" I'd never even asked what his injuries were. "They took out a kidney?"

"Jus' one outta two. Doctor Bob, he say they more worried about my brain waves, but everything seem okay. He say—"

"You know it's my fault this happened, don't you?"

"Don' know nothin' like that. But, hey, I be fine now. Layin' around waitin' for nurses to come give me a bath an' stuff. Not bad, hey?" He grinned and started to laugh, but that made him cough and he couldn't stop coughing and his shoulders hunched up and the pain was obvious in his face.

I just stood there until he stopped. "Have you been pressing the button for your pain medication?"

"I do the yoga thing, mon." He was short of breath. "Try to pay attention. Feel *inside* the pain."

"So, you should just suffer, because—"

"Plus the dope make me sleep all the time."

"Well, you were sleeping when I got here this morning, anyway. So what's the difference?"

"Not sleepin', big mon. Pretend sleepin'. Hear everything." He grinned again, which brought on more coughing, and more pain.

"Please," I said, once he'd settled down. "Don't laugh."

He closed his eyes for a moment, then opened them. "You help the fuzzies, big mon, like they say?"

"Maybe."

"They lookin' to catch someone from what? Couple years ago? That be way over, mon. Why not catch *today's* bad guys?"

"Five years ago. Cops killed a drug dealer and his girlfriend

129

in a shootout at his place. But three cops were shot, too. One died; one can't walk. They think there was another shooter involved, and they want the missing shooter. They wanna know what happened."

"Sometimes people find out what happened from long time ago, they find out they don' wanna know."

I stared at him. "They . . . they don't think that way."

"They say you help them, they help you get your license back." He reached for his water glass. "What license that?" When he swallowed, he winced in pain.

"Hit the damn button, Yogi."

"I hit it when you leavin'," he said. "So what license?"

"Law license."

His eyes widened. "Hey, mon. You a lawyer?" He seemed disappointed.

"I was. They took away my license."

"Shoulda made you happy, mon."

"What have you got against lawyers?"

"Got nothin' against nobody, big mon. You wanna help the fuzzies 'cause you wanna be a lawyer again . . . that's cool, mon. Each gotta do his own."

"I don't really *want* to help them, and I'm not sure I really want to be a lawyer again."

"But you gonna do both." He grinned, and I thought he was going to laugh, but he stopped himself. "An' peoples say I the one tink funny."

"If I help the cops, it might also help me find out who attacked you."

He seemed more amazed than ever. "For why you wanna do that, mon?"

"Because first I'm gonna tear his ass off, and then I'm gonna have him tossed in jail. That's why. I told you. It's my fault this happened to you."

130

"This here happen 'cause I be smokin' outta my brain, mon. Didn't see the fuzzies comin' up."

"What? You mean it was *cops* who did this?"

"Maybe just one, I don't know," he said. "But I'm on the ground and I hear the radio thing and he answer it."

"Would you recognize his voice again?"

"Prob'bly. But, hey, mon, I been beat up before. Fuzzies, dopies, whatev—"

"Did you know you had my business card in your pocket?"

"Nope. Where I get that?"

"Exactly. I didn't give it to you. And there was writing on the back of it. It said, 'Use your head, asshole, or there's more to come.' "

"You tinkin' someone tellin' me not to help you?"

"Maybe. But more likely the message was for me, that if I don't stop trying to get my license back, more people are gonna be hurt—same as you."

"So it's easy like pie, mon. You stop, and nobody get hurt."

"But you've *already* been hurt. You lost a goddamn kidney, for chrissake."

"Doctor Bob say I got another one an' it be workin' fine. Pretty soon I be workin' fine, too, somebody go to jail or not." He smiled. "So you go on do whatever. But 'cause you tink it gonna make *you* feel better, big mon. Keep me outside it."

"Yeah? Well, just seeing the pain you're in pisses the hell outta me. Whoever did this . . . What about payback, or justice, for God's sake?"

He shook his head. "That justice thing, mon, that be way too huge for me. If everything gotta equal out, like on a scale . . . what I'm gonna pay? So I jus' do my yoga thing. Stand on one leg an' tink how a tree stand; tink about peace an' shelter an'—" He grimaced, then started coughing again and when it was over he grinned—or tried to. "Right now I

131

tinkin' 'bout the dope button, big mon." He took a deep breath, and another shudder of pain went through him. "Feel kinda wore out, you know?"

He told me what to push to lower the head of his bed and I did that, and put his water on the bedside table. He closed his eyes and I turned to leave, but then thought of something. "Hey, Yogi," I said. "Those cops say anything interesting before I got here?"

He opened his eyes. "Uh-uh. They only here 'bout three, four minutes before you. They don't speak nothin'. I feelin' they don't like each other, but they don't speak nothin'." His eyes closed again. "Gotta go now."

I stared down at him for a while, and then left. What had happened to him was my goddamn fault, and I wasn't about to let it drop. I'd find out who did it, and see they paid in full.

I guess I'd have felt better about my mission, though, if the victim himself hadn't just dismissed the whole concept as a dumb idea. And not just dumb, but selfish, too.

CHAPTER

24

I WENT DOWN TO THE FIRST FLOOR and back to the parlor where I'd met Dr. Tyne, and where I remembered there was a telephone on an end table by a sofa.

I called Breaker Hanafan. "Great work," I said. "Only you and me and the cops know where he is. Of course, since it's you and the cops I'm mostly worried about, you—"

"I know, I know. That Theodosian guy and some state dick. Tyne called."

"Dr. Tyne called *you?*"

"Not me directly, for chrissake. The guy's on the up and up . . . so how would he know me? Anyway, he called. Said they put a lot of pressure on him in a hurry and he couldn't turn them away." He paused, and by his breathing I knew he'd taken a drag on a cigarette. "So," he finally said, "you talk to them?"

"Uh-huh."

"What'd they want?"

"They know you're the one got him moved, and they figured we were working together somehow. They called you my friend."

"What'd you tell 'em?"

"I denied everything, especially the 'friend' part. I'm very convincing when I'm telling the truth."

"What's their interest in . . . in the patient?"

"I don't think they have any. It's me they wanted to see." I waited, but he didn't press for an explanation. "So," I said, "you'll be moving him somewhere else?"

"Move him where, for chrissake? I mean, we're not talking here about paying off some neighborhood quack to patch up a bullet hole and keep his mouth shut. Recovering from major fucking surgery like he had means you need a real hospital. At least for a week or so." He paused and I imagined him lighting up a new smoke. "Christ, it's always the same. You spend a goddamn fortune and you still don't have the control you want."

"So anyone who flashes a badge can walk into his room?"

"Not anymore. Not unless they got a warrant, or unless you or I agree. We got that straight with Tyne. The loony little son of a bitch is no good to me dead. My people will still be around, and hospital security will be right there, too." He paused. "I'll get him moved again as soon as Tyne says okay. Trust me."

"That's asking a lot," I said, and hung up.

TRUST WOULD NEVER BE A WISE REACTION to anything Breaker Hanafan said, terminal illness or not. Still, I knew he'd be anxious to move Yogi as soon as he could. Inverness Clinic was a legitimate hospital and he'd get good care there, and be relatively safe from whoever had beaten him up. But Breaker would want him more secluded, more easily available, to make sure I lived up to our so-called done deal.

Time was short, and I'd have to get busy and show I was taking a run at getting Breaker's former grandson-in-law shut up in the slammer. One possibility was to press forward with my reinstatement petition and force Jimmy Coletta to testify about what happened the night he was shot. He'd tell the truth—I was convinced of that—which might put Kilgallon away and make Breaker happy. It would probably help identify the bastard who'd kicked the shit out of Yogi's kidney, too; and I wanted to know that, even if Yogi couldn't care less.

Except I didn't *want* to force Jimmy to testify. I really felt he was a changed man—something I hadn't seen that often—and I couldn't come up with any good reason why the new Jimmy should go down, just because the old Jimmy deserved it. I certainly wasn't about to destroy the man, and the work he was doing now, just to make Breaker Hanafan happy. I wanted to keep Breaker's hands off Yogi, sure, but I had no more interest in bowing to that son of a bitch than I had in bowing to the Supreme Court of Illinois.

It was a dilemma with no apparent solution, and I had nothing to do but slog ahead and figure it out as I went along.

CHAPTER

25

FOUR COPS HAD DROPPED in on Lonnie Bright the night my client Marlon Shades was out in the alley loading dope and the shooting began. One of them—Jimmy Coletta's brother, Sal—had been carried away in a body bag. Two others, Richard Kilgallon and Jimmy, I'd recently spoken to. That left one more. His name was Arthur Frankel, and on my way home from Inverness Clinic I'd go through Highwood, and there was just a bit of a chance I'd find him there.

Frankel had resigned from the police department exactly a year to the day after he'd gotten his medal from the mayor for "outstanding courage and devotion to public safety" in connection with the Lonnie Bright shooting. He'd suffered a through-and-through to the thigh, which wouldn't have been so bad if the slug hadn't nicked the femoral artery. He could have bled to death on the scene, but stayed conscious and kept pressure on the wound until the paramedics got there. With a graft from one of his veins to repair the artery, he came out nearly as good as new.

When he left the department he went into the restaurant business with his cousin. The cousin had been a lawyer, but—at about the same time Frankel was being honored— the cousin had admitted to taking fifty thousand dollars from the trust account of a brain-damaged client. He'd agreed to a voluntary disbarment, paid the money back, avoided indictment by an eyelash, and gone to work tending bar in a place down the street from Wrigley Field.

I'd learned all this from Barney Green—who wouldn't

have told me his sources if I'd asked. He even knew that when Frankel and his cousin bought their first restaurant they came up with a pretty big down payment. That kept their monthly nut small enough so they could meet their other expenses and still make a bit of a profit.

Two years later they were incorporated and owned two trendy restaurants on the near north side. Then one night the cousin rode his jet ski full throttle into a concrete breakwater a quarter-mile out from the North Avenue Beach. Whether it was the alcohol or the coke—the autopsy showed plenty of both—that tipped the scales and got him out there on the lake in his street clothes at three in the morning on the Fourth of July, didn't make a whole lot of difference. Either way, he left Frankel sole owner of the business.

Now there were four restaurants: three in the city and one that just opened in Highwood, a town with about five thousand residents and, from all appearances, a restaurant for every five of them.

I GOT THERE ABOUT twelve-thirty. The place was called *Le Chantier*, which probably had something to do with its country French motif. I didn't really expect to find Frankel, but I elbowed my way through the crowd gathered in the waiting area inside the front door and stepped past the hostess station.

A wide archway opened into the main dining room. Maybe the food was supposed to be French, but just then they were serving a Sunday brunch buffet and the place smelled pretty much like Denny's to me. Way more expensive, though. Crowded, too; and noisy, with chattering women in chic outfits and carefully casual hairdos, and confident-looking men in sport coats and slacks. The hostess collared me right away and I talked her into getting the manager for me.

137

His name was Edward Alberto, and he walked me away from the dining room and into the bar, where the only customer was a man sitting alone nursing a bottle of MGD and watching a ball game on a TV with the sound turned way down. The two bartenders were busy, though, making Screwdrivers and Bloody Marys for the waitstaff to carry out to tables. Alberto was nice enough—a fortyish, dark-haired guy in black pants and a sort of blousy white shirt—but he'd never heard of any Arthur Frankel, and wondered in a New Jersey accent whether there was some reason why I expected the gentleman to be dining there just then. "If it's an emergency," he said, "we could page—"

"No need." I showed him my PI license. "He's . . . uh . . . a witness to an automobile accident. He owns this restaurant." Alberto looked surprised, but didn't say anything. "And since the place is new, I thought he might be hanging around, making sure you and your people had your act together."

He frowned. "The staff here is hand-picked by me, and well-qualified. We . . ." He let it go, apparently realizing I wasn't being critical. "As far as I know," he said, "*Le Chantier* is owned by AF Enter—"

"See?" I spread my hands, palms up. "AF. Arthur Frankel. Simple."

He nodded. "I suppose AF could be someone named Arthur Frankel," he said, "but I've certainly never met him. I was hired by a couple of people who called themselves 'corporate staff.' So, you—"

"Would Mr. Alberto come to the front, please?" A pleasant female voice came over the intercom. "Mr. Alberto to the front?"

"Sorry," he said. "Probably someone claiming they made a reservation . . . which they didn't, of course."

He turned and headed toward the restaurant's entrance

and, figuring I might as well go home, I started after him.

"Hey, buddy." The call came from behind me.

I thought it was one of the bartenders, and turned around.

The guy sitting at the bar raised his bottle. "I'm buying," he said. He stayed seated, but I guessed him to be about five-nine; overweight, maybe one-ninety-five. He had light brown hair—and not much of it—combed straight back over the top of his head.

"Thanks, but . . . it's a little early for me." Not exactly true, but I wanted to get home and catch the Lady as soon as she showed up.

"Don't wanna waste a trip, do you, pal? Thought you wanted to see the owner."

"Yeah, but . . ." And then I read the look on his face. I walked his way, nodding back over my shoulder. "That guy's good," I said. "The manager, I mean, he really—"

"That's 'cause he was telling the truth." He kept his voice low. "Why would I ever wanna talk to the guy who runs my restaurant?"

CHAPTER

26

HE NODDED TOWARD THE STOOL beside him, and I sat down.

"I'm Art Frankel, all right," he said, "but how the hell would I pick out a good restaurant manager?" he said. "Maybe I know a *little* more than Ditka and M. J. and those other guys that just sell their names to places." He smiled a little. "But mostly I leave the hands-on stuff to the experts."

The bartender came over and rattled off the names of a dozen beers and I ordered a Berghoff.

"So," he said, "I'm the owner, and so far no one here knows me, and I like it that way."

"My lips are sealed," I said.

"And you know what else?" he went on. "I haven't witnessed an automobile accident in over five years." He waited while the barman came back and set down my beer, then added, "So, you wanna show *me* that ID?" That last came out with a whole new tone of voice—pure, one-hundred-percent cop. Somewhere along the way, the smile had disappeared, too.

I'd been lied to so often in the past few days I was gun shy, but right then I recognized him as Frankel for sure, even if he looked a little different than when I'd seen him collect his medal four and a half years earlier. I handed him my PI license and he stared down at it for a long time.

"Remember me?" I finally said.

He looked up. "I recognize the name. I don't think we ever met." He handed the card back. "Guy lets a cop killer walk, I don't have much interest in meeting him. Except . . . in a dark alley, maybe."

"Lucky for me we're in a classy place like this, then."

"If you say so." And that's when—if he'd had as little interest in me as he claimed—he should have sent me on my way. But instead, he asked, "So what is it you want? Am I s'posed to tell you how much I admire a man who keeps his word?"

"I'd like to know what happened that night at Lonnie Bright's house."

"Read the police reports."

"I have, over and over. I still wonder what happened." He didn't answer, so I went ahead. "The reports say Sal Coletta and his partner, Richard Kilgallon, saw Lonnie in front of his house arguing with an unknown male. Lonnie was waving a gun around. Then you and Jimmie Coletta happen along. When Lonnie and the other guy see two unmarked squad cars, the other guy splits and Lonnie runs inside. Sal Coletta and Kilgallon follow him in. You wait by their car on foot to call for backup if it's needed, while Jimmie drives around to the alley to cover the back of the house." I paused. "That's how the reports say it all started. I pretty much have the story memorized."

"Uh-huh."

"And so far it's total bullshit, on its face." He leaned toward me, but I raised my hand to keep him quiet. "That doesn't bother me. A little bullshit when you're out hassling a known drug dealer? All in the public interest." I drank some of the Berghoff, while Frankel lit up a Lucky Strike. "Except, according to the report, things took a bad turn. All of a sudden you hear shooting from inside and you call for help and then run inside because your buddies are in there and they're in trouble. It's a two-flat and you run up the stairs and the lights

141

all go out and there's lots of screaming and shooting, and the next thing you know you're sitting on the hallway floor upstairs, squeezing your thigh to try to keep your blood inside your body. It takes a little while, but help arrives, and pretty soon the paramedics. In the darkness and confusion, you say, you never even saw who shot you, and you don't recall firing several rounds yourself."

"They said I probably squeezed the trigger involuntarily when I was hit."

"Right. That happens sometimes. Anyway, you and Jimmie are taken away and the dicks and technicians are left to go over the scene, and they find bodies and blood everywhere, and slugs embedded in bone and flesh and plaster—most of them too flattened out to be tied to any particular gun. Kilgallon tells them he was behind Sal Coletta when they went in, and the two of them had ordered Lonnie to stop, but when they get upstairs he suddenly turns on them and opens fire. And there's another man up there, too. He's hidden in shadows, but he has a weapon. And Lonnie's girlfriend has a gun, too, and . . . Well, by the time it's over there was a lot of shooting and if the specifics are confusing and unclear the dicks don't find that surprising. The man in the shadows was gone and Kilgallon, the only one on the scene still standing, was in a pretty bad mental state."

"You wouldn't understand that if you've never been through it."

"But everyone *did* find it understandable," I said. "The assistant state's attorney on Felony Review that night went over everything and signed off on it. And the police department found its officers' use of lethal force justified." I sipped a little more of my beer. "Funny, though. Everyone knows Lonnie's a dealer, but all they find is a burner and a tiny bit of crack. Otherwise, no drugs. And no money."

"Funny?"

"Yeah. I mean, no drugs, no money, and still for some reason Lonnie turns and fires on a couple of cops who just chased him inside his own house, when he knows there are more cops outside."

"Who can say what a fucking dopehead like Lonnie would do? They found the shit in his system."

"Just a trace, though, and it seems such a crazy thing to do." I watched Frankel as I spoke, but he just kept switching his gaze from the TV to his cigarette and back, with an occasional glance at his watch, as though he was bored. "Anyway," I went on, "there aren't many houses on the block that aren't boarded up and abandoned, but the coppers do their best. There's page after page of go-nowhere interviews of potential witnesses, and pulling in snitches and known associates, but nobody turns up clue one about the missing man. And that's about it for the police reports."

"Not quite," he said, still not looking at me. "You left out the parts you didn't think were important—like Sal Coletta going down with three slugs buried in his chest, and his brother Jimmy shot in the back . . . left to sit on his ass the rest of his life."

"Right," I said. "Also the part about the extra hole in Lonnie Bright's head, and his girlfriend's not being as lucky as you . . . and bleeding to death before she got to the ER."

"A dog and his bitch. They left the world a better place." He tapped his cigarette on the edge of a little foil ash tray on the bar. "The other animal got away. And if it wasn't Marlon Shades himself, Marlon could've told us who it was."

"You don't know that."

"Yeah I do," he said. "Otherwise you'd have let him talk. And if you had any balls you'd have told everyone what he said when they ordered you to, especially when they told

143

you there *was* no fucking privilege. It's people like you made me decide to quit the department. People who don't give a shit."

"You mean if I had any balls I'd have caved in and done what I was told? Instead of what I thought was right?"

"You wouldn't know what's right from your own asshole, counselor."

The conversation was decomposing pretty quickly. "I'm not a lawyer," I said, switching topics, "not till I get my license back."

"Which you're trying to do now. I know all about your fucking petition. Me and a few others already got letters from that attorneys' commission." He took a drag on what was left of the Lucky Strike, then punched it out in the ashtray. "That's why you're really here. To find out if I'm gonna testify against you."

"The question did cross my mind."

"The answer's yes. I'm gonna tell 'em how my leg's never worked right since that night, and how they oughta lock you up again and this time leave you rot till you tell what that chimpanzee said to you, so the cops can either close the case—if he was the shooter—or find the other monkey if he wasn't." He stood up. "Yeah, I'm gonna testify." He walked out of the bar, dragging his foot across the floor as he went.

Funny thing. I'd been there in the crowd when he got his medal that morning in the Daley Center Plaza. He'd been in uniform, maybe twenty pounds lighter, and he'd gone up those steps and across that temporary stage with hardly a trace of a limp.

CHAPTER

27

WHEN I GOT BACK to my place there was a message from the Lady, saying she was home, but would be leaving again at four o'clock.

Layla opened the door when I rang and led me to the parlor. I thanked her and she nodded, and I'd have sworn she gave me just the hint of a smile before she turned and left. The Lady poured me some tea.

I'd have preferred brandy, actually, but I took the tea. We both sat down and I sipped a little and tried not to make a face.

"Oh dear," she said, and stood up again. "You've never liked that tea, have you." She walked to a table across the room and came back with two fingers of brandy in a snifter—way more than she usually offers—and handed it to me. "With my apologies," she said.

"Thanks." I drank half a finger.

"You're welcome." She sipped her tea. "I understand you were concerned about me."

"Concerned? Jesus, I couldn't sleep all last night waiting for you to come home. After all, you—" I stopped, wondering why I was so mad at her. I wasn't her son, and even if I had been, what business would it have been of mine what she did? "It's just that I had things to talk over. I asked for you and . . . and then kept thinking you'd be home any minute. I didn't know where you were. At least you could have picked up a phone and . . ." I gave up and went back to the brandy.

"I should have called you to report that I wasn't coming home?"

"Well, I mean, not that it's my business what you do, Helene, but this is a bad time, you know?"

"A bad time for you, yes. And as I recall, one you specifically chose to endure."

"But you could be in danger, too. I thought you understood that. People are trying whatever they can to convince me to withdraw my petition. They jumped Yogi and ruptured one of his kidneys, and he's not nearly as important to me as you—"

"Yogi? I'm afraid I don't understand."

"That's not surprising, because you haven't been *available*, for God's sake."

She should have thrown me out on my ass, of course, but she didn't. She just drank her tea, and watched me drink too much of her brandy, too fast, and listened as I went through everything that had happened since we'd talked Wednesday night. That was three and a half days of happenings, and it took a while. I worked my way through it all very carefully, and as I did, a few of the pieces started falling together. Other things—and especially how Maura Flanagan fit into the picture—were still way up in the air. When I finally finished I stood up and started for the brandy, then realized it would be my fourth hit, and sat down again. Damn, that stuff was potent.

"I believe that's quite prudent, Malachy," the Lady said, and I knew she meant not going for more of the juice. "One thing still remains very unclear to me," she went on, "perhaps because it's unclear to you."

"What is it?"

"That supreme court justice. Why *ever* is *she* involved?"

"Good point," I said. "I was wondering that my—"

"Does she *know* any of these people?" she asked, more to

146

herself than to me. "Did she ever work for the police department? Was she married to a policeman?" She looked up at me. "Didn't you tell me, the last time we talked, that she's always been in public service?"

"What I said was she's been feeding at the public trough all her life, something to that effect. Like her family before her. She's been on the supreme court two years now, after being on the appellate court less than a year. Spent a year or so before that as a lawyer for the park district. Before that she was with O.P.S. for a couple years, and with the county and . . . Damn, that's—"

"What is O.P.S.?"

"The police department's Office of Professional Standards. The unit that investigates charges of police brutality, and the use of firearms by any police personnel."

"And that's where she was at the time of that shooting?"

"I don't know. Her name's not on any O.P.S. reports. Although . . . I'll have to check that out." I thought hard, which was a struggle, with the brandy fighting back. "God, Helene, maybe you're a jeezus. I mean a genius."

"Maybe," she said, "but I doubt it." She stared at me, then poured out a fresh cup of tea. "Drink this. I think you need it now."

I drank the tea and we talked some more. Mostly about Maura Flanagan, and how she'd been married and then gotten divorced and gone back to Flanagan, her maiden name. And how I seemed to recall reading somewhere that she was glad she'd done that because it was an Irish name, which she admitted was helpful when she ran for the supreme court against a guy named Radzinski.

Before I knew it the Lady was standing up and telling me it was getting late and she had to dress for a party at the woman's shelter she runs in Uptown. One of the residents had just gotten her GED. We said our good-byes and I left and headed down the drive toward the coach house. I remembered I'd never found out where she'd been the night before.

Not that it was any of my business.

STARTING UP THE STAIRS to my place I felt light-headed, and by the time I reached the top I was definitely dizzy. Then Dr. Sato's tea must have decided the best way to deal with the brandy was to convince my system to reject the whole mess. The plan kicked in and I had to hurry back down to the bathroom in the garage.

It was past four o'clock and I hadn't eaten since breakfast—and that was just some toast and jam—so when I finally got through with what quickly turned into the dry heaves, I was pretty washed out. Hungry and thirsty, too, but afraid to send anything down there for a while. I was supposed to play that night at Miz Becky's, but called in sick. Becky didn't seem very disappointed, and that sort of response was why I didn't blow off the gig very often.

I lay on the sofa and dozed on and off for what seemed like a half-hour or so, and finally got up and made some coffee. I was staring into my mostly empty refrigerator, pondering a supper of toast and jam, when the front doorbell rang. It would have been a good time for one of those intercom systems, but . . .

I slipped a windbreaker over my T-shirt, took the Beretta from the shoulder holster hanging on the hall tree and dropped it in the jacket pocket, and headed down the stairs. They seemed unusually steep.

It was Layla, carrying a large box with two hands. I pulled open the plateglass door and saw the words *Tag's Bakery* on the side of the box. "A cake?" I asked. "Is it someone's birthday?"

"It's not a cake," she said. "It's some supper. For you. Be

148

careful and don't spill it. It's soup. I mean, it's in a covered container and all, but . . . Anyway, there's some bread, too, and half a stick of real butter." She held the box out toward me. "Here, take it by the bottom."

"Okay," I said, taking the box, "and tell the Lady thanks."

"The Lady?" She looked confused. "Oh, you think . . ." She smiled. "She doesn't know about it. She left at four o'clock, like about three hours ago."

"What?" I looked at my wrist and remembered I'd left my watch on the kitchen table.

"Uh-huh, and the soup, I made it myself. The bread, too. I'm going to cooking school and, you know, I'm practicing." She spun around, and was gone before I could think of anything to say.

CHAPTER

28

SHERIDAN ROAD TO LAKE SHORE DRIVE, then south. The drive
along the lakefront, from Evanston to the Loop, was a pleasant one on that warm, sunny Monday.

The previous night, after I'd washed the dishes Layla
brought over and put them back in the cake box, I sat for a
while looking out the coach house window. At about eight
o'clock the Lady had pulled her big old Lincoln Towne Car
up to the gate. The woman who let her in wasn't Layla. Too
bad. I could have taken the dishes down and thanked her.
The bread had been a little chewy or something, but tasted
pretty good; and all the soup needed was a little more salt
and pepper, which I added.

Anyway, I enjoyed the drive, and wished the world were
as friendly a place as it looked right then.

At Barney Green's office a paralegal sat down and showed
me—for the third time in as many months—how to use the
computer to retrieve information about cases filed in the Circuit Court of Cook County. She was always very patient and
I'd try to look as if I was paying attention, but once the information I wanted turned up on the screen I'd lose interest
in how it got there. This time I thought I had a challenge for
her. I knew that "Flanagan" was Maura Flanagan's maiden
name, and that she'd gone back to that name when her divorce was finalized. What I wanted was her married name.

It took the paralegal all of sixty seconds: Liederbach. I could
verify it with a call to the police department's Office of Professional Standards, but there wasn't much doubt that Maura

Flanagan was the "M. Liederbach" who, as assistant administrator, had directed the O.P.S. investigation into the use of firearms by police officers at Lonnie Bright's home. It was she who, despite a police version of events that any impartial investigation would have found questionable at best, declared the use of deadly force "justified," and closed the case in just a few weeks, when similar cases dragged on for months.

The search for the unidentified man in the apartment who'd gotten away seemed to fade pretty quickly, too, while the supreme court and the media concentrated on me. Sal Coletta's widow and the whole Coletta family, among others, kept up a relentless crusade about forcing me to tell what Marlon Shades had said. They didn't know that Marlon's information was the last thing Jimmie Coletta and the other two surviving cops wanted out in the open.

For their part, it seemed neither Lonnie Bright nor his girlfriend had family or friends interested or capable enough to raise any stink. What few neighbors Lonnie had were happy to be rid of him and his drug house. All anyone wanted to say was how nobody saw or heard a thing, and how everyone wished the man who'd escaped would have been shot down, too.

Many months later, when the supreme court finally let me out of jail, the incident was out of the public mind. Marlon Shades had finally resurfaced, but he had a new lawyer by then and I never saw him again. There was no reason for me to poke my nose into the affair, even though I knew the real story hadn't been told, and probably never would be. I hadn't blamed Lonnie Bright's neighbors for thinking the cops had done a service to the community.

But Maura Flanagan Liederbach? She should have known better, and she probably did. And that was probably why—five years after she'd shut down that shooting investigation in record time—she was so worried about my reinstatement case.

Maura and I would have to chat.

CHAPTER

===

29

STEFANIE RANDLE WAS AS CUTE AS EVER, but there were dark shadows under her eyes and her shoulders sagged as she led me down the hall at the disciplinary commission.

Renata hadn't withdrawn as my lawyer, but she'd filed a notice giving Stefanie permission to talk to me directly, since Renata was engaged in trial and temporarily unavailable. So it wouldn't appear odd for Stefanie to meet with me.

When we got to the conference room she dropped into a chair and I sat across the table from her. "You're not sleeping well," I said.

"I'm not sleeping at all."

"Has your boss talked to you about my case? About not filing objections?"

"He hasn't mentioned it. But there's . . . well, something else. Something personal."

"It's your husband, right? I mean your ex-husband. He's—"

"I told you. It's personal. It's got nothing to do with your case, or what I told you."

"Richie's never shown much interest in your daughter. Missed most of his visitation days. Now, though, you want to move out of state, start a new life." Her eyes widened in surprise, and I kept going. "When he found out he started raising a stink. Suddenly he's a daddy who can't stand the idea of not seeing his little girl every week. It's bullshit, of course. He's just trying to mess up your—"

"How do you know all this? My plans have nothing to do with you."

"Maybe. But Richie Kilgallon happens to be right in the center of my case. For more than one reason. I talked to him a few days ago."

"What? About me and my daughter?"

"Actually," I said, "that didn't come up."

"But then how . . ." She poured herself a glass of water from the shorter of two carafes on a tray on the table. "He hates to be called Richie, you know. It infuriates him."

"I know. I try never to call him anything else."

"You should be careful. Richard's an angry, disturbed man." She shrugged. "But I don't think you worry that he'll hurt you, do you?"

"He's mostly a mean drunk," I said. "And no, I don't worry about it." I picked up the taller carafe from the tray. "Is this one coffee?" She nodded and I poured myself a cup. "I could make one of your problems go away, you know. I could simply withdraw my petition."

"I wouldn't ask you to do that," she said. "Not for me."

"I'm not withdrawing it, and if I did, it wouldn't be for you."

"Gee, thanks."

"At least, not mainly for you. I wouldn't mind helping you."

"And I wouldn't mind *someone* helping me, for once." She was absolutely serious. Her voice broke and she seemed about to cry. "A little help once in a while would be a nice change."

She had to be pretty far down to allow such an open display of self-pity, and I busied myself with tearing open a packet of powdered creamer—which I hate—while I thought of some way to respond. "Someone is," I finally said, dumping the white crap into my cup and stirring it around.

"What?" She looked up at me. Her eyes were wet, but she'd managed to stop short of crying. Obviously embarrassed, she

153

pulled a little pack of Kleenex tissue from her jacket pocket. "What do you mean?"

"Someone *is* helping you."

She blew her nose and dropped the tissue into a waste-basket against the wall behind her. "Really. You mean *you?*"

I shook my head.

"It's sure not my divorce lawyer," she said. "She doesn't even return my calls. Of course I haven't paid her bill yet, either." She gave a weak smile. "So, whoever this mysterious person is, I hope he knows what he's doing, and has a lot of *clout,* or something."

"I don't know that I'd call it 'clout,' but he's got plenty of power, all right. He's close by, knows exactly what you've been going through, and wants to help. He'll get the job done, too, one way or another, and you won't have to pay him. In fact, you'll be getting a lot more from him in the future."

She stared at me, obviously surprised. "You're not kidding, are you?" Then her eyes widened even further. "Jesus, Foley," she said, "you're not talking about . . . about *God,* are you? Because—"

"God?" My turn to be surprised. "Not hardly." I wasn't even sure I should have brought up Breaker Hanafan, so I shut up and sat there.

She tried to wait me out, but couldn't. "Look," she said, "you show up here unannounced and I think maybe you have some news. But all you tell me is, first, you could help me by withdrawing your petition—but you won't. Then you say some mysterious kindly being is watching and helping me, and—"

"I didn't say 'kindly,' not at all."

"But anyway, it's not you, and it's not God, and . . . wait a minute. Do you mean my—" She stood up and gave a toss of her head, fanning her hair out like a model in a Clairol

154

commercial. A great move. Impatient and sexy both. "If you're just going to play games," she said, "I have lots of work I could be doing."

"Ah," I said, "the old Stefanie." I stayed seated, searching for the right word. "Snippy," I tried. "Is *snippy* a . . . well . . . a sexist adjective?"

"You bet it is." She looked like she might slap me, but then she smiled—a sudden, genuine smile. "I guess you're not going anywhere." She sat down again. "So, what are you here for?"

"I need to talk to Maura Flanagan, and I'm trying to figure out how to do it without causing more problems. For you, I mean."

"You can't talk to her. The court will believe you're trying to influence one of its members, and have one more reason to deny your petition."

"I don't care what the court believes. I thought I established that long ago. I want to confront Flanagan with her special interest in my case, but not let her know you eavesdropped on—"

"I didn't *eavesdrop*. I overheard."

"Uh-huh."

"Anyway, she's not going to tell you why she cares."

"I said I want to confront her, not ask her. I already know what her interest is."

"You do? What is it?"

"She was part of—" I stopped. "The less you know, the better off you are."

"But I'm only in trouble if she discovers I heard her warn Clark Woolford that our office better not raise an objection to your reinstatment. I'm sure you're not going to tell her that."

"Right," I said. "But you still don't have to know *why* she's interested."

155

"Except that I *want* to know." She leaned forward. "I mean, I'm the one who let you in on what she told Mr. Woolford, so you owe it to me to tell me how she's involved."

In fact, she'd only told me because she was scared out of her wits and wanted me to tell her what to do, but chivalry kept me quiet about that. "I *owe* you?"

"Well . . ." She let the word trail off, and there was a new look, a sort of humorous twinkle, in her eyes. "You *sort* of owe me."

Maybe the look wasn't so much humorous. Maybe seductive, or whatever. Anyway, why not tell her? Maybe she could be of some help. Maybe I just felt like telling her and seeing what she thought. Lots of maybe's. Maybe I just enjoyed talking to her.

"You told me you read the police reports about that shooting," I said. "You find anything odd?"

"Actually, I focused on what happened afterwards, the parts about you and your client. How he was supposed to turn himself in and you were to take him to the police station, but he didn't show up. And then how, later, you wouldn't say what he told you. And what eventually happened to you."

"You didn't read about the shooting itself? About what happened when the police got to Lonnie Bright's house?"

"Oh, I read everything. As to the incident itself, I read the reports and I guess . . . well, my main thought was they weren't very clear. But I decided that was because, out of the four policemen who were actually there when it happened, one was dead and two were taken to the hospital. So the initial description came from whatever the detectives could get from . . . from my ex, from Richard. And somewhere in there it said he appeared to be in shock, and not entirely coherent."

"Right."

"Plus there were descriptions of bullets and shells and whatever else they found on the scene. A tiny bit of cocaine, or crack, or something." She frowned. "But you asked about anything 'odd,' so I guess what struck me was why would that man—Lonnie Bright?—why did he just suddenly turn around and start shooting at the policemen? I mean, it seemed so . . . so dumb."

"Absolutely," I said. "Dumb." Which this woman was not.

"Then I thought, since they'd seen him with a gun, maybe he was afraid a weapons conviction would send him to prison for a long time. Still, though, it—"

"Lots of arrests. No prior felony convictions," I said. "The weapon was registered. Don't forget, this was a guy who probably knew as much or more about the criminal justice system—from personal experience—than you and I. He'd have known that with a halfway decent lawyer he'd walk on an 'unlawful possession' charge."

"Then I was also thinking, since he was a drug dealer, that maybe he and the other guy—the one who got away— maybe they were doing a drug sale and the police burst in and that's why he shot."

"Cops didn't say that. And they found no drugs, no big sums of money."

"Maybe the man who got away took all that with him."

"Pretty lucky guy, huh? All kinds of shots fired. Three people dead, two wounded, and he's right in the middle of it. And still he gathers up the money, and the cocaine—or whatever—and walks away without a trace."

"So then, what's your theory on why Lonnie Bright started shooting?" She paused, then added, "Or maybe you *know*. Maybe your client told you."

"All my client knew was where he was and what he was doing when it all went down." I paused. "By the way, that's the most I've ever told anyone about what he told me." I poured a new cup of coffee, without the creamer. "My theory is that Lonnie Bright didn't start shooting at all."

"Really. But would it make any more sense for his girl-friend to start it? And if it was the other guy up there, he'd be the first one the police would shoot back at, and—"

"And he'd be dead. Right." I paused. "It wasn't the girl-friend who started the shooting. And there *was* no *other* guy."

"So, you're saying . . ." She sipped water from her glass. "You're saying the police shot first, then falsely claimed there was someone else there who got away. God, I mean, that's a really serious charge. That means they simply shot Lonnie Bright, then they all lied about everything. I mean, when they finally got statements from the two officers that were wounded, they said pretty much what my . . . what Richard told them."

"Right," I said. "After they'd seen all the reports already. And maybe even had lawyers of their own. Would they lie?" I shrugged. "Would Richie Kilgallon lie to keep himself out of trouble?"

"Richard? He'd lie for no damn reason at all except he felt like it. But why the story about an extra man? I mean we all know sometimes cops shoot too soon. Then they explain they thought the victim was armed and dangerous."

"Right," I said. "As in: 'That soup spoon in the victim's hand, it sure *looked* like a gun.' "

"But in this case the man they shot, Lonnie, actually *did* have a gun, registered to his name. And even if he had no prior felony convictions, everyone seems to agree he was a bad guy. So why the story?"

"Lonnie had several gunshot wounds, but the bullet he died from went through the center of his forehead. There's some indication in the pathologist's report that that was prob-ably the first slug he took. That could have been followed up on. But it never was."

158

"I only sort of skimmed through the pathology reports." She stared at me. "So, just what *is* your theory?"

"My theory is that four cops went to Lonnie Bright's house. One or more of them went upstairs and deliberately put a bullet in Lonnie's brain. The forensics lab couldn't tell for sure whose gun that bullet came from, just that it wasn't Jimmy Coletta's. My theory is that murdering Lonnie was planned, but that then something went wrong. Maybe they didn't know anyone else was up there. The girfriend was, though; and she had a gun, the semiautomatic they later had to pry out of her hand. Fact is, she had a record of violence worse than Lonnie's. Anyway, she opened fire. The cops returned fire. More people got shot. Richie managed to call for help, and when help arrived it was all over but the bleeding."

"And then all three surviving cops lied about someone there who got away?"

"Not to repeat myself, but would Richie Kilgallon lie?"

"The fact that someone might lie doesn't prove that he did. Besides, the police turned up bullets on the scene that couldn't have come from any of the guns they found there."

"I know. Two slugs dug out of the hallway wall. I can't explain that for sure. Maybe they were old slugs. Maybe they had nothing to do with that night."

"So what's your theory about why a police officer murdered Lonnie in the first place?"

"One pulled the trigger. Maybe they all murdered him." I drank some coffee. "They were narcotics detectives. Lonnie was a drug dealer."

"I don't think you're saying they killed him just because they don't like drug dealers."

"No."

"So? Go on."

I shrugged again. "Heroin, speed, coke, acid—all these chemicals and their various formulations. Most of us can't even keep track of them. What everyone knows, though, is that there can be more money involved in one illegal drug transaction than most people see in their lifetime—and it's all cash."

"And you think the cops were doing a drug deal with Lonnie."

"It's a plausible theory."

"Did your client tell you this?"

"Marlon Shades didn't tell me one thing that I plan to tell you or anyone."

"Okay." She seemed to be thinking. "You don't believe there was any unknown person up there who got away."

"That's my theory."

"So then, where did the drugs go?"

"And the money, too," I added. "I don't know."

"You won't say?" she asked. "Or you really don't know?"

"I really don't know." I did have a theory on that, too, but to explain it I'd have to tell her what Marlon Shades had told me.

"God, what a mess!" She shook her head and poked at the pen that lay on the table in front of her, as though studying it. I didn't think she saw the pen at all, though, and I was hoping I knew what was going through her mind. "There's a part of me," she finally said, "that wishes I hadn't convinced you to tell me what you think happened."

"You didn't *convince* me to tell you," I said.

"You mean you planned to tell me all along?"

"I was thinking about it on my way here," I said. "But I wasn't sure, not until we talked, and you figured out who your secret helper is."

"Wait a minute." She frowned. "I didn't say I figured anything out."

"No, but I think you did."

"Well, is it . . . my grandfather?"

160

"You didn't hear it from me, or he'd be very unhappy with me."

"But I never even met him. I—"

"Wait." I held up my hand. "You said one part of you wishes I hadn't told you my theory about Lonnie Bright. So tell me about the other part."

"Other part?"

"Yeah, the part that's glad I told you." I paused. "Tell me about the part of you that wants to help me find out if I'm right."

CHAPTER

30

No question about it. Stefanie couldn't help hoping I was right about what happened at Lonnie Bright's. She'd understood at once that if I was, and if it ever got out in the open, her no-good ex-husband would be up to his ear lobes in bad-smelling stuff. And way too busy to worry about Stefanie and her plan to move back home to Albany, New York, with their little girl.

On the other hand, she had difficulty believing Breaker Hanafan would want to help her. She'd learned as a child not to talk about, or even think about, her mother's father, Francis Gilmary Hanafan. She'd never seen him, never communicated with him in any way. When other kids, or teachers, pressed her for information, she'd say he died before she was born. When she came to Chicago for law school, she'd had a vague notion to find out more about him. But at first she was too busy with classes and exams, and eventually with a job and a kid and a major headache for a husband. There was a touch of fear, too, knowing Breaker supposedly had "underworld connections." So, if anyone ever asked, she stuck with the story she'd used all her life, and claimed her maternal grandfather was "deceased."

She knew I had no reason to lie about it, but couldn't believe Breaker actually cared what happened to her. I told her he'd gotten it into his mind somehow that it was up to him to punish Richie for what he'd done to her. I told her how badly he wanted Richie in prison—skipping the part about wanting him "bent over a bench"—and how he'd leveraged me into getting enough dirt on Richie to put him there. I didn't tell her the leverage was his threat to kill Yogi, or that her caring grandfather planned to flat-out kill Richie himself if I didn't succeed before the cancer had him too far gone to do it. I didn't mention his medical condition at all.

"Oh," I said, "about your being followed? Or in danger? I mentioned that to Breaker. So if someone does follow you, or bother you, it's *them* I'd worry about . . . not you."

Her hand went to her throat and her eyes widened. "My God!" Despite her shock, though, she seemed happy about it, too. "Do you think I should . . . contact him or something?"

"That's your decision," I said. "But I don't see what help it would be. The man's moods are, let's just say, erratic. I'm not even sure it's *your* interests he's concerned about. Or if it's simply to satisfy some need of his own."

"You make him sound like . . . like someone I don't want to know."

"Which is what the people who knew him well taught you as a child," I said. "But for now, I'm just hoping you'll help me to help him help you." I shook my head. "Does that make sense?"

"I guess so. I mean, this whole thing scares me to death," she said, "but I'll do whatever I can. How will your talking to Maura Flanagan bring out what really happened the night of the shooting?"

"I don't know," I said, which was the truth. "I'm just gonna put pressure on her, then wait and see what happens. The first problem, though, is how to get close enough to her for a private conversation, without getting arrested in the process."

We kicked it back and forth awhile, and finally came up with a plan. On the one hand, we were in luck because Flanagan was to be back at the disciplinary commission for a meeting on Wednesday, just two days away. On the other hand, it wasn't a very good plan. But, hey . . .

ON THE WAY OUT, I filed a notice with the commission's clerk that I'd subpoenaed Jimmy Coletta to appear and give a deposition on the coming Friday. Then Stefanie let me use a phone, and I called my own number to pick up my messages.

My main strategy was to keep the ball rolling. I'd had the subpoena served on Jimmy over the weekend, along with a letter from me. It was a polite, lawyer-speak letter—in case it ever got public—stating that we might be able to "obviate the necessity for sworn deposition testimony" if we met in person to discuss the issues. I gave him my phone number and wrote that the meeting could be "at any such time and place as is convenient to you," but by Tuesday at the latest. "If this good-faith attempt to avoid the time and trouble of sworn testimony is not acceptable," I concluded, "the deposition will go forward as required by law."

The only message on my machine was Jimmy's response. He said he'd meet me that night at the same south side gym where we'd talked the previous Thursday. He said to call him, and left his number. "That's the gym," he said. "I'll be there all day." He sounded tired, stressed out, impatient.

Feeling pretty much the same, I punched out the number. A man answered. "Beale here."

"I want to talk to Jimmy Coletta."

"Who's this?" He didn't sound friendly.

"Just get Mr. Coletta."

"Y'all ain't talkin' to nobody, 'less y'all tell me your name."

"Foley," I said, "now just—"

"Hold on."

I waited a few minutes and Jimmy came on the line.

"Who was that?" I asked.

164

"Who was who? Oh, you mean answering the phone? Preston Beale, the janitor. He thinks he runs this place." There was some cheering in the background, then silence, and I imagined Jimmy getting someone to close a door. "Tomorrow I have physical therapy, all day. I can't miss it. But I'll meet you tonight, here at the gym. Eight o'clock."

"It's just one-thirty now. I can be there in forty-five minutes, maybe less."

"No, I can't. We're having sort of a tournament."

"I can watch. We'll talk between games."

"Listen to me, will you? There are too many people around now. Come at eight o'clock. Except for my . . . my driver, everyone will be long gone by then. I don't want anyone to know we're talking. Don't you understand?" Tired, stressed out, impatient. For sure. And frightened, too.

"I understand perfectly."

Jimmy Coletta had been a bad cop. Then he'd taken a terrible blow, survived, and grown into a different person. Now he was afraid the new life he'd painfully constructed for himself and his family over the last five years was about to be suddenly demolished, and the pieces hauled off to a landfill.

I was scared, too. My fear was that Jimmy might be right, and that I'd be the one wielding the wrecking ball.

CHAPTER

31

THE CAVALIER WAS IN a parking garage a few blocks east of the disciplinary commission, on Randolph, and I had six hours to kill before my meeting with Jimmy Coletta. I walked back to the car and slid into the driver's seat.

Ten minutes later, I was still sitting there, thinking.

I climbed back out, slipped off my sport coat and laid it on the roof of the car. I got the Beretta out of the trunk, snapped it into a shoulder holster and slipped the harness over my Chicago Symphony Orchestra Radiothon sweatshirt. Just then a white Cadillac DeVille came around the corner from the next level up, and a gray haired, wide-eyed woman slowed to a stop and stared at me.

"FBI," I said, and gave her a stern, governmental glare. She drove away.

I put the jacket back on, slid an extra seven-round magazine into the left pocket, and closed the trunk. Back in the driver's seat I checked my watch. Great. Now I had only five hours and forty-five minutes to kill. Maybe I'd go find a forest preserve and sit in the parking lot and stare out the windshield.

The advantage of doing that was it would bore the hell out of the guy hiding behind a newspaper, about a block away on Randolph in what looked like the same car Yogi had tipped me to a week earlier, a dark green four-door Crown Vic. The disadvantage was that I'd be equally bored, and I'd still have to shake him off before I drove out to see Jimmy.

I left the Cavalier where it was and departed the parking garage on foot, by way of an alley that opened onto State Street. At Barney Green's office I told his secretary I needed a car. I'd have to come up with a client to send Barney pretty soon. He was way ahead of me in our exchange of favors.

IT WAS SEVEN-THIRTY—HALF AN HOUR early—when I pulled up in front of the Ellison Community Center in Barney's wife's car, a mocha-colored Lexus LS400. She was in Paris for the week and the rental agency Barney uses couldn't deliver anything right away that he thought I'd fit into comfortably. Barney's big on comfort, and I didn't remind him my usual ride was the Cavalier. I also didn't tell him I'd be leaving the car unattended on a barren, rundown street in Englewood.

I parked a car-length back from a full-sized Ford van with disability plates, and right beside the *No Parking* sign. I couldn't imagine anyone would care. The gym was on the west side of the street, at the north end of the block. To the south there was a wide vacant lot, then a couple of boarded-up two-flats, and finally, on the corner at the far end of the block, an apartment building with a tavern called the Tahiti Inn on the first floor.

Directly across the street from the gym was a factory building sprayed with intricate gang graffiti at ground level, and a faded sign higher up that said *Borkman Tool & Die*. South of that was a fenced-in parking lot for factory employees. In the glow of the street lights I could see tall weeds growing up through the broken concrete behind the chainlink fence. My guess was that no one had worked at Borkman Tool & Die for a decade or two.

Before I parked I'd circled around for a while, getting a feel for the neighborhood at night. When I was there Thursday it had been a gray, stormy afternoon, the streets empty and depressing. Now, after dark on a warm evening, the feeling was altogether different. Not any less depressing—at least to an outsider like me—but filled with frenetic noise now: kids hollering and dogs barking on overcrowded residential blocks; raucous laughter and ear-pounding music from too many bars on streets where there should have been shops and businesses; and behind it all the din of traffic on 63rd Street—two blocks to the south—including wailing sirens that never seemed to stop. The atmosphere seemed somehow strangely brighter with the sun down, a psychological brightness charged with tension and hysteria, ready to erupt into rage and violence at any moment.

Then, again, maybe most of that came from me.

Twice I'd driven past the Tahiti Inn, a dingy-looking bar with a little neon palm tree in the window. The odors of beer and reefer hung heavy in the air and there must have been twenty people milling around outside the place—most of them young men, many wearing identical athletic warm-up jackets. Whatever nation the jackets announced—whether "People" or "Folks" or some other alliance—didn't really matter much. Those certainly weren't all Steelers fans out there lounging on the hoods of double-parked cars; drinking, smoking, trying to outshout the deafening rap that poured out the bar's open door. Just your average bunch of palm-slapping, crotch-grabbing gangbangers, celebrating a warm Monday night and wondering why that white motherfucker in the LS400 keeps driving by . . . and refuses to look intimidated.

Now, though, I'd completed my final circuit and there was nobody nearby when I got out of the Lexus at the gymnasium end of the block. No lights showed behind the tall windows high above the sidewalk. Except for the Ford van—which I'd seen Thursday and which had to be Jimmy's—I'd have wondered whether he was even in there waiting for me.

There were three sets of double doors facing the street,

heavy wooden doors with small frosted windows about chest high, protected by steel grates. I tried the middle set first because high up beside them was a push button. They were locked, so I pressed the button.

If a bell or a buzzer sounded inside somewhere, I couldn't hear it. I waited, then tried again. No response. Finally I pushed and held it for a long time, pressing my ear to the door. No sound but distant traffic, and the shouts and curses and monotonous, mind-numbing rap floating up the block from the Tahiti Inn.

I tugged again, but the doors hadn't magically unlocked themselves. I gave up on the middle set and tried the pair to my right. Locked, of course. Damn! I was early, sure, but still I was angry that Jimmy wasn't watching for me, and then right away I got worried, with the two feelings leapfrogging each other for first place in line. At the third set of doors I pulled on both handles—yanked hard, without hope—and one door flew open so easily it almost broke my nose.

I stepped inside and let the heavy door swing closed behind me. The only light in the small lobby area came from one low-watt bulb in the ceiling. The other two pairs of doors weren't just locked; they had short thick chains wound through their panic bars inside. I had to assume the chains came off when the building was in use. My set of doors had no chain, but the one I'd pulled open could be deadbolted to its partner from either outside or inside. Security was a big thing in Englewood.

I stood for a moment, inhaling the familiar odors of sweat and dust and cleaning compound, then crossed the lobby and went through an open doorway into the gym itself. Just a hint of the outside street lighting filtered in through the tall windows, but as my eyes adjusted I was able to see that the bleachers on both sides had been folded up against the walls. I didn't see any people, but—

Ka-chunk.

Barely audible. From behind me, out in the lobby. I froze for an instant, my right hand already reaching up under my jacket, resting on the Beretta. I stepped to the side and peered around the edge of the doorway into the lobby, but there was no one there.

There were no more *ka-chunks*, either. No sounds except someone walking by on the sidewalk outside, and the far-away noise from the Tahiti Inn. I was pretty sure now that I knew what I'd heard. I walked back across to the door I'd come in by, and pushed against it with my left hand. It moved maybe a sixteenth of an inch before it caught up on its dead-bolt, now slipped into the slot of its partner door. I was locked in, from outside.

Whoever they were, either they were very good—because I hadn't spotted any tail—or they knew I'd be there and were already waiting. That would have meant Jimmy had told them, so I preferred to think they were very good. Or maybe they had someone watching him. That was even better. I didn't have to blame either Jimmy or myself.

And where *was* Jimmy? His van was still there, or at least I hadn't heard it drive away. And the driver he'd said would be with him . . . where was the driver? Had *he* tipped somebody off I'd be here? And why the hell lock me inside the building, with Jimmy or without him?

The questions were endless . . . and useless. I looked around. Both double doorways from the lobby into the gym, opposite the doors to outside, were wide open. To my left, on the south wall, there was a pay phone. The handset was hanging where it belonged, but its cord was pulled out of the bottom of the box and hanging toward the floor.

To the right of the phone was a door that reminded me of the classroom doors in my grammar school. Golden oak, with a large window in the top half. I walked over and tried that door and it wasn't locked, and I wasn't sure I should be happy about that. I went through, into a wide corridor which went forward just a few yards and then made a sharp right turn. The dismal light from the lobby bulb didn't make the turn, so the rest of the hallway was very dark. I stood at the corner a long minute, leaning into the darkness. I thought I heard faint snatches of music—*real* music, not rap—but it was very far off and most likely coming from outside the building.

I went back into the lobby and from there into the gym again. On the wall just inside was a bank of light switches in a recessed metal cabinet, and I flipped them all on, one by one. Most of them turned on lights in the gym or in the lobby. The others, assuming they were connected to live wires, activated fixtures I couldn't see.

With the lights on the gym looked smaller, but no less vacant, than it had in the dark. There were two more sets of double doors on the opposite wall and I walked across and tried them, but they were locked. On my way back to the lobby I paused at the switch panel and assured myself again that every switch was in the "on" position.

Then, with an uneasy feeling about what might be waiting for me, I went back to the only unlocked door I'd been given, and went through.

CHAPTER

32

PAST THAT FIRST SHARP TURN the corridor ran along the south wall toward the rear portion of the building, behind the gym. It was well lighted now and I moved quickly, the Beretta in my hand. Brightly colored posters, taped to the wall on my right along the way, warned me not to play on railroad tracks, not to smoke, not to take drugs, and never to try to solve my problems with a gun. Three-out-of-four wasn't bad, I thought.

I heard the music again, piano music. Still very distant, but I could tell it wasn't barroom music—not unless the patrons favored Brahms. At the end of the corridor I stepped into another lobby, this one running from south to north along the west side of the gym. The lights were on. The air was stale and chilly, easily ten degrees cooler than outside. The music had stopped.

The ceiling in the gym itself had been very high, but here it was only about twelve feet. At the far end, jutting out from the north wall, was a wide stairway that went up to a landing, then turned west and went up some more. So there were at least two floors, maybe three. On the wall to my right were the sets of doors I'd already tried from the gym side and found locked. To my left were three rooms with their doors standing open and hand-printed signs that labeled them *Tutoring*, then *Crafts*, then *Tots*. I went to the rooms one by one and turned on the lights, and there was nobody in any of them.

I was checking the Tots room when the piano music

started up again—the same piece as before. It was coming from inside the building. Someone practicing; someone very good. I didn't think it was Jimmy; he just didn't seem the type. Besides, from the sound of it I guessed the piano to be up on the second floor. Without an elevator—and I didn't see one—he'd have a hell of a time getting a wheelchair up there.

I was wrong, though, about where the piano was.

Beyond the Tots room were a men's and a women's rest room—both unlocked, both empty. Then, finally, I came to two closed, windowless doors farther down, near the stairs. The first had a small plastic sign that said *Office*. There'd be a phone in there, for sure. But that door was locked, and by the time I'd found that out I didn't need to read *Music Room* on the last door. That room must have had some sound-proofing, because that's where the distant-sounding piano was.

I stood off to the side of the door and knocked. The music stopped short and there might have been a few muffled words spoken, or maybe not. Then nothing, so I knocked again—very hard.

"Yeah? Who's there?" It was Jimmy Coletta. Loud and aggressive, like a cop. Not silent and dead, like I'd expected. "Who's there?" he repeated.

"It's Foley." I was starting to breathe again. "Open the door."

"Open it yourself. Why would it be locked?"

I holstered the Beretta and opened the door. "Maybe," I said, "so some dope-smoking, Brahms-hating Gangster-Disciple doesn't come in and complain about the noise."

The room was maybe twelve by twenty feet, with thick soundproofing material on the walls and ceiling. An electric heater sat on the floor, making it very warm. There were several small children's chairs, some black metal music stands and an upright piano that had been painted beige about fifty years ago. Jimmy sat in his wheelchair, holding a plastic bottle of drinking water. A woman sat at the piano, but was turned and facing me in the doorway. She was a brown-haired, fair-skinned woman—plain but attractive at the same time—in dark pants and a red sweater.

Jimmy held up his wrist to show me his watch. "You're fifteen minutes early."

"Sometimes that's helpful," I said. "Although this time, I don't think so."

"What do you mean?" he asked.

"Wait," I said. I nodded toward the woman. "So you're the driver?"

"Driver and wife," she said. "Suzanne Coletta." Her smile seemed more nervous than friendly.

I glanced around the room. "No windows," I said. "You need some air in here."

"Ventilation system's not working," Jimmy said. "Money's kinda tight in these neighborhoods."

"We closed the door because the rest of the building's so cold," Suzanne said. She stood up. "But you're right. It's very stuffy in here."

"And hot," I said. Actually, it smelled like a post-game locker room.

We went out into the lobby. Me first, then Jimmy in the chair, then Suzanne. "All the lights are on," she said, obviously surprised.

"I turned them on," I said. "You know, you shouldn't leave the front door unlocked like that."

"What are you talking about?" Jimmy said. He swiveled his chair to face me. "Didn't the janitor let you into the building? Mr. Beale?"

"No one let me in. One of the front doors was unlocked."

"It couldn't have been." His amazed look seemed genuine.

174

"But it was," I said. "The panic bar was locked in the down position, so you could just pull the door open from outside. You oughta be careful. The gangs are—"

"They've never bothered us; not yet, anyway. We usually all leave together. Mr. Beale's the last one out and he locks up. But tonight I said I was meeting someone and we'd let the person in and let the door lock behind us when we left. He said no, he'd have to let you in and hang around until we left. Said it was his . . . his rear end on the line if the door didn't get properly double-locked. I said fine. I didn't think it would be a problem." Jimmy paused. "He's an old guy, y'know? Thinks the place belongs to him and—"

"He was gone," I said. "And the door was unlocked. Do you have a key?"

"We have just the panic bar key." Jimmy shook his head. "I guess we better go release the bar now, so no one else wanders in."

"Not necessary," I said. "The door's locked. With the turn bolt."

"You mean . . ." He seemed confused. "We don't have *that* key. Only Mr. Beale has that . . . and I suppose the director of the center."

"Yeah, well, I think someone got to your man Beale. Either paid him or scared him enough to make him help them." I explained how, after I was inside, someone locked the door behind me. "Beale knew it was me who called you. He told someone, and . . . Anyway, at first I thought no one was here. But then I followed the music." I turned to Suzanne. "I play, too, a little. But you play beautifully."

"Not really." She blushed and looked away, toward the Music Room. "That's a wonderful old piano, despite how it—"

"She has a gift from God," Jimmy said. "She'd be playing at Carnegie Hall if she hadn't married me." He wasn't sounding like a cop anymore. He reached out his hand and she took it. "I never paid attention before," he said. "All those years. But now the Lord's given me time to sit and listen, y'know, and—"

"Look," I said, wondering how we'd gotten off in that direction, "someone locked me in here . . . for a reason. I thought they wanted time to get away. I was afraid that when I found you, you might be . . ." I looked from Jimmy to Suzanne.

"You can talk in front of her," Jimmy said. "She knows everything. I mean what happened when I got shot. Every last thing." He paused, as though to make sure I understood what he meant, then asked, "You thought I might be what?"

"Be dead," I said. Suzanne gasped, but I went on. "You're not, though, so why'd they lock me in?" I looked around. "Before we talk, maybe we should figure out how to get out of here."

"There are some rear doors," Suzanne said, "although Mr. Beale always chains those, too." She turned and headed toward the stairway, and then past it. "Here."

I followed her to an alcove on the other side of the stairway, and another set of double doors with panic bars. And chains. I turned back to Jimmy. "Any more exits?"

"I understand there's a fire escape on the second floor," he said. "And one on the third. But . . ." He gestured and I turned and saw that the entry to the second half of the stairway, up from the landing, was blocked by a padlocked iron gate. "We've never been upstairs."

"I'm getting a little nervous," Suzanne said. She crossed her arms and hugged herself, from more than just the cool air. "I mean, the kids are all right with my sister, and I guess we'd be safe in here until they open up in the morning, but what if someone steals the van." I figured the Lexus a more

176

likely target, but kept quiet. "Or even just vandalizes it. We can't afford to—"

"Hey, hold on," Jimmy said. "Don't forget, we pledged to leave the future in God's hands. He's doin' all right so far, isn't he? Besides, we can use the cell phone to call someone and—"

"We can't, though," she said. "I left the cell phone in the van."

"That's okay," he said, and I was amazed at the patience in his voice. "Your sister will call when we're late. When we don't answer, she'll get worried and call the police and they'll come and find us." He paused, then turned to me. "The only problem is, everyone'll know *you* were here, which is what I wanted to avoid." He spun around and wheeled toward the south end of the lobby. "Let's go try the front doors. First they were open; then they were locked. Maybe now they'll be open again."

But they weren't.

There were voices, though, outside. Male voices, apparently two; approaching from the south, the direction of the Tahiti Inn. Intoxicated, mostly unintelligible voices. Arguing, but not shouting. Then a bottle hit the pavement and broke. I was hoping they'd pass on by. But they stopped right outside the door, and I heard just the word I didn't want to hear.

"Lexus, man. Fuckin' Lexus. Go for like fifty G or some'n'."

I was thinking he low-balled it for an LS400, but what would I know?

CHAPTER

33

I STOOD WITH MY EAR to the locked door and listened. Help-less, hoping they'd move along. But they didn't. Their voices dropped and I couldn't hear what they were saying, but I pictured them walking up and running their hands over the Lexus.

Finally, one spoke up in a louder voice. "Gots to go, man. Shirley be—"

"Fuck Shirley, man. This here moth'fucker be worth some'n'. Wait here. I go git Zorro. Zorro got a lift man do it without a scratch."

"Nah, man. I gots—"

"Five, ten minutes, man. An' y'all fat ass best be here or Zorro see to it y'all won't be worryin' 'bout no Shirley or nobody else." His steps disappeared back toward the Tahiti.

"Fuck you, fag," the other man said, "and Zorro, too." But he said it softly, and he wasn't going anywhere.

IT DIDN'T SEEM LIKE five minutes later that I was outside the building.

We'd talked about breaking into the office to get to the phone. But I didn't want the police involved. Besides, they might not get there in time to scare off Zorro & Co., and Barney's wife would be highly pissed if her LS400 was gone.

Every window I could find was either glass brick, or re-inforced glass in panes too small to get through, with heavy-duty iron frames. Except those high windows in the gym, where there were large panels of frosted, pebbled glass. So

178

Suzanne and I had opened up the bleachers on the west side of the gym and I stood on the top row to reach the bottom part of a window on the north end of the building, around the corner from the Lexus.

I pretty much destroyed a heavy brass fire extinguisher breaking through the thick glass. It was reinforced, too, like the other windows, with what looked like chicken wire embedded in it. There wasn't that shattered glass sound when it broke, so probably no one would hear it way around the corner. The outside window ledge was twelve or fifteen feet above the ground. I had to hang by my hands and drop the rest of the way, landing on dirt, fortunately, not sidewalk.

It must actually have taken me more than five minutes to get out, though, because by the time I rounded the corner there was already a man in the driver's seat of the Lexus, and one in the backseat. A third man was opening the front passenger door.

I was mad as hell, and yelled something—God knows what—and a head turned and stared out the back window at me. The man by the passenger door turned, too. The building's outside lights were on now and I could see him clearly. Tall and thin and dressed in black . . . and damn if he wasn't wearing a Zorro hat. He had a thin mustache and light brown skin full of pockmarks and scars. He was smiling, with possibly the most disturbed-looking smile I'd ever seen.

The Lexus' engine kicked in just then—so much for high-end security systems—and I thought Zorro would get in the car and they'd all drive away. But instead, he said something I couldn't hear, smiling and keeping his eyes on me all the time, and the man in the backseat got out. He was short and fat and dark-skinned, with long braided hair and one of those gang jackets.

"Get away from the car," I said. "You'll be much happier if you do, believe me."

179

" 'You'll be much happier if you do, believe me.' " Zorro parroted my words, in a mocking, imitation white man's voice.

"Exactly," I said.

"Uh-uh, man. We takin' this car." In his own voice now, mean and cocky and filled with contempt. "Y'all go on an' run back home now, where you belong, or we take care o' your white ass first."

I could have turned away and let them take the damn car, but I felt insulted and frustrated and in no mood to back off. As it turned out, it wouldn't have made any difference to them if I had—but I'd have been better off.

"Better call out your driver," I said. "The two of you aren't enough."

Zorro's hand dipped into his pocket and came out again, and a blade flashed in the light. "Oh, we got plenty."

Even as he spoke, my own hand went under my jacket toward the Beretta, but his grin widened and something about the way his eyes wandered off my face reminded me . . . counting Zorro and his "lift man," there should have been four of them. And I suddenly knew where the fourth man must be.

I stepped to my right, ducked and pivoted, and the narrow side of a two-by-four, that might otherwise have crushed my skull, glanced off my left shoulder. His momentum carried the attacker forward and he was in front of me. As he struggled to regain his balance, I shoved him hard in the back and he stumbled toward Zorro and the fat man.

Zorro slid out of the way. His smile never wavered as he came at me with smooth, supple movements—like a deranged cat—slicing the knife back and forth, carving Z's out of the narrowing space between us. He moved more quickly than he seemed to, and I jumped backwards—and crashed hard into the building behind me. He reached in and slashed

180

at my face and I raised my left forearm and felt the slice of the blade across my wrist.

He paused. "Do it hurt, man?" he asked, and then smoothly closed in on me again.

I pulled the Beretta and shot him in the chest.

The rest happened in seconds. Zorro down on both knees, crying and moaning and coughing up blood. Not smiling now. "Fucking hospital," he kept saying. The driver had never left the Lexus, and the other two dragged the wounded man between them and loaded him into the front seat and slammed the door.

"Wait!" I yelled. "Call 911. The paramedics. They'll know what to do." I was certain I wanted Zorro to live more than they did—maybe even more than he did himself. "Wait for the goddamn ambulance!"

But they didn't wait. The two of them scrambled into the backseat and the Lexus roared away. I ran out into the middle of the street, chased it a few steps, but then stopped and stood there and watched, hoping they knew where they were going, hoping they'd get there in time. They drove very fast and I could see they had a green light and clear sailing at the corner.

Just as it passed through the intersection, though, a blinding white light filled the interior of the LS400, like a strobe, silhouetting two dark heads through the rear window. The white light faded at once into orange, as the back of the car seemed to leap up off its tires. Then, with its rear end humped up in the air, the car exploded a second time, bursting now into red and yellow, blue and orange and white all at once. In the shimmering light I saw a thousand fragments of debris—human and automotive alike—falling through the air, already on their way down.

How long does it take for a car to blow up? One second? Two? But these were seconds that took forever, until what was left in the intersection was a flaming mass that wasn't a car at all anymore. It was twisted metal and molten fiberglass; plastic and fabric and rubber, burning, billowing up into thick black smoke.

And the flesh and hair and bone burning with it? Not the flesh and hair and bone intended; but human, nonetheless.

CHAPTER

34

I STOOD A MOMENT AND WATCHED, but sirens were already drawing near and I went back around the corner to the community center's rear doors. The city was repairing curbs on that street and they'd started putting in forms for the new concrete, so there was lumber lying all around—including lots of two-by-fours. It must have been one of those that almost split my skull.

I pounded on the locked rear doors with a two-by-four until finally Suzanne answered. "Who is it?"

"It's me. Get Jimmy close up to the doors."

"I'm right here," he said.

"You heard the explosion?" I asked.

"Yes. It sounded like—"

"It was the car I came in, a Lexus. I parked it behind your van. Whoever set the bomb figured I'd eventually get out of the building, but locking me in would give them time to place the device and get away. It had some sort of delayed switch. The car'd been running several minutes before it blew. The guys who took it . . . they were in it."

"My God!" Suzanne said.

"Before the explosion," Jimmy said, "I heard a gunshot, too."

"It's that kind of neighborhood," I explained. "Gangs, taverns, fights. Lots of gunshots, all the time."

"Yeah," he said, "I guess so."

"I'm leaving. You don't want everyone to know I was here, do you? That you'd agreed to talk to me?"

183

"No," he said, "but it was *your* car that was blown up, so there's no avoiding—"

"Not my car. I borrowed it. Maybe the real owner will report it stolen—which it was. The only people who know I was here are whoever locked me in and placed that bomb. They won't bring it up."

"I don't want you to lie to protect me," Jimmy said. "There've been too many lies already."

"You'll have to make your own decision about what to say. But the truth is you didn't let me in, and we didn't get a chance to talk. Anyway, when can we meet?"

There was silence, and then, "Maybe Suzanne and I should think it over again."

"It's such a difficult decision," Suzanne said. "What it might mean, not just for us, but the kids, and—"

I didn't want to go there. "I better be on my way. I'll find a phone and call 911 and tell them someone's locked in here. And . . . Jimmy?"

"Yeah?"

"You'll want to have the police check everything."

"I don't understand," Suzanne said. "Check what?"

"What he means is the van," Jimmy said. "We should ask bomb and arson to check it for explosives."

A CROWD HAD ALREADY GATHERED at the corner. Fire trucks and ambulances were screaming up; squad cars from every direction. Everyone wanted the best possible view. Pretty soon there'd be press and TV people. I mean, hell, there were dead bodies to be seen, right? Or bits and pieces of them anyway.

As for me, I didn't want to see any more. What I'd seen already would be playing itself out for me in my head—over and over—for a long time. I turned and walked west a couple of blocks, then south. I was pretty conspicuous in that neigh-

184

borhood, but if anyone noticed me, they stayed away. The way I felt, I must have looked like someone to stay away from.

On Sixty-third Street I found a phone outside a little all-night grocery and called 911 about someone locked in the gym. When I hung up a cab driver was just coming out of the store with a cup of coffee. He wanted to go view the carnage, too, not take me for a ride. But I offered to double the fare to Evanston and he couldn't resist. He wanted the money upfront. I gave it to him. I'd have given him double that again if he'd demanded it.

I just wanted to go home. The Cavalier could wait in the parking garage where it was. I'd call Barney Green to tell him about the LS400, and to see if his people had had any luck finding what I needed for my upcoming chat with Maura Flanagan. And I could ask him who to get to check out the Cavalier. Maybe he'd know a security firm that had nitrate-sniffing dogs.

CHAPTER

35

WHY I WAS SO ANXIOUS to get home I don't know, because all I did was smear some antibiotic ointment on the cut Zorro opened on my wrist, call Barney Green, and then lie on my couch and watch a car full of people burst into flames, over and over.

Tuesday I moved around in a fog, doing what I had to do, and then Wednesday—still pretty much sleepless—I was back at the disciplinary commission. This time I was stuck in a tiny, windowless room by myself with piles of documents, on the pretext of going through them to make sure I had all the same records the commission had.

Paging through piles of paper was the sort of mind-numbing task lawyers did a lot of, or—if they were in a firm with junior lawyers—made someone else do a lot of. That was why I'd never have asked for my license back except to please Lynnette Daniels, and why I'd have dropped the idea the minute she left, if some creep hadn't tried to frighten me into doing just that.

Now, though, I had additional motives for staying with it: like to find out who beat Yogi up, to protect Yogi from Breaker Hanafan and get my hundred grand for putting Richie Kilgallon in the pen, to liberate Stefanie from Richie . . . and maybe even to help Jimmy Coletta get on with bringing a bit of hope to some kids who otherwise had none.

The trouble was, of course, that Yogi didn't give a damn whether I caught his attacker, or even whether I protected him or not; Breaker's money I could live without; Stefanie was an adult who should handle her own domestic problems; and Jimmy and company were responsible for the whole damn mess in the first place. So much for my motivation.

But what the hell, the car I'm supposed to be driving explodes, scattering what were meant to be bits of my body like confetti all over the south side. How could I walk away from that? Not to mention my shattered and irreplaceable Expulso toilet bowl.

Those were some of the thoughts going through my head as I sat there and stared at the stacks of file folders in front of me. I had no intention of looking at any of them. The only papers I cared about just then were the ones in the large manila envelope I'd picked up at Barney Green's office and brought with me.

In the center of the envelope I'd printed the words "The Honorable Maura Flanagan," and below that "Personal & Confidential." I'd stapled my business card up in the return address corner, with a note written on the front of the card: "We'll do lunch. Today. Vincent's, Beaubien Court."

It had been eleven-fifteen when Stefanie met me in the reception area and took me to my little cubicle and left me there. It was twelve-ten when she knocked and opened the door. "Find everything you need?" she asked.

"I don't know," I said. "I think—"

She closed the door and I was alone again. What she'd just told me was that the meeting of the Illinois Blue Ribbon Committee on Revised Ethical Rules for Attorneys, with Maura Flanagan present for the supreme court, would be taking a break soon, and that Stefanie knew this because the catered lunches had just arrived.

I slipped the large envelope down the front of my pants, then went to the door and opened it. Sure enough, in the hall just a few feet to my right, were two metal carts. One held the food—two platters of sandwiches, another piled with fruit and cheeses fanned out in display, and a fourth full of cookies and what looked like brownies—all held down tight under clear plastic wrap. The other cart was loaded with cans of soft drinks, an ice bucket, and two large carafes for hot beverages. Beyond the carts two women in white aprons were standing and chatting softly.

I nodded to the caterers and turned to my left, where the hall deadended at a closed door. Behind that door was the Blue Ribbon Committee. The last time they met they'd adjourned about noon, according to Stefanie, but had lunch brought in so they could get back to work quickly. There'd be fifteen or twenty of them, she'd said, all very important people, top guns in the legal community from around the state. "Gosh," I'd said.

And I said the same thing again when the meeting room door opened and the caterers started toward their carts. "Gosh," I said, moving quickly, "those look heavy. Let me help."

Before they could object I was pushing the cart full of food down the hallway with one hand, and pulling the drink cart behind me with the other. At the same time people were trickling out of the meeting room, headed for a cigarette or a rest room before lunch. They looked pretty ordinary for very important people, especially when they flattened themselves against the wall to avoid being hit by a fast-moving, apparently out-of-control food cart.

Up ahead, just inside the door, was a cluster of top guns who'd thoughtlessly chosen that inconvenient spot to stop and chat. "Comin' through!" I called. "Comin' through!" I made it very clear I wasn't going to stop, and they scattered.

I'd worked up a bit of speed by then, and as I entered the room I faked a little stumble over the threshhold—there was no threshhold—and pushed the cart even faster, toward the floor-to-ceiling windows opposite the door. "Oops, sorry!" I called, and then had to swerve, of course, to avoid the windows. The front cart caught the corner of the long conference table full of papers and started to tip, sending the platters of food sliding. The cart itself stayed upright, though—despite my best efforts—and only one platter of sandwiches actually crashed to the floor. The drink cart didn't tip over, either, but the carafes teetered dangerously when the cart banged into my hip. I reached out toward one of them, but somehow couldn't steady it and—darn!—it went crashing to its side, sending hot coffee cascading over the side of the cart and onto the conference table, where it spread out and streamed down to the floor.

"Gimme a hand here!" I called. When the sandwiches hit the floor, the taut plastic wrap must have split open and what looked like sliced turkey and maybe tuna salad and mayonnaise and God-knows-what were all over the carpet, with steaming coffee soaking through the whole mess.

There was a lot of talk and confusion, with the catering ladies fussing and yelling for towels—and blaming *me*, of all people—and a whole blue ribbon committee of take-charge people crowding around, snatching coffee-sodden documents from the table and mostly getting in each other's way.

I pulled the envelope from my pants and headed toward the far end of the long table. A man and a woman stood near another door at that end of the room, both of them staring at me. I recognized Maura Flanagan from a photograph, and had a feeling the man was Clark Woolford.

"Justice Flanagan?" I said, and when she nodded I handed her the envelope. I leaned in close to her. "Ask for Mister Remorseful," I whispered, and then went out the nearby door.

It was a different hallway, but it led back to the same reception area where Stefanie had met me an hour earlier. I stopped at the desk. "Tell Ms. Randle I had to leave. It's those people," I said, nodding back behind me. "They're making such a racket I couldn't concentrate."

VINCENT'S WAS ON BEAUBIEN COURT, directly across from the building lobby, so Maura Flanagan—assuming she showed up—could get back to her meeting quickly if she wanted to. It was the sort of downtown restaurant where the drinks—outrageously expensive—were large and strong enough to give you a buzz while you convinced yourself that "just one" at lunch couldn't hurt. The place was quiet, dimly lit, and far enough from city hall and the courthouse that people could be pretty sure the U.S. Attorney hadn't taped a microphone to the underside of their table. In their fearless struggle to save the world from crooked politicians, judges, and lawyers, even the Feds couldn't bug every table in every restaurant in the Loop. Could they?

A thin, sleek-looking guy in a black suit, with blond hair pulled into a ponytail, led me to a secluded nook and a table for two. I told him I was "Mr. Remorseful" and my companion would be along shortly. His complete lack of reaction made me wonder what kind of place I was in. I ordered coffee and a bowl of minestrone, which arrived almost at once, and then waited fifteen very long minutes before Flanagan showed up.

She'd have looked like an ordinary middle-aged woman in an expensive blue business suit—maybe silk—and a white blouse open at the neck, but there was an air of authority about her—or was it arrogance?—that kept "ordinary" out of the picture. Her hair showed just enough gray around the edges to convince you the black was natural. The manila envelope stuck up from a leather handbag slung over her shoulder. I could see it had been torn open.

The blond ponytail was escorting her over and when they got close I looked up, but didn't stand, didn't greet her at all. He held the chair for her and she sat down, smiling and telling me how happy she was to see me. I drank my coffee and stared at her. The waiter was already standing there, and she ordered a Diet Sprite with lime, and chicken salad. He turned to me and I told him the minestrone had been delicious and all I needed was more coffee.

When the waiter left there was a long silence and finally she said. "You really *are* crazy."

"No," I said, "really, the minestrone isn't bad at all, and I hate to eat a large meal in the middle of the—"

"You listen to me, Mr. Foley. You've got a petition pending before the court. I could have you charged with attempting to tamper with a judicial proceeding."

"Gee whiz," I said, "and we were getting along so well."

She shook her head. "My time is valuable," she said. "If you have a point, get to it. Why did you ask me here?"

"I didn't ask you. Read my note again. I *required* you to be here."

"What do you want?"

"I see you opened the envelope."

"Yes. Those are confidential documents. What is it you want?"

"Confidential?" I said. "Notices of IRS liens, subpoenas, releases of the liens? All public records. One just has to know where to look." And, once I'd told them the sort of thing I was hoping for, Barney's paralegals had known.

The waiter was back with her Sprite and chicken salad, and a refill of my coffee. When he was gone again, she said, "Tell me what you want, or I'm going back to my meeting at once."

"Feel free," I said, waving my hand in a dismissive gesture. "I got the important half already."

She didn't go anywhere. "I don't understand," she said, and for the first time there was a note of unease in her voice. "Important half of what?"

191

"I think you *do* understand." I leaned forward. "You see, Maura," getting personal, watching her flinch a little when I did, "I've verified what I thought, that those back taxes and interest and penalties you and your ex-husband owed, and the fact that you were able to pay them all off, at just the time you did . . . that that's a worry to you. And that I, in particular, know about it, that's an even bigger worry." I leaned back in my chair and watched her.

She sipped at her Sprite while she thought. "Look," she finally said, "you can't—"

"Wait," I said, interrupting to keep her off balance. "Time is short. You need to get back to your meeting. The worry's the first half. The second half is . . . what are you willing to do about the worry?"

"This is starting to sound like blackmail."

"See?" I said. "You *do* understand." I realized Flanagan could have been wired, even if the table wasn't, but that seemed a slim possibility. "Actually, though, it's not your traditional blackmail."

"Really."

"Your traditional blackmailer demands something, in exchange for his promise to keep quiet."

"And I suppose you're not demanding anything?"

"Oh, I'm demanding something, all right," I said. "But I'm not promising to keep quiet."

CHAPTER

36

A FEW MINUTES LATER Maura Flanagan was gone, and the waiter hustled over at once. "I'm surprised," he said, picking up her nearly untouched plate. "Most people really like our chicken salad."

"She was late for a meeting," I said. "She's a very important person."

I'd told Flanagan I knew that six or seven years ago her ex-husband had been the subject of a tax fraud investigation. The taxes had to do with his construction business, and she was listed as vice-president and secretary of the company and had cosigned all the tax returns. I said I knew her ex had made a bundle, mostly on public works projects, but had turned out to be a compulsive gambler who couldn't stop to save his life—or hers.

I told her I knew the investigation dragged on and on and she became a target, too. The IRS was talking a couple of million dollars and, even though the fraud case was shaky and the couple had no money, the government had way too many auditor-hours invested to drop the case. Criminal charges were on the way. So, guilty or not, she'd been facing enormous legal fees to defend herself, and the result would almost certainly be some sort of guilty plea. That meant the loss of her law license and a very promising career, and maybe even some time at the women's prison in Lexington, Kentucky.

Some of it I made up, of course, but obviously I was close enough, because she kept on listening. It didn't take me long to get to the punch line: "Then you suddenly came up with almost two hundred thousand dollars. Not what the IRS was looking for, but enough so they could save face. So you settled up with them and got them off your back." I paused, then added, "That was right after the Lonnie Bright shooting."

If something showed up in her face just then, it was gone as quickly as it came, and she didn't say a word.

So I gave her my demand. "I want to know who gave you the money to close out that O.P.S. investigation so quickly. If you tell me, I can't promise to keep it to myself. I can only promise I'll try to keep your part out of the public eye. I'll do my best. That's the deal."

"You'll try? You'll do your best?" She took a sip of her water, then shook her head from side to side, slowly. "That's it?"

"It's the only deal you've got," I said. "Otherwise, I keep pushing until I get what I want anyway, and I don't have to worry about keeping you out of it. So . . ."

I let my voice trail off, and that's when she'd leaned forward a little and smiled. Anyone looking on would have thought she was especially pleased with me. But her voice was taut with anger and something that might have been hatred blazed in her eyes. What she said was, "Your story is absolutely untrue, Mr. Foley. All of it." She took her purse from the floor beside her and stood up.

"You have my card," I said, pointing at the envelope sticking up from her purse. "Call any time. But call by noon tomorrow."

"You'll be goddamn lucky, you son of a bitch," she said, still managing to hold the smile in place, "to keep your sad sorry ass out of jail that long." Not exactly the language you'd expect from a supreme court justice, no. But I could understand. She was a little upset.

Besides, she was, as her campaign posters had once so boldly proclaimed: "One tough broad."

I LEFT VINCENT'S and took the el to Diversey and walked west to where I'd parked that morning, in the lot of a Wonder Bread thrift store. I went inside and bought a package of day-old sweet rolls and took them out to the car. I was driving a two-tone—blue over rust—1990 Buick Electra that Barney Green had gotten for me from God knows where. It had Arkansas plates and Barney said it belonged to a shirt-tail relative of his. And maybe it did.

It wasn't that the Cavalier had blown up. I'd had it checked out the day before and when they said it was clean I'd driven it home and parked it in one of the bays under the coach house. At its age it could use the rest. And driving a different car gave me the illusion I could hide.

The Electra was way more confortable, too, and—rust notwithstanding—it drove like a dream. I went west to the Edens and then headed north.

Barney and his wife had taken the demolition of the LS400 pretty well. There was insurance coverage, of course. And, although Trish had loved her Lexus to death, it *had* been nearly a year old, after all. She'd been looking at a new Mercedes, maybe one of those cute little SUVs. Barney and Trish were a perfect match. They were both good parents, thoughtful, generous to a fault, and easy to get along with. On top of that, Barney loved to work his ass off twenty-four hours a day, and Trish loved to buy stuff.

I drove all the way to Lake Bluff, parked on the street, and walked about a mile to Inverness Clinic, where no one gave me any trouble at the guard house. The nurse let me peek through the door at Yogi, to prove he was there. "He's asleep and you can't talk to him," she said. "He's had a setback, but he's much better today. I'm sure by tomorrow you'll be able to visit with him."

"You tell him I'll be here tomorrow," I said. "Tell him he has my word on it."

At four o'clock I was downtown again. I'd checked for messages and there was nothing from Maura Flanagan. The only call had been from Lieutenant Theodosian. He wanted a meeting.

It was a clear, warm afternoon and Theodosian was sitting on a park bench near Buckingham Fountain, reading the paper in what was left of the sunlight as the shadows of the tall buildings west of Michigan Avenue crept toward him. We were less than two blocks, actually, from where Yogi had intervened when the masked goon was pounding on me.

"This seat taken?" I asked. I was carrying two coffees and a paper sack and I set them down beside him on the bench.

He closed up the *Sun-Times*. "Feel free," he said. He reached for one of the coffees. "Got any sweetener?"

I sat down at the other end of the bench and took a couple of packets of sugar from my pocket. "This natural stuff will have to do. And I couldn't carry three coffees, so your friend Uh-Smith is out of luck." I nodded toward another bench, about twenty yards away, where Theodosian's state-cop partner was pretending to study his little notebook.

"He's got a name," Theodosian said. "It's Frick. Which rhymes with *prick*. Which is what he is. But he's a good copper. He started this cooperative task force thing, ICOP, five or six years ago. I'm just on loan, temporarily. Except for Frick being such an asshole, it's interesting, a good break from the same old bullshit."

"Always things involving bad cops and narcotics?"

"It's confidential. I won't say yes and I won't say no," he said. So it was yes, the first piece of information he'd given me so far.

"You wanted to see me?" I asked.

"Frick thinks we oughta touch base every few days. So . . . anything new?"

"Nothing."

"Haven't heard from anyone? More threats, beatings, whatever?"

"No such luck," I said. I pulled the package of day-old sweet rolls out of the paper bag and tore it open. "Hungry?"

"Uh . . . sure." He took a roll and bit off half of it, then made a face and tossed the other half on the sidewalk, where it was immediately pounced upon and fought over by about a hundred ravenous pigeons. "Kinda stale," he said.

"The sticker on the package here says they're only a day old. The birds sure seem to like 'em." I washed down my second roll with some coffee. "They *are* a little dry, though."

"You're taking Jimmy Coletta's deposition Friday." I must have looked surprised, because he added, "You filed a notice. It's a matter of public record." He paused. "I thought we agreed you'd keep us up to date on anything happening." So that was the reason for the meeting—to let me know they didn't like being left out of the loop. "A deposition's a pretty significant thing," he added.

"Maybe *you* agreed I'd be an open book," I said. "But I didn't. Besides, depositions never go forward on the day they're first set for. This one's no different. Meanwhile, I'm trying to talk to Jimmy informally to see if he plans to testify against me. He hasn't exactly told me to go screw myself, since that's not in his new vocabulary. But he won't talk to me, either."

"Jimmy's one of the things I don't like about this investigation. I can't help thinking those four guys—or some of them, anyway—were rotten. And if he was in on it . . . well, shit." He shook his head. "It's not just the wheelchair and all. I mean, I think he's for real. Him and his wife are struggling just to keep the boat afloat and still, except for when he's

197

working out, he spends most of his time on that youth program of his."

"I was out at that gym in Englewood," I said. "Last week, Thursday. He wouldn't talk to me then, either." I didn't mention my second visit, just two nights ago, or the car bomb. I'd have had to answer a lot of questions about that. And for what purpose?

"He's got another site, too, on the West Side." Theodosian sipped his coffee. "It's not just wheelchair basketball, but helping kids get back in rehab who got discouraged and quit. He's got a few back in school. He's started a nonprofit corporation."

"I know," I said. I finished off another roll. "He really believes helping those kids is the work the Lord called him to do."

"That's why I don't like it. Because if Jimmy Coletta was part of some deal to buy or sell dope, or rip off Lonnie Bright or kill the cocksucker, we're taking him down with the rest. What do we have if we don't have a police force people can trust?"

"That's five years ago. Old news to most people."

"Five years ago or last week, it's all the same. It's an open case and—" He stopped short, and nodded at me. "This ICOP thing, it's confidential, you know?"

"Who would I tell?"

"The thing is," he went on, "that other shooter, up in Lonnie's apartment, your client mention him?"

"Nice try," I said. "But what my client said is—"

"Yeah, I know. Anyway, someone must have been helping him. Otherwise, why couldn't we find him? Scumbags like that aren't exactly famous for being geniuses." He shook his head. "This incident's sure not old news to someone. They're worried, which is why your petition is stirring up so much oppposition."

"Maybe it's simple. I want my license back, but I still won't

198

say what Marlon Shades told me. Maybe people aren't *worried*; maybe I've just reminded them how I wouldn't cooperate back then—and still won't—and they don't like it." I looked at him. "Makes *you* mad as hell, doesn't it?"

"Damn right it does," he said.

I chugged down the last of my coffee. "Frick have a first name?"

"Yeah. Warren. Warren Frick."

"What does he think about Jimmy?"

"He thinks Jimmy's a lying, phony-assed piece of shit. He thinks everybody he targets on is a lying, phony-assed piece of shit." Theodosian shook his head. "And you know what? In the time I been with him? The prick's been right every goddamn time."

"Yeah? What about me? Does he think—"

"Hold it." Theodosian stood up. He was looking at Frick, who was on his feet now, too, with a cell phone to his ear. "Gotta go. Talk to you soon."

I watched the two of them stride off, apparently in a hurry. I broke the last roll into four pieces and threw them toward the pigeons who'd been hanging around, beady-eyed and hopeful. Theodosian and Frick walked straight west, across Columbus Drive toward Michigan Avenue, until I lost sight of them. Then I walked in circles for a while before heading back to the Electra, hoping everyone had lost sight of me.

Interesting. I'd once gone through the police reports and listed everyone shown anywhere who had anything to do with the Lonnie Bright investigation. One name had appeared just once, on a case report filed by one of the first investigators to arrive. He noted that he'd been approached on the scene by a man in plainclothes whom he didn't recognize. He'd asked for identification before he referred the man to the lieutenant in charge. The man had shown him an ID issued by the state police. The man's name was Warren Frick.

CHAPTER
37

I STILL HADN'T TOLD THEODOSIAN about Maura Flanagan. I'd given her until noon the next day to respond and—whether she called me or not—if by then she hadn't had me thrown in jail, I'd know I was on the right track. If she was smart, she'd call me. If she wasn't smart, she'd call the person she got the money from.

I used a phone at a gas station and checked my answering machine. Two messages. One was from the Lady. It was Wednesday and she hadn't seen me since Sunday and wondered how I was doing. The other was from Stefanie, asking "how things went with the wicked witch."

Two callers. One was a woman old enough to be my mother and, though I felt closer to her than anyone else in the world, I'd just learned she had a life I knew nothing about. The other was a bright, attractive, available woman—who hoped to God I'd help her get out of town and far away.

I left a message with the Lady's voice mail. I told her I didn't realize I had to report to her on my whereabouts, then said I was kidding and not to expect me for a few more days. I called Stefanie and told her machine that I'd know by the next afternoon how the meeting had gone.

I walked back to the Buick, thinking it might be nice on occasion to have someone to tell the whole truth to. Then, taking side streets all the way, I went to church.

WELL, NOT EXACTLY to church, but to the rectory, the priests' home. The church itself—Saint Ludella—was next door, a hulking mass of soot-grayed stone that I'd seen the inside of just once. That was a couple of years ago, when I was keeping my eye on a priest named Kevin Cunningham and it turned out he'd needed way more help than the little bit I'd been able to give.

Saint Ludella parish was on the West Side. The neighborhood hadn't changed for the better as far as I could tell. In fact, it made the streets around the community center in Englewood, where Jimmy Coletta coached basketball, look good. Englewood had its share of gangs and graffiti, rundown housing stock, and boarded-up storefronts. Around Saint Ludella's, though, they had all that, plus rubble-strewn, vacant spaces which still remained after whole blocks had been burned to the ground in the fallout from Martin Luther King's assassination, more than thirty years ago.

Many of the worst housing projects in the world were there; some being emptied out now; some already torn down. Here and there—standing out like a shiny new car in a yard full of junkers—a supermarket had appeared, or a Walgreen's. There was money to be made even on the West Side. But good times never really trickled down very far here. Brutal gang warfare and the drug industry still gobbled up nearly all the young men and spat them out into the grave or, maybe worse, into prison. Kids scrambled over too many stripped, abandoned cars that slouched on their axles at the curbs in front of too many frame houses that leaned too far to the right or the left. There wasn't much grass, there weren't many trees, and there was very little hope.

You had to start somewhere, though, so planting trees around the senior citizen housing across the street from the church was one of the latest projects of Casimir Caseliewicz, the priest who opened the rectory door when I rang the bell. He made me walk across with him to look at the trees. He called himself Casey because—or so he liked to joke—he'd long ago forgotten how to spell his real name. He was the pastor of Saint Ludella's. If he had his way he'd be the pastor there until he died, or until gentrification—still far to the east, but looming up like a cloud of locusts—finally arrived to rehab the few houses worth saving and row-house the rest of the land.

"Hell yes, I'm still here," Casey said, once we'd settled down to coffee in the rectory kitchen. "I'll stay until those damn blood-sucking developers—God have mercy on 'em, they know not what they do—drive out all the poor people."

Not your typical priest. Although . . . how would I know? I just knew his way of speaking always caught me off guard. It was rough and coarse, yet sprinkled with pious phrases he really seemed to mean. But then, Casey himself was rough and coarse. He was built in the shape of a Wheaties box, six-foot-five in his stocking feet and in the house he never wore those big black boats he called shoes.

Wherever Casey went, he nearly always wore the same outfit—faded black pants, a faded black short-sleeved shirt—with a slip-in roman collar for dress-up occasions—and black shoes and socks. Even his crew-cut was faded black. I asked him once if he wore the same shirt and pants every day, or if he had spares that were identical. "Don't ask," he said, "don't tell."

So we drank coffee and reminisced about past times, like how he'd gotten shot that night outside Kevin Cunnigham's summer cottage, and the time he was tied to Lammy Fleming's kitchen chair when the building went up in flames. We laughed a little, and finally he looked at his watch. "Well," he said, "I gotta be leaving pretty soon."

"Oh, sorry. Maybe I—"

"One of those police community relations meetings. You know, where the police get up and scare the hell outta the old people about how things are getting worse all the time and everybody oughta stay home with their doors locked day and night." He reached to his shirt pocket but it was empty, so he must have been trying to quit smoking again. "So what's up, anyway?"

"Well," I said, "I was wondering if I could move in here for a few days."

"Hey, great idea!" Not even a hint of hesitation. "Let's go get your stuff." He stood up, but when I didn't move he sat back down. "What else?"

"Nothing really." I got up from the table to get more coffee.

"What *else*, dammit?"

"I just wanted to tell you . . . tell somebody." I took the carafe from the coffee maker and turned back toward him. "I shot a man a couple of days ago."

"Damn." He stared at me, his eyes squinting beneath bushy eyebrows going gray. "Is he . . . I mean did he . . ."

I sat down and refilled both our cups. "He's dead."

"Holy crap. Lord have mercy on him." He slapped at his empty shirt pocket again. "Is that why . . . I mean, are you hiding out?"

"No. Well, yes. But not from the police. Or maybe from *some* police."

"That certainly clarifies things," he said.

"I don't think anyone knows I shot the man. I don't even know if I killed him."

"You said he was dead."

"I know. I shot him and his friends dragged him into a car and drove off, and someone had put a bomb in the car and . . . and the car blew up."

"Holy Christ! I mean, Lord have mercy on his friends, too. So someone else had it in for this guy, too. Besides you."

"I didn't even know him. Mine was self-defense."

"Thank God. That is, I knew that, of course. That's the only reason you'd—"

"Whoever planted the bomb in the car didn't have it in for

him, either. He and his buddies were *stealing* the car, and . . ."

"And what?"

"And it was my car."

"Jeez, Mal."

"And that's why I need a place to stay."

JUST SHORT OF SEVEN-THIRTY Casey left for his meeting and I got on the phone again. First I confirmed my meeting later that night with Jimmy Coletta. He was coaching at his west side site, which made it convenient for both of us. Then I called for my messages. Bingo! Maura Flanagan. She wanted to see me. Tonight, if possible. At her place.

I called the number she left, but got her answering machine. "I'll be there tonight," I said, "but I have another committment first. I'll call when I'm on my way."

Casey had given me a remote control for the garage, which was attached to the rectory and opened onto the alley out back. The rectory was built to house as many as six priests, but he was the only priest there now.

"I finally got a janitor, though," he'd told me. "Him and his wife and baby are living here. Until they can find an apartment. It's been about six months and they've . . . well . . . they've kinda taken over the third floor."

"Uh-huh," I'd said.

"But they're real quiet, and they never have any visitors. He speaks a little English, but she only speaks Nigerian. *Ibo*, I think. I'm pretty sure they're in the country illegally. But what the hell, it's nice to hear a baby cry once in a while."

I'd be staying in the housekeeper's room, on the first floor behind the kitchen. The place hadn't had a live-in housekeeper since long before Casey was pastor, but the room was there, complete with a telephone, a sofa bed, a TV set, and a tiny bathroom. I pulled around to the alley and parked in

204

the garage and brought in the gym bag I leave in the trunk with my stuff for emergency exile from home.

I rummaged around in the refrigerator, and had a supper of hot dogs and decaf and chocolate-mint ice cream. After that I made a few more phone calls, but mostly I just sat. I tried taking a nap, but that was no use. Awake or asleep, I kept seeing the same man. He sat on the ground and turned his frightened face up to me under his black Zorro hat. Blood kept bubbling out of his mouth . . . and tears ran down his pockmarked cheeks.

AT NINE O'CLOCK Casey came back home. He said he was going up to bed, and I told him he was expecting company at nine-thirty.

"I am? Hell, I don't have to stay down here and *talk* to whoever it is, do I?"

"Only a little. You're his excuse for stopping by, but . . . what do you do if you have a visitor in a wheelchair?"

"Well, the church is wheelchair accessible, but not the rectory. I think, though, that the two of us could carry just about anyone up those front steps."

"Except that I can't afford to be seen, and it's possible someone's following him."

"Well, then, I'll meet him out front and wheel him between the buildings to the stairs down to the basement entrance. It's only five or six steps down and you can help me. We'd be out of sight there."

"Deal," I said.

I told him it was Jimmy Coletta who was coming and that, in case anyone ever asked, the reason was so Jimmy could look over the facilities, to see whether they were appropriate and available for a handicapped youth program he was trying to expand.

"Is that true?" Casey wanted to know. He didn't like to lie.

205

"That's the only reason you know of," I said. "And he'll be back someday to follow up on his visit . . . if I can keep him out of jail."

It wasn't long before the van pulled up in front, with Suzanne driving. We got Jimmy down the side steps and into a basement meeting room, where a long, battered table took up most of one wall. A large coffeemaker stood on the table, and beside it a carton of paper cups. An ancient refrigerator whirred noisily in the corner, and there were ten or fifteen old metal folding chairs scattered around. The floor was clean, but the room smelled like roach spray and cigarette smoke and old coffee.

"Not exactly elegant," Casey said, clearing the way for Jimmy's wheelchair, "but at least it's not being used tonight. Two nights a week they have AA meetings in—" He stopped. "Oh, can I get you something to drink? Pepsi or something? Don't have any beer or booze around."

"That's okay, Father," Suzanne said. "We don't drink alcohol."

"Really?"

"We're evangelical," she said. "It's against our relig—" She stopped and looked embarrassed. "We don't practice Catholicism anymore, Father."

"Not to worry. You got lots of company," Casey said, obviously trying to put her at ease.

"I never went to church anyway," Jimmy said, "but I sure used to drink, way too much. Before I was born again in the Holy Spirit and accepted the Lord into my life." He said it matter-of-factly, neither ashamed of it nor pushing it.

"You drank too much?" Casey laughed. "Well, join the club. I'm a recovering alcoholic. What I call a fallen-away drunk. But back when I was a *practicing* drunk I was a full-blown, pee-down-my-leg, crap-in-my-pants, fall-on-my-face drunk. Pardon my French, but it's God's truth. And I don't

206

wanna ever forget it. 'Cause I could be one again, dammit, any day of the week."

There was a long, embarrassed silence, until Jimmy finally spoke up. "It's okay," he said, and he looked right at me. "Sometimes the truth isn't pretty."

Casey got drinks out of the refrigerator—three cans of Pepsi-Cola—and handed them out. "I'll be upstairs," he said. "Just holler when you're ready to go."

CHAPTER
38

THE THREE OF US sat there in the rectory basement and waited. Suzanne pulled her chair up closer to Jimmy. She looked at the unopened Pepsi can in her hand as though wondering where it came from, then set it on the table.

We heard Casey close the upstairs door, and then Jimmy spoke up. "You keep telling me you'll protect me," he said, "but I keep wondering why I should trust you. I don't know why you would care what happens to me."

"I told Marlon Shades I wouldn't talk," I said, "and I went to jail to keep my word. That's why you should trust me." I leaned in toward him a little. "But I never said I'll protect you. What I keep telling you is I'll do my best to keep you out of this if I can. And that's what I'll do . . . my best." I popped the top of my own Pepsi. "Why do I care? I guess it's really why I *don't* care. I know what you were doing that night and I still don't see any reason for you to go to jail— not now—or lose your disability benefits because of a conviction. For what purpose? Justice? The law? Maybe protecting you is illegal. Some might even say it's immoral. I don't much care about what people say."

"So then why are you stirring up trouble?" Suzanne asked. "If you don't care, why not just let things be?"

"I have my own interests, other promises I've made; some of them to myself. And I like to keep my promises. Besides, sooner or later it's not going to work to 'just let things be.' The case is still an open case. People are working on it."

"Working on it?" she asked. "What are you—"

"Wait, Suzanne," Jimmy said. "What he means is it's a homicide case. A man got away—a cop killer—and the case will stay open forever. Or until they catch him. And if they do," he added, "then all the other . . . circumstances will come out."

"Maybe someday they'll put it all together," I said. "If that happens, and if you go to jail, it'll be because of your own actions. I can't change what you did. But I have no interest in taking you down. None. If you fill me in on the details, maybe I can wrap up what I need to do, and keep you out of it. *Maybe*. That's the best I can offer." And maybe I had no business holding out even that much hope. "Otherwise, I just keep flailing around and whatever I churn up goes public."

"I don't know, Jimmy," Suzanne said. "Maybe we shouldn't have come. Maybe—"

"No," he said. "We agreed. I can't just sit and wait any longer. It's eating away at me. I don't want to go to jail, or lose my disability. But we both know that someday that might happen, whether this man has anything to do with it or not. Maybe he can help; maybe he can't. But I need to take some action that *might* protect us."

"But . . ." She paused, then let it go. "You're right," she said. "We agreed, and we're together in this." She was strong and smart, and she loved this man in his wheelchair.

Jimmy turned to me, took a deep breath, and began. "One of the hardest things for these poor kids I work with is to face reality. As for me, I've already faced my paralysis, and now I've got to start facing the rest of it." The words came out in a rush, as though he'd rehearsed them so he'd be able to get started. "On the night—"

"Wait," I said. "Let me go first, all right? Then you can fill in the blank spaces."

He looked at me. "Okay," he finally said. Suzanne just stared down at her hands in her lap.

"When a suspended lawyer files a petition for reinstatement to the bar, the disciplinary commission notifies lots of people," I said, "people who might have something to say about it. So the cops who were there that night at Lonnie Bright's—and their friends and relatives—they all heard about my petition. Right?"

Jimmy nodded.

"And everybody expects them to object. After all, I lost my license because I wouldn't reveal what Marlon Shades told me, so why should I get it back again until I tell? I make it clear, though, that I still won't tell, and I insist on a hearing. The cops and their relatives are notified that if there's a hearing they'll be subpoenaed to testify against me, to describe the damage that's been caused to so many families, and how I could help bring them some closure, if I'd just obey the supreme court's order. Maybe my information would help catch someone who participated in shooting three police officers, murdering one of them and putting another . . ." I sipped some Pepsi.

"In a wheelchair," Jimmy said, but he didn't look at me.

"The thing is, though, for the three living cops—and let's assume it's all of them—for these three cops maybe the truth is the one thing they're afraid *will* come out." I paused. "Stop me if I get too far off base, okay?"

"Yeah. Okay." Jimmy's voice was barely audible.

"Of course, these cops don't know for sure what Marlon told me. But if I didn't reveal it before, they ask themselves, why should I now? And if I don't tell, and if they all stick together, they're in the clear. They have a meeting, maybe, to talk it over. And then there's a new problem. If there's a hearing, and if they have to testify, maybe they *won't* all stick together. In fact, one of them says he *won't* lie, says he's

210

different now. Or he *doesn't* say it and they know it anyway. He won't lie, and he especially won't lie under oath. Jesus wouldn't lie—even to save himself—and neither will this born-again Christian. He doesn't want to go to jail, but he's a man who lives by what he sees as God's commandments. He'll tell the truth."

"If he's *asked*," Suzanne said. "Remember that." She looked like she might cry.

"That's what I figured," I said. "Anyway, the truth these police officers don't want known is that they were selling cocaine to Lonnie Bright. And worse than that, that they murdered him. They figured why give the coke they had to Lonnie Bright, when they could take his money and keep the stuff and sell it to someone else."

"Wait a minute," Jimmy said. "I—"

"Well, let's say everyone didn't know what everyone else was thinking. But anyway, who'd care if Lonnie was shot down? Decent citizens would be glad to be rid of one more middleman in the delivery of death to kids. Lonnie's competitors would be happy. The cops who could sell the same coke twice would be happy. Of course they couldn't do this very often, or who'd deal with them? But this time, hey, why not?"

Jimmy cleared his throat. "You—"

"If I'm pretty close to right so far," I cut in, "don't say anything."

No one said anything.

"Maybe Lonnie's looking to rise in the world, so he's cutting his . . . his business associates . . . out of the deal," I said. "Anyway, the cops know he's gonna be at his place by himself, which is what's gonna make it so easy. They arrive and get their money, and then one of them puts a bullet in Lonnie's brain. But surprise! Someone else *is* there. Fay Rita, Lonnie's lady friend. Who knows why? Anyway, she's hiding and

211

watching. She's a psychopath herself, and she's got an automatic and when Lonnie takes the bullet she's too slow to stop it, but she starts shooting everyone in sight. Eventually the cops take her down, but by the time it's over three out of the four cops are shot too. The fourth one, Richard Kilgallon, calls for help and when help arrives he's wandering around on the sidewalk out front—like in a daze, or in shock. He talks about Lonnie and his girl friend, and some other man with a gun, too. A man no one's ever able to identify."

Suzanne was crying softly now.

"I'll stop there," I said. I hadn't mentioned Marlon Shades at all. "Your turn."

Jimmy nodded, and took a deep breath. "That night, all I knew was—"

"Wait," Suzanne said. "Are you sure?"

"Yes." He reached his hand out toward her. "I . . . I *need* to."

She took his hand. "I know," she said. "I know you do." She brushed her lips across the tips of his fingers and then let go of his hand.

CHAPTER

39

"ALL RIGHT," Jimmy said. "Okay." He paused, then pushed on. "I don't know to this day—at least I don't know for *sure*—what my brother and Richard Kilgallon, my brother's partner, planned. I mean, about killing anyone. All I knew was that the two of them had got their hands on a trunkload of co-caine and that some guy named Lonnie Bright—I'd never even heard of Lonnie before—was gonna buy it. I hadn't been assigned to narcotics very long, but I . . . I'd been pretty sure for a while what Sal was into. That night he was gonna bring me in for the first time." He shook his head. "When I think back on it now, it's even hard for *me* to understand."

"What do you mean?" I asked.

"Well, at the time I knew it was wrong. I mean I was a cop, a sworn police officer. But somehow, back then, its be-ing wrong didn't matter much. Other guys were doing it. Not everyone, you know, but . . . Plus, you get to thinking, hey, the drugs are there anyway. Everywhere; an endless supply, so . . . Well, the excuses don't look so good now. But all I knew about was the sale."

"You're sure of that?" I asked, mainly to make him say it again, to watch him.

"I didn't know about any plan to kill anyone. I really didn't. I was to stay downstairs with Marlon Shades and— Oh, what you said was right, about Lonnie doing this deal on his own. Sal told me that. He was surprised Lonnie's nephew, Marlon, was there." Jimmy stopped, looked at me. "You didn't men-

213

tion Marlon, but you know he was there, right? He must have told you that."

I just shrugged.

"Right," Jimmy said. "You're not saying. Anyway, we met Lonnie and Marlon in the alley. Nobody knew that Lonnie had his girlfriend and another guy hiding upstairs. Anyway, Lonnie checked out the coke in the trunk of Sal's squad. When he was satisfied, he said the money was upstairs, and Sal and Richie went with him to get it. Art Frankel—he was my partner—was out front with our car. Sal told me to stay down there in the alley and help Marlon unload the cocaine out of the squad car and into Lonnie Bright's car."

"How much?"

"Pounds? Kilos? I don't know. Maybe twenty-five, thirty kilos. It was packed in little clear plastic bags, and then put in some plastic shopping bags. I thought it was strange when Sal pulled me to the side and told me to help Marlon with the loading and then bring him upstairs in a hurry. I said to forget Marlon and once it's unloaded I'd just bring the car around front and we'll all get outta there. But Sal said we didn't want Marlon running off with any of the stuff. He told me, 'You get that skinny little nigger's ass up—' " Jimmy stopped and stared down at the unopened Pepsi can cradled in his hands. "I'm sorry, God help me, but that's what he said."

"Take a deep breath," Suzanne said. "Take your time."

"Right. So, like I said," he went on, "it seemed strange because if we had the money, who cared what Marlon did? But I said sure. The thing is, though, I didn't help Marlon at all. I figured that was scut work, beneath me." He shook his head, remembering. "That made Marlon mad and he took just two bags at a time, and he moved pretty slow. Sal should've backed his squad up to Lonnie's car, trunk-to-trunk. But he didn't, and Marlon had to haul them around and—"

"Wait," I said. "Was there plenty of light?"

"Hardly any at all. The only lights were from the trunk lights of the two cars. The alley lights were out. The first floor was vacant. Anyway, Marlon just had two more bags to go, when all the sudden there was a shot upstairs. Then right away more shots. I left Marlon there and ran up the stairs. But by the time I got up to the second floor it was real quiet again. The back door to the apartment was open and I stood there a few seconds, with my gun in my hand, wondering what to do. Then I thought I heard someone moving inside. It was dark in there and I figured someone might be waiting for me. So I ran back downstairs and . . . and there was more shooting upstairs. And then it stopped again."

"Where was Marlon?" I asked.

"Marlon was gone. Both trunks—Lonnie's car and the squad—were still open. I was scared. I couldn't think straight. I was afraid to call in because I didn't know what happened. Plus, you know, we'd be caught with the coke. I looked in the squad and the two bags were still there. I ran to Lonnie's trunk and all those bags were still there, too. And then I heard someone behind me, back by the back stairs of the building, and I realized someone must have come down from upstairs. I remember I still had my weapon in my hand, and I'm pretty sure I raised it up and started to turn." His voice was shaking.

"Relax," I said. "Take your time."

"Right. Okay. So I was turning around from Lonnie's trunk and I saw someone on the steps, but just like a glimpse. Everything happened so fast and . . . and I was shot right then, sort of in the side of the back, but I don't remember hearing any shot, or feeling any real pain. I just remem-

215

ber . . . it's hard to describe. Like something hit me hard and I was scared. Somehow I knew I was shot and I thought I was gonna die, and I was scared to die. I stood there, and I lost control, you know? My bladder. And then I started falling. I think I fell half into the trunk." He stopped and breathed deeply. "And that's it. That's all I really remember until later, in the hospital, when I woke up."

"Nothing else?" I pressed him, but he shook his head. "When you were able to be interviewed you told the detectives that your brother and Kilgallon ran up the front way after Lonnie, because they'd spotted him with a gun. You said Frankel stayed out in front and you drove Sal's car around to cover the back of the building. You heard some shooting and you started up, but someone was running down in the darkness and knocked you back down the stairs, and then followed you down and shot you. And that's all you remembered."

"Yes," he said. "That's what I told them. That's after I read what the others said. I had to keep the drug deal out of it. I lied."

"If you were over by Lonnie's car when you were shot, why did you say—"

"Because where they said they found me was by the bottom of the steps. That was only a few feet from the car, anyway."

"But actually you were looking in Lonnie's trunk. When you turned, did you see the person coming down the steps?"

"Not really. I heard him and I started to turn and I just saw a vague figure, almost like a shadow. And he shot me. It all happened at once."

"And you fell and you don't remember *any*thing after that?"

"Well, I mean, I *sort* of remember feeling and hearing little bits of things. Being lifted or dragged, then later being picked

216

up and put on a stretcher. Sirens, voices. I'd be aware maybe for a few seconds, and then out again. I think I remember the ambulance bouncing. But I'm sure they put me under on the way to the hospital."

"I was there when he woke up," Suzanne said, "after surgery. He didn't really wake up even then. He recognized me, said my name, but he doesn't remember that, either. Then there was more surgery. And it just went on and on."

"Did you talk to either Kilgallon or Frankel before you gave your statement to the detectives?"

"No, I didn't. I had a lawyer. Someone sent him. His advice was not to talk to them, just read their statements. He said he assumed my statement would be consistent with theirs. I was depressed and angry and afraid. I said what I said, and it wasn't true."

"When did you finally talk to either Kilgallon or Frankel?"

"Never," he said. "That is, I never talked to either of them again about that night, or what happened. Neither one ever came to see me in the hospital, or at home. I saw them on a couple of public occasions, but we didn't really talk. We never have."

"Not even recently?" I couldn't believe there'd been no communication.

"No, but I know what you're getting at." He paused. "The lawyer came to see me, about a month ago. The same lawyer I had after the shooting. I didn't call him this time, either; he just came. He wanted to discuss any letter I might send to the disciplinary commission about you, or any testimony I might give. I told him I wasn't sending any letter, and I wasn't going to testify. He said they might subpoena me and I told him that if somehow I was forced to testify, I . . . I'd just tell the truth. He got the point."

"Did he suggest that you lie?

"No. He just left."

217

"What happened to the money?"

"I don't know. The guy who shot me must have taken it. And the cocaine, too, I guess. I figured he moved me away from the trunk to get at it and—"

"The doctors," Suzanne said, "they thought the bullet was lodged near the spinal cord and then shifted later. They said if Jimmy'd been immobilized before . . . if he'd been moved properly, maybe he wouldn't . . ." She was crying.

"We don't know that, honey," he said.

"How much did you get when the whole deal was over?"

"What?" He looked as though he didn't understand the question.

"Well, you got some of it. What was your share? How dumb do you think I am?"

"Look here, you—" He stopped, shook his head. "Nothing. Not dime one. I never—"

"Okay, I believe you." And I did. "But that night, you never actually saw any money?"

"No, but Lonnie Bright said he had it, and I'm sure he did. I mean, I didn't know him, but Sal sure believed him. And the man would have had to be crazy not to have the money. He—"

"Wait," Suzanne put in. "I really never thought of it, but maybe that's why he had his girlfriend up there, and that other guy. Maybe he wasn't meaning to buy at all. Maybe it was a trap to—"

"No," Jimmy said, and made me more certain than ever that he was telling me the truth. "He'd have known better, Suzanne," he explained. "He had two cops up there with him, me in the alley, and Art Frankel on the street out front. With our radios. No way he'd think he could ambush four cops."

"Right," I said. "And if he managed to pull it off, how would he explain what happened? It'd be hard to get rid of

218

four dead bodies and two squad cars." I shook my head. "Uh-uh, he had the money. How much was it supposed to be?"

"Five hundred thousand dollars. And I think that was cheap for the amount of coke that was there."

"Jesus!" I said. "So there was half a million in cash upstairs, and at least that much in coke downstairs, and some lucky person got away with it all."

"No, not lucky," Jimmy said. "That was Satan's money, the wages of sin. It cost my brother his life, and me my legs."

"Who was it?" I said. "Emerson? Thackeray? Somebody back then. He said that's the trouble with money. It usually costs way too much."

CHAPTER

40

AT TEN-FIFTEEN CASEY AND I carried Jimmy up the outside steps from the basement. I went back inside and upstairs, while Casey went with Suzanne and Jimmy out to the van. They were both exhausted—and it wasn't just physical. Besides, I had another appointment to keep.

I watched from a front window of the rectory as Casey swiveled Jimmy's wheelchair this way and that on the front sidewalk and pointed in various directions, before wheeling him onto the van's lift platform. Finally, Suzanne got Jimmy into the van and they drove off.

"What was all that turning and gesturing about?" I asked, when Casey was back inside.

"I was showing him the church, and the school buildings, and the old convent. Whatever might be useful for his youth program. That was for my sake, y'know? In case anyone ever asks what he was doing here, God forbid. I don't think he was paying attention, though."

"No," I said, "probably not."

We went to the kitchen for coffee and I used the phone there to call Maura Flanagan. Again I got her answering machine. That seemed odd, since she'd wanted to see me that night, and I hung up without saying anything.

I called my own number, but there was only one message, the one from Flanagan that I'd already heard. I listened again. She sounded awfully worried.

I SUPPOSE I SHOULD HAVE gone to bed and seen what the morning would bring. That was Casey's suggestion. But I didn't. I'd had enough of Zorro's sad, dying face looking up at me, every time I closed my eyes.

I drove too fast and I don't know what I thought about while I was driving. I might not even have remembered to park the Buick far from my destination and walk the rest of the way, except that I pulled off Lake Shore Drive and onto the narrow, crowded streets of Lincoln Park and realized at once that I probably couldn't find a spot near Maura Flanagan's house if I wanted to. I finally parked on a dark street that said *Permit Parking Only*, and had to walk a long way.

With just two short blocks to go, I turned the corner onto Flanagan's street—and stopped in my tracks. My heart stopped beating and for an instant I couldn't get my legs to move. When they did start working again, I turned and re-traced my steps, forcing myself not to run. Just an easy, nat-ural, rapid pace, all the way back to the car. I got into the passenger seat and slid off my jacket and the shoulder holster and got back out. I put the jacket on and stowed the Beretta in the trunk, then headed back to Maura Flanagan's.

I'd been too far away to tell just where the action was cen-tered, so all those flashing blue lights and squad cars, and the people milling around, didn't have to mean it was Flanagan's house where something bad had happened. But her address was an even number, so it was on the west side of the street—and the cops were keeping the curious on the east side.

Still, it didn't have to be Flanagan's house. Maybe her next-door neighbor came home drunk and beat the shit out of his wife—surely not unheard of in upscale Lincoln Park. Or maybe someone robbed someone at gunpoint; or maybe they were having a midweek, midnight block party and that's why the street was blocked off.

It didn't *have* to be Flanagan's house.

CHAPTER

41

"IT'S THAT JUDGE'S HOUSE," the man said.

We were standing on the sidewalk at the south end of Maura Flanagan's block, near the corner. The man nodded and pointed across the street and several houses to the north. "That one," he said. He was a small, dark man with an Indian accent . . . or Pakistani, maybe. He could have been the owner of the two-million-dollar brownstone behind us, or the driver of the cab parked illegally just around the corner. But it was cold out and he wore a white dress shirt and no jacket, so I guessed homeowner. I'm a detective.

"The female," he added. "Judge Flanagan, I think, yes?"

"It's Justice," I said.

He peered up at me. "You mean what happened? It is justice?"

"No. I mean it's not *Judge* Flanagan. It's *Justice* Flanagan."

"Ah." He nodded and pursed his lips as though I'd said something terribly wise.

A couple of cop cars—a blue-and-white and a tan un-marked—backed down the street our way, turned around in the intersection, and drove off. People were wandering away. The action was dying down.

"What happened?" I asked.

"That I do not know," he said. "But she is dead. They—"

"What? You don't know that!" The words came out too loud and he stared at me and stepped backwards. "I mean," I said, struggling to control my voice, "did you see her?"

"No. They came out of the house with one of those bags

222

with a zipper, like one sees on TV programs."

"So you don't *know*, for God's sake."

"Word spread through the crowd that a policeman said it was her. That's how—" He stopped. I must have had a kill-the-messenger look on my face, because he backed away again, moving inside the iron gate toward the brownstone. "It is cold," he said, looking past my shoulder as though afraid to look directly at me. "I must go." He turned and hurried up the steps.

"Hey," I said, "I'm sorry. Can you—"

"I must go." On the porch landing he turned, but still kept looking past me.

I spun around. "Damn," I said.

They were two uniformed cops; both black, both with their right hands resting lightly on their holstered weapons. The taller one leaned toward me a little. "Malachai Foley?" he asked.

"Mala-*key*," I said. "Key, key, KEY! Dammit."

"Yes, sir," he said. "Investigator Brasher would like to talk to you, sir."

"Yeah? Tell him to have his people call my people." But it was no use. They just stood there, waiting for me to move. "Who's Brasher, anyway? Where is he?"

The cop spread his arms as though indicating the entire block. "Violent Crimes Division, sir. He's in charge of the scene. He's in that car." He pointed down the east-west street toward the tan unmarked car that I thought had driven away. The blue-and-white was parked in front of it. "He asked us to bring you to him, if it was okay with you."

"And if it's not okay with me?"

"He said to bring you anyway."

BRASHER WAS A BIG MAN and had a big, homely, intelligent-looking face. He sat in the back seat of the detectives' car on the left side, behind the driver—who was also in plainclothes—and I sat on the right. That was after the taller uniformed officer patted me down, of course, and passed my wallet to Brasher.

He went through everything in the wallet, and handed it back to me. "You carry a lot of cash," he said.

"I'm a cash-and-carry sort of guy," I said. "No credit cards."

"I noticed."

"Am I under arrest?"

"Nope."

"Then why the search of my body and possessions?"

"Obviously consensual," he said. "I didn't hear any objection."

"Is that it?" I said, and opened the door beside me.

"How well did you know Justice Maura Flanagan?"

I closed the door. "How well *did* I know her?"

"That was my question."

"Is she dead?"

"How well did you know her?"

"I hardly knew her at all. She called me earlier tonight. Left a message on my machine asking me to come and see her. I called back and said I would."

"Really?" His surprise was phony. They'd have listened to her messages. "And what did you talk about?"

"I left a message on her machine, said I'd be there."

"What did you talk about," he said, "*after* you got there?"

"I didn't get there. I was on my way when two large uniformed police officers grabbed me at gunpoint, threw me up against the side of a car, and searched my body in an intrusive, embarrassing way. They took my wallet, which they gave to a man in civilian clothes, who pawed through it before he gave it back to me. I was kept in custody with no explanation." I stopped. "Just kidding," I said. "Why the interrogation?"

"It's not an interrogation; it's an interview. You're not a

224

suspect; you're a witness. You're not in custody; you're co-operating with a police investigation."

"What was I a witness to?"

"You were one of the last people," he said, "to see the victim alive."

"So she *is* dead."

"Very."

"You said 'victim.' What happened to her?"

"Her heart stopped beating," he said.

"Not funny," I said. "What makes you think—"

There was a rap on the front passenger window. The door opened and a man leaned in and said, "Excuse me." It was Theodosian. "Could I talk to you for a minute, Brasher?" he asked.

HALF AN HOUR LATER I was sitting in a back booth at an all-night restaurant just south of Lincoln Park, on Clark Street. Theodosian sat across from me and we were both drinking coffee. The waitress returned with a burger and a piece of lemon meringue pie for me, nothing for him. I wasn't that hungry, but I wanted something to do and say, while I figured out how open I wanted to be with Theodosian. The waitress refilled both our coffees, said to holler if we needed anything, and left.

"Where's your partner?" I asked.

"Furlough."

"Really," I said. "He was at Lonnie Bright's, you know, after the shooting. He's mentioned in a report."

"I don't remember that, but I'm not surprised. ICOP was new. It was his baby and he was all over the West Side that year, trying to show the brass he was accomplishing something. Actually, most people thought he was a pain in the ass."

"And he's on furlough now?"

"That's what Chicago cops call it. I don't know about the state guys. Maybe they call it vacation. I mean, he didn't even tell me he was gonna be gone." He stirred some sugar into his coffee. "Frick the prick."

"For how long?"

"I don't know. A week, I think."

"He picked an interesting time to take off," I said.

"What's that mean?"

"Nothing, except . . . you know . . . he missed Flanagan's murder."

"That's not his jurisdiction. Anyway, it's by order of his commanding officer. Otherwise the sonovabitch never *would* take time off. It's a break for me, I tell ya. Frick practically invented the word 'workaholic.' "

"I don't see you taking it easy," I said, and bit into my burger. "Thanks for getting me out of there."

"It's only temporary. Personally, I don't think you're the murdering type. But Brasher has a job to do. He and I go back a ways, and I told him I needed to talk to you, bad, about something else that couldn't wait. I said I'd transport you to Area Three myself. He's got plenty to do, anyway." He sipped some of his coffee. "What I want to know is how does Flanagan fit into your situation?"

"She doesn't. Not as far as I know. She's one of the justices who'll decide my case, but otherwise . . ." I shrugged and spread my hands to show my bewilderment. Mustard dripped to the table from the half-eaten burger in my right hand. "Oops."

"And nothing else, huh?" He didn't seem to believe me. Maybe my obfuscation skills were slipping. "Let's see," he went on, "first someone shoves a note with a dismembered spider through your slot with your mail and threatens to pull off *your* limbs, too; then that little friend of yours gets the living shit kicked out of him, carrying a business card that seems to implicate you; and now a supreme court justice gets killed and the dick on the scene tells me there's a message on her machine saying you're on your way. Am I reading too much into it, or is it all coincidental?"

I shrugged. "I think that note on the business card in Yogi's pocket was another warning to me. Flanagan, though, is different. If there's a pattern, I don't see it."

"Why'd she call you up then, ask you to come and see her?"

"Brasher tell you that, too?"

"He said that's what you told him."

"Right." I finished off the burger and pulled the pie closer. "But my answer to your question is still the same," I said. "The connection I know of is that Flanagan's on . . . she *was* on . . . the supreme court. She called me and I might have found out something else, but I was just getting to her place when I saw all the activity. Then Brasher had me picked up. That's it."

Theodosian drank the last of his coffee. "I don't know." He shook his head. "I don't think Brasher's gonna believe your story."

"Why?" I said.

"Do you know what a *fake book* is?"

"What?"

"A fake book. Do you?"

"Sure. Musicians—especially piano players—use them. They're books with the music—and sometimes the words—for pop tunes, old standards. Usually hundreds of tunes in one book. They print the melody only, and above that the chords, so you can read the melody and *fake*, or improvise, the arrangement from the chords. I've got half a dozen of 'em. Otherwise, I'd have to memorize a thousand—" I stopped. "So what's that got to do with anything?"

"Brasher'll go after my ass if he learns I told you, but he

said they found a music book on a piano in Flanagan's place. He said it's called *Columbia's Colossal Fake Book.*"

"Sure, I've got a copy of that one. I used to use it all—"

"This one's a beat-up copy, according to Brasher. Cover's half torn off." Theodosian stood up and dropped a couple of dollars on the table. "You didn't hear it here, okay? But this one's got *your* name written up in the corner of page one."

CHAPTER

42

RENATA CARROWAY DID HER USUAL TAKE-CHARGE lawyer thing. She met me at Area Three Headquarters, told me to keep my mouth shut, and demanded to know from Brasher whether I was a suspect. When Brasher waffled, she told him I was exercising my right to remain silent.

She didn't tell Brasher we knew about the fake book on the piano because he'd know I must have gotten that from Theodosian. She insisted, though, that he tell us whether they had anything that actually put me on the scene. He refused to say, and she glared at him through her glasses and dared him to lock me up on whatever evidence they had—which I happened to think was a bit rash. But it worked and I was out of there by two A.M., no charges filed.

We left in Renata's car and, driving back to mine, I told her the fake book could have been taken when my house was broken into. "Or maybe it was in the pile of music I always leave at Miz Becky's."

"Uh-huh," she said.

"Besides, would I kill her and forget to erase my message off her machine?"

"People have done dumber things," she said. "In fact, you yourself have—"

"Well then," I said, "I have an airtight alibi for most of the evening."

"Really," she said. "And why didn't you tell me that before we went in to talk to the police?"

"Because I wasn't going to tell them where I was, or with who."

When she stopped calling me names, she said, "Whom."

"What?"

"You won't tell them where you were, or with *whom*." By that time we'd gotten to where I'd parked the Buick, and she stopped. "I'll call you," she snapped, "when I hear from Brasher."

"I'll tell *you*, though, where I was. Don't you want to know?"

"What good will telling *me* do?"

"Well, at least you'd see I'm not making it up. You—"

"I *know* you're not making it up, dammit. I also know you're always honest with me, and you're the most irritating, most idiotic client I have."

"Thank you."

"I'm tired now, and my child has the flu and I have to get home. Good night."

I got out and watched her drive away. I liked Renata, a lot. And I knew she liked me, too—sort of.

I drove around until I was certain no one was following me and then I drove to Saint Ludella's and parked in the garage. I got the Beretta out of the trunk and took it inside the rectory with me. There was a note on the kitchen table from Casey, saying the janitor and his wife and baby were gone somewhere, until Monday. "P.S.," he'd added, "I put clean sheets on the sofa bed and towels in the bathroom. And don't forget, God loves everyone, even you and me."

I went into the housekeeper's room, put my jacket and the holstered gun on a chair, and lay down on the bed in my clothes. The mattress was still only two inches thick and just as uncomfortable as it had been the last time I'd tried to sleep on it, a couple of years ago.

I lay there and knew I'd never get to sleep and wished I could believe in God because it would have been nice to have someone to say thank you to for Casey. And for Renata, too. And for . . .

I must have fallen asleep around that time and to my knowledge I didn't see Zorro looking up at me—or the sudden terror in his eyes, or the blood foaming up on his lips— until almost nine o'clock. Which is when I woke up.

WHEN I STUMBLED into the kitchen Casey was sitting at the table reading a thin book with what looked like a leather cover, but seemed too small to be a Bible. He didn't look up, but said, "Help yourself," and pointed toward the coffee-maker.

"Thanks."

Maybe it was something in my voice, but he lifted his head, then, and stared at me. "God, you look terrible," he said. "Go back to bed."

"Can't sleep."

"Well then, go back and clean up a little. I'll make breakfast."

"You don't have to do that. Edna not around anymore?" Edna was the woman who used to come in and cook five days a week.

"Getting over the flu," he said. "Supposed to be back in a few days. Anyway, I have to eat, too. I've been waiting for you to get up."

I showered and shaved and changed clothes, and went back to the kitchen. Casey had orange juice, scrambled eggs and sausage, and thick slices of whole wheat bread on the table, and we both dug in.

"Got any salt?" I said, after a few bites.

"In that cabinet," he said, pointing. Then he laughed. "I

knew you'd wanna add salt. These eggs, they're not exactly real eggs, and the sausage is meatless. Edna's got me on this healthy diet."

"Hot dogs and ice cream part of it?" I asked, remembering my supper the evening before.

"Nope." He scooped himself some more not-exactly-real eggs. "I cheat a little when she's not looking. You gonna be around today?"

"In and out, probably. I'll be careful, though. Don't wanna get you in trouble with the Cardinal."

"Not to worry," he said. "I've had my ass in a sling with him since he arrived on the scene. That's how I like it."

"Really?"

"Sure. That way he tries not to think about me, and I get to stay right here at Saint Ludella's—not that there's a helluva lotta priests standing in line to replace me here." He shoveled down the rest of his food. "Gotta go. Monthly meeting at the alderman's office."

"The alderman?"

"Yeah. He'll be there, and the police commander, local school administrators, clergy, social workers . . . other community activist and political types. We're supposed to share ideas about how to make the neighborhood a better place." He got to his feet. "Most of 'em wish I wouldn't show up."

"Really?"

"Yeah, my ass is in a sling with *them*, too." He grabbed a black windbreaker off the back of his chair. "Which proves that *some* of my ideas—like maybe they should stop talking and actually *do* something about housing, public safety, jobs, and education—must be right."

"Have a great time at the meeting," I said.

As he headed down the hall toward the front door, he called out, "I won't need my car today. The keys are in that drawer with the can openers and stuff."

"That's all right," I called back, "I have—"

The front door slammed. I finished my breakfast and washed the dishes and studied the evidence until I figured out which cabinet and drawer each piece went in.

I knew Casey would have been up since six-thirty, and said mass at eight o'clock in a little side chapel in the church for just a few people. He never listened to the news or read the paper until after breakfast. "What's not a buncha fluffy crap is too damn depressing," he'd once told me. So he wouldn't have known about Maura Flanagan's death.

But he did get both the *Tribune* and the *Sun-Times* delivered to the door, and I found them on a table in the hallway, still folded inside their plastic sleeves. Both had front page headlines that screamed the murder of a supreme court justice, but not much in the way of hard news about what happened. Both said police had no one in custody, but were pursuing several avenues, including looking at cases before the court recently in which a losing party might have been angry. In other words, the cops claimed to be clueless.

I knew, though, that they had at least two clues, and that both of them pointed my way.

There was nothing in the papers about my phone message on the answering machine, though, or my fake book. What they had was that Flanagan had lived alone on the first floor of a two-unit condo building. The second floor was being renovated and was vacant. She'd been seen by a neighbor arriving home in a cab about six o'clock. Sometime later a call came in to the desk at the local district station—so it wasn't taped—from someone claiming they heard screams and a gunshot from inside the house. The responding officers found her dead. She'd been shot once "in the upper part of the body," police said.

My own theory was that Flanagan had told the wrong person about our conversation. Whether she'd called me on her own, or the person made her do it, I might never know. Whoever it was, though, must have decided he couldn't trust her to keep quiet much longer, so he shot her . . . probably in the head.

Unfortunately, I couldn't go to Brasher and present my theory. I'd have to reveal the whole story, including Stefanie's overhearing the conversation between Flanagan and Stefanie's boss, Clark Woolford; Flanagan's being paid off to close the O.P.S. case; and the drug deal between Lonnie Bright and the cops.

Of course, if I established all that, Richie Kilgallon would end up in jail—maybe even death row—and that would make Breaker Hanafan happy and keep him away from Yogi. The problem was I couldn't prove any payoff without Flanagan, and she was dead. More importantly, I couldn't prove any drug deal without Jimmy's testimony, and I wasn't going to be a part of destroying him. He'd been part of the deal, yes, but I was convinced he hadn't known Lonnie would be killed.

I'd had a hand in too many deaths in the last couple of days. Maura Flanagan was the latest. But before that, if I'd have just pulled on Zorro and backed him off me, not been so quick to squeeze the trigger, he and his buddies—or some of them, anyway—might not have been inside the Lexus when it blew up. Better them than me, for sure; but still, I didn't want any more part of people dying.

I SAT IN THE KITCHEN trying to fit the pieces together. At noon I called my phone to retrieve my messages. There were two of them. The one from Brasher said he wanted to talk to me. The one from Renata also said Brasher wanted to talk to me. Renata said she hoped my alibi would stand up.

I was a suspect in the murder of Maura Flanagan.

CHAPTER

43

I CALLED RENATA. "You don't have caller ID, do you?"

"Not at the office. Where—"

"Good. I'm far, far away. I *do* have an alibi, and it'll stand up if we ever need it. But in the meantime, if they ask whether you've heard from me you can say yes and that I said I'd turn myself in and cooperate. That's all. Nothing about the alibi. Okay?"

"So," she said, "when will you be here?"

"What?"

"You're wanted for the murder of a justice of the Illinois Supreme Court, for God's sake. No way you can stay underground for long. You said you're turning yourself in. When will you be here?"

"I'll get back to you on that," I said, and hung up on her.

The next call was to Jimmy Coletta's home. Suzanne answered and I said, "it's Foley. You have caller ID?"

"No. That costs—"

"Just wondered. Look, whatever you hear on the news or anywhere else—and tell Jimmy, too—don't talk to anybody about the meeting we had. Whether or when or where or anything. Okay?"

"Of course," she said. "Why would we?"

"Because you or Jimmy might think it would be helpful—helpful to me—to tell someone. But it won't, believe me."

"What are you talking about?"

"Just don't forget. And one more thing. Don't let Jimmy talk to anyone about . . . about the past. Not the police or anyone. Till you hear from me. Do you understand?"

"Yes, but—"

I hung up on Suzanne, too. That seemed to be one of the things I did best.

Casey'd be home soon and I had to be gone by then. If the cops somehow learned he was helping me they'd be all over him. He'd have to tell them I was there the night before—which was my alibi in a homicide case, sure—but he'd have to say Jimmy and Suzanne were there, too, and I didn't want that. I was doing my best to keep Jimmy out of it. I'd promised.

I gathered up my stuff and was headed out the back door into the garage when Casey's voice boomed from the front of the house. "Mal?" he called. "Mal? You here?"

I closed the door softly and left.

I suppose in my mind I'd been picturing the world as a pretty dark and dreary place, because when I backed the Buick Electra out of the garage I was surprised to discover the sun was high and the alley bright. I had to drive slowly at first, to avoid two bone-thin, ragged dogs, snarling at each other across the bloated body of a huge, dead rat. More proof that what makes a treasure worth the risk must—like beauty—lie in the beholder's eye.

Meanwhile, in the swirling fog of my own mind's eye an idea was taking shape, a notion of what must have happened that night at Lonnie Bright's—where some people had seen a treasure worth the highest risk of all. With the idea came the hint of a plan for what to do now. I really needed more time to think it through, but Renata was right. Time was a luxury I didn't have.

THE FIRST ITEM ON MY AGENDA was a visit to Breaker Hanafan. It was time for the bastard to dip his hands a little into his own dirty work.

Breaker let me in right away. He already knew I was a

suspect in the murder of Maura Flanagan. He knew a lot of things before most people did. Then I told him what I was going to do and what I wanted him to do. He didn't think much of the idea. But, then, who would have?

"If it works," I said, "your ex-grandson-in-law Richie Kilgallon goes to jail for a very long time—or at least as long as he can survive there. And if it fails," I added, "what the hell, you always have your back-up plan." Which was that Richie didn't go to jail to be sodomized and brutalized, and Breaker would simply kill him. "So, when you boil it down, you got nothing to lose."

He shook his head. "When you boil it down," he said, "your so-called plan is that you get that fuckin' sonovabitch Kilgallon and the other guy together in a room, right?"

I nodded.

"And one of 'em's just stupid enough to admit he committed a crime. And then the cops come along and throw his sorry ass in the shithouse." He waved his hand at me. "Bullshit."

I shrugged, and kept silent.

"Even if it made sense," he said, "how would I know it'd be fuckin' Kilgallon who talks and goes to jail?"

"You're missing an important point," I said. "They're *both* stupid enough to admit they committed a crime. It's just that one admits to a worse crime than the other. Anyway," I concluded, "it's the best we got. Time's short . . . for both of us. I'll be picked up by the cops. And you? Hell, you look strong as a bull, but . . ."

"I *feel* good, too," he said, "for now." A touch of something, maybe fear, came into his eyes, but he shook his head as though tossing it away. "Fuck it!"

"Right." I struggled not to feel sorry for the murderous bastard. "So," I said, "take it or leave it."

He sat there awhile, and then he took it. Maybe he knew there was something I was holding back. And maybe he just didn't care.

237

CHAPTER

===

44

I WORKED OUT a few details with Breaker, then left and drove southwest on Interstate 55 and stopped at a truck stop near a town called Summit, about fifteen miles from the Loop and, as far as I could tell, no higher up than anywhere else in Cook County. I had coffee with a guy hauling a load of Jeep Cherokees to Omaha, borrowed his cell phone, and called home. There was one new message on my machine, one the cops probably knew was there.

"Hey, Mal." It was Barney Green. "Just wanna say I'm on your side. But you oughta hurry up and meet with the police. They're talking to everyone they can find who knows you. Asking where you might be, what you're driving, what your habits are, where you might go. So, what I mean is, it's just a matter of time. Me, I told them what I know, including that you were sure to come in and cooperate. Have Renata set it up, okay? God bless, buddy." He hung up.

In other words, Barney wanted me to know he'd told the cops I was driving the Buick Electra he'd gotten for me. If he hadn't told them, and I got picked up in it, he'd be in deep trouble, and in no position to help me anymore.

I ditched the car in the lot of a nearby Holiday Inn, with the key under the floormat. There was a pay phone in the hotel lobby and I called one of Arthur Frankel's restaurants in the city. He wasn't there, so I tried another one and he was. We talked and he agreed to meet me at his restaurant in Highwood the next night, and to get Richie Kilgallon there, too.

It wasn't quite that easy, of course. I had to tell him I knew what happened at Lonnie Bright's, and that I'd never told anyone yet, but I'd tell the world now if he didn't do what I said. I told him that if I was arrested between now and to-morrow night I'd easily prove to the cops that I couldn't have killed Maura Flanagan, and that once they let me go I'd see that he went to jail, and that if he knew what was good for his sorry ass, he'd . . .

That sort of thing.

Eventually he agreed. The next day was Friday and the dining room at *Le Chantier* closed at eleven, he said, and the bar at midnight. By one o'clock the staff would be gone, and we could meet at one-thirty. The only hitch was he said he hadn't talked to Kilgallon in years, and couldn't guarantee he'd be there. I borrowed Breaker's line about being bent over a bench in Stateville and said maybe the two of them could get adjoining benches if he didn't make sure Richie showed.

Frankel was a tough enough guy, but he could be scared, like just about everyone else. When I hung up I felt a surge of optimism—for maybe five seconds.

A METRA COMMUTER TRAIN RUNS through Summit and there's a station there. I rode a near-empty evening train back into the Loop, took the el to Rogers Park, and walked to a six-flat building on Glenwood, near Pratt. It was past six o'clock. The sun was just down, but it wasn't really dark yet. Inside the tiny vestibule, I pressed the button for the second floor, south, Stefanie Randle's apartment. She didn't answer.

I walked to a bar on Sheridan Road and, two cheeseburgers and two Sam Adamses later, it was quite dark out and I walked back and she answered. I announced on the inter-com who I was, and she buzzed me in.

She stood in her open doorway on the second floor landing, running her hand through her hair as though it needed straightening out or something. "My God," she whispered, "what are you doing here?" But even as she said it, she let me in and closed the door behind me.

She had on black stretch tights that went down to her bare feet and a white shirt that went halfway to her knees and might have looked like a man's dress shirt except it had little flowers—embroidered, I think—sprinkled across her decidedly feminine chest. The apartment smelled like popcorn.

"You're wanted by the police," she said.

"Do you think I killed Maura Flanagan?"

"Don't be absurd."

"So that's why I'm here."

She said her daughter had seemed to be coming down with the flu, or a cold or something, when she picked her up from daycare, and she'd put her to bed. She raised her forefinger to her lips and led me down a long hallway, through a darkened dining room full of little-girl-type playthings and big-girl-type computer stuff—but no place to eat—and into a small kitchen. The ceiling light was on and the room was neat and spotless. A tea kettle sat on a lighted burner on the stove and the odor of popcorn was stronger here, along with the smell of bleach—or was it fabric softener?

She turned. "Really, what are you *doing* here?"

"I'll tell you," I said, "but . . . may I sit down?"

"Oh." She seemed startled. "Yes. Um . . . do you want a cup of . . . tea or something?"

"Coffee?"

"Instant decaf?"

"Tea's fine," I said. I sat on one of two chairs at a little white wooden table set against the wall, and watched her stretch up to get two mugs from a cabinet. She put a tea bag in each mug. Plain, ordinary Lipton's. The kettle started to whistle just then and she turned off the gas at once and made the tea. She was awfully pretty and I reminded myself she was leaving town for Albany and there were thousands of other attractive women within a twenty-mile radius. Millions, maybe.

"All I've got to serve with the tea," she said, "are some ginger snaps. My daughter loves them, but I don't."

"I don't either." I tried to remember if I'd ever *seen* a ginger snap. "You said you'd help me. I realize things are a little different now, but—"

"Wait," she said. "Let me go make sure she's asleep."

She was back in a couple of minutes and I'd have sworn there was something different about her and decided it was fresh lipstick, and the hint of a floral scent. I also decided I'd made a mistake and I should get the hell out of there. But I didn't. I just sipped my tea and said, "Wouldn't you like to sit down, too?"

She sat down and stirred artificial sweetener into her tea.

"I don't want to be a bother," I said, "but I'd like to spend the night with you."

MY CHOICE OF WORDS had been careless. Maybe unconsciously too accurate, in fact. But we'd gotten that cleared up right away. It was a two-bedroom, one-bath apartment, and I slept in my clothes on the couch in the living room. In the morning I pretended to be asleep and listened to her move around the apartment and get her little girl up. They went back to the kitchen and, ten or fifteen minutes later, Stefanie came to the living room door. "Mal?" she whispered.

I lifted my head and opened my eyes.

"We'll be going out the back door," she said. "I don't want her to see you, obviously. Like I said last night, everyone in the building works days, so it should be pretty quiet." She paused. "Um . . . we'll be back about six."

241

"Don't worry, I'll be long gone," I said. "How's she feeling?"

"What? Oh, she's barely awake yet, but fine, I think."

"Good. And Stefanie? Thanks."

She smiled. "No problem."

I heard them go out the back door. I thought about Stefanie for a while; and then about Lynette Daniels and how nice it must be in Taos in April, and wondered whether I should fly out there when this was all over. Then I thought no.

Then I hoped I'd be around when this was all over, to see if I still felt that way.

CHAPTER

45

AT NOON I was sitting at one of Stefanie's front windows, looking down through a soft steady rain at Glenwood Avenue. Pretty soon a dark blue Bonneville approached from the north and parked beside the fire hydrant right below me. There was a perfectly legal space right across the street, but the Bonneville would have had to go down to the corner, turn around, and come back. You couldn't expect a busy guy like Fat Wilbur to go to all that trouble. He got out of the Bonneville and crossed over to the northbound side of the street, where he stood motionless in the rain, his huge body seeming to fill the vacant parking space.

A minute later a Jaguar came from the south and stopped. It was a green four-door sedan, and must have been one of those extended models Jaguar makes, because Fat Wilbur managed to fit into the backseat. It was Breaker Hanafan's car. It had dark tinted glass all the way around and I wouldn't have been able to see the driver, except that he lowered his window as he pulled away. It was Breaker himself. He didn't look up.

I went downstairs. The key was in the Bonneville and I moved it to the legal space across the street. Then I went back up to Stefanie's apartment, made myself another cup of instant decaf, and returned to the window. I killed an hour watching for—and not seeing—anything unusual. That left about eleven hours of down time ahead of me. I found a pizza in Stefanie's freezer compartment, one with no mold, and wrote her a nice note of apology while I heated it up. I left the note with a twenty-dollar bill on the sink and went to the living room to eat the pizza, watch TV, and try to nap.

No matter how boring CNN got, though, I couldn't sleep, so I spread a newspaper out on the kitchen table and took the Beretta apart. I'd already cleaned it after my encounter with Zorro, so there was nothing to do but stare at the parts and put them back together again. I thought about Yogi and how I said I'd visit him on Thursday. Now it was Friday and no way could I show up there, or even call. I worked out for an hour, mostly just stretching. From the sound of things Stefanie was right and the building was empty, but still I didn't want to make much noise.

There were lots of things I didn't want to do. I didn't want to think about Zorro; I didn't want to wander aimlessly from room to room through Stefanie's apartment; I didn't want to sit in the window and nourish my paranoia. And I certainly didn't want to keep going over my so-called plan for that night at *Le Chantier*.

If I kept going over my plan, for God's sake, I might come to my senses.

I'D PROMISED to be long-gone by six, so at five-thirty I left Stefanie's. The rain was still falling—quiet, gray, ceaseless. The Weather Channel had told me about fourteen times during the afternoon to expect steadily dropping temperatures and rain throughout the night, possibly broken later on by a thunderstorm. So the weather, at least, was something to be happy about, because people don't pay as much attention in the rain.

On the other hand, I had to drive slowly and carefully, just the opposite of the hyped-up way I felt, because I didn't want to be stopped for a traffic violation, and then arrested for murder. I needed some reassurance, so I drove to Devon Avenue and headed west. At Ravenswood I went north a block and deliberately drove right past the Twenty-fourth District police station. In fact, I drove around the block several times. Each time a cop car fell in for a while behind me, and then drifted off to go about its business, it further convinced me that no one was especially interested in a dark blue Bonneville with Illinois plates.

I left the city, headed north. It was still more than seven hours to one-thirty, and Highwood was only a half-hour drive. The streets seemed filled with cars whose drivers had never seen rain before. It was a nightmare, even apart from the feeling that I had to keep looking for something suspicious in my rearview mirror.

At a discount store I bought a raincoat—cheap and plastic and big enough to fit over me and my jacket—and a black knit ski cap with a built-in mask that I could roll down over my face, and made me feel like a terrorist when I tried it on. Then I went to a movie I'd never heard of, starring a guy from a TV sitcom I'd never seen and—after the movie— vowed I never would. Then, it was salad and coffee from the drive-through window at a McDonald's; after that more driving in the rain, stopping now and then under a service station canopy for a few gallons of gas but mostly to stretch my legs, and driving again, with a couple of washroom breaks in there somewhere.

AT TEN-THIRTY I was in Highwood. It was a busy night there, with lots of cars going both ways on the main thoroughfare, Green Bay Road. Most of them crept along, the drivers peering out through what had turned into a monsoon, looking for a particular restaurant or club and where they might park once they found it. I drove past *Le Chantier* several times. It was on the edge of town, right next to Ricci's Nursery and Garden Supplies, nearly two blocks from Green Bay and its cluster of eating and drinking spots. Set apart, yet near to

245

enough bars and clubs that were open till two and three a.m. so that cars and people coming and going wouldn't draw attention.

Le Chantier seemed to be doing great. There was a well-lighted parking lot, and valet parking at the door so you didn't have to walk in the rain. It looked warm and cozy through the windows. The restaurant was a wide, single-story building, and was butted up in the rear—and apparently attached—to a much larger frame structure, like a rectangular barn, two or three stories tall. There were a couple of smaller buildings or sheds beyond that, visible through the rain under the glow of a few dim security lights on tall poles, but the whole area back there was blocked off by a row of evergreen trees and a tall chainlink fence.

Freshly painted, with most of its many windows clearly part of a recent renovation, the restaurant was housed in what must once have been the store and front office part of a lumber yard. That was my guess, anyway, mostly because of the sign high up on the wall behind and above the restaurant section. The faded paint was illegible in the darkness, but I'd seen it the previous Sunday.

HIGHWOOD LUMBER & BUILDING SUPPLIES

As Frankel had said, the dining room closed at eleven. Most of the dinner crowd seemed to be gone by then, anyway, and after that the lights in the windows to the left of the front entrance gradually dimmed to almost nothing. The bar, though, visible through the windows to the right of the entrance, kept going strong until midnight.

A few patrons hung on past that, but eventually they left and the lights in the bar, too, went out. By twelve-thirty the bright outdoor *Le Chantier* sign, and the parking lot lights, had all been switched off. Only a handful of cars remained, all gathered at the far end of the lot. Employees, obviously. Over the next half hour they came out, too, the last one being the manager, Mr. Alberto, who locked the door behind him. Once they were gone the lot was empty and lit only by spill-over from a security light in front of Ricci's Nursery. Dim night lights glowed through the windows on both sides of *Le Chantier*'s darkened entrance.

Those Weather Channel people seemed to have gotten it right. The wind was rising a bit, so maybe thunderstorms were on their way to punctuate the mind-numbing rain. And the temperature was dropping, too. I knew, because by then I'd parked the Bonneville several blocks away and stationed myself behind the row of evergreens by the fence beyond the edge of the parking lot. A sign on the fence warned me that the buildings and property behind it, the abandoned lumber yard, were vacant and unsafe, and that the fence was equipped with an electronic alarm system. Trespassers would be arrested and prosecuted. I kept my distance.

It was one-fifteen and I'd been standing there in the dark and watching for half an hour. My new plastic coat kept the rain on the outside, but also kept the perspiration on the inside and soaking into my clothes. Surprising how a person can sweat and still be shivering from the cold. For a moment a desk stacked high with legal papers, in a warm, dry office, seemed a little more tolerable than usual. But only a brief moment, and only very little.

At one-twenty-five by my Timex Indiglo, a Chevy Corvette—old, but in mint condition, and don't ask me what year—pulled up and parked near the restaurant entrance. A man got out and ran through the rain to the door. It was Arthur Frankel. He dug into the pocket of his trench coat, came up with a key to his own restaurant, and let himself in. An out-side light above the door went on. I waited.

Several minutes later, a cab pulled up beside the Corvette.

A man paid off the driver and got out. It was Richie Kilgallon, in a hip-length black leather coat and what looked like blue jeans. The cab drove away and Richie made a dash for the entrance. It wasn't locked, and he went inside. I waited some more.

Several minutes later I was still waiting, but nothing more happened. Something was supposed to happen, dammit, according to my plan; but nothing did.

What was supposed to happen was that Breaker Hanafan would drive up and Yogi would get out of his car. Breaker had told me that Doctor Tyne said Yogi was weak, but gaining strength and able to walk short distances. I'd take Yogi inside, with my Beretta handy and with Breaker and his muscle outside as backup. Not that I trusted Breaker, but we at least shared a similar interest in Richie Kilgallon's future and . . . well . . . he was the help I had available. Which right about then didn't seem to be quite enough.

What else was supposed to happen was that I'd get Frankel and Richie both talking and Yogi would listen and tell me if he recognized either voice as the voice of the cop who'd pureed his kidney and left him to die on the street. Not that Yogi gave a damn about vengeance, but I thought some *quid pro quo* was in order and I figured Yogi would at least tell me who it was.

Then, once I'd accomplished item one on my agenda I'd send Yogi back out to Breaker and move on to item two. But ten more minutes passed and I realized that item one wasn't going to happen—and that I wasn't going to have my backup.

I walked through the rain to the door of the restaurant. It was unlocked and I went inside.

CHAPTER

46

IN THE DIM LIGHT inside *Le Chantier*, Arthur Frankel was standing behind the hostess station. He'd ditched the trench coat and had on a dark-colored crewneck sweater. He closed the cover of a large book which might have been used to keep track of reservations and seating.

"You're late," he said. He switched off the tiny desk lamp and then the only light came from the exit sign behind me above the door. That, and what little spilled out through the archway from the dining room, past Frankel and to my left. The bar area, on the right, was a separate room and that door was closed.

I took off the plastic raincoat and dropped it on a bench seat beside me. My pants were soaked from the knees down and my feet were wet and cold and I stamped them on the floor to stir up the circulation a little. "Kilgallon here yet?"

"Why do I have the feeling," he said, "that you know that already?" He turned. "Follow me, and—"

"Bring him up here." Anywhere he and Kilgallon wanted to meet, I didn't.

I walked past Frankel and into the dining room. For brunch last Sunday there'd been placemats on the round, glass-topped tables, and with all the bright light and windows and plants, there'd been the feeling of eating on a patio. But now the tables were spread with clean white cloths, ready for more formal dining the next day.

"I'll pick out a nice table in here," I said.

"But in the back we'll be more comfortable." As if comfort

were a factor. "And," he added, "the dining room has all those windows. Someone might—"

"Nobody's around," I said. "Besides, are you expecting something illegal to happen? I mean . . . it's not like we're dealing drugs or something."

He opened his mouth, then closed it. He turned around and, dragging his foot, went across the room and through a set of swinging doors into the kitchen.

Picking a table for four in the middle of the large dining room, I removed the salt and pepper shakers, the tiny flower vase, and the white cloth, and put them on a nearby chair. The glass tabletop was pebbled, not smooth and slippery, but transparent enough to see hand or leg movement through it. I sat down, but then got up again right away and took one of the four chairs, the one for the person to my right, and stuck it at another table. I wanted the two of them sitting close together.

Then I sat down again, laid the Beretta on the glass in front of me, and rested my hands, palms down, on the metal rim that ran around the edge of the table, one on either side of the gun. The light in the room, from one tiny ceiling bulb, was too dim to cast much of a reflection on the windows, so if I looked to my right I could see through them, out to Frankel's Corvette. Across the room straight ahead of me was the archway we'd come through and, beyond that and out of sight, the hostess station and the waiting area. Off to the left were the kitchen doors.

Just then those doors swung open and Frankel came limping through; and behind him, Richie Kilgallon. Richie still had his leather coat on, and a bottle of beer in his hand.

I didn't move. When they got close they stopped, side-by-side. "The fuck is this?" Richie asked, nodding down toward the gun.

I left my hands resting where they were. "I like to have

250

everything out on the table," I said, "like the fact that we're all armed and we all know it."

"Really," Richie said. "And you want me to put mine on the table, too?"

"I don't care what you do with it. As long as you don't reach for it. While we chat."

"And if we don't like talking across a gun?" That was Frankel.

"Then we don't talk. And my sense is you *want* to talk, or we wouldn't all be here. So, sit down."

Frankel sat down to my left and Richie started to move the third chair around the table to sit across from Frankel—and to my right.

"No," I said, not lifting my right wrist from the table, but wagging my index finger, then pointing it. "*Across* from me, Richie boy."

"Fuck you, Fo—" He stopped short and stared at the Beretta in my hand, pointed up at his face. He pulled the chair back and sat down across from me. "So," he said, and grinned, "I guess the heat make you 'the man' now, hey bro?" He put his sarcasm into black dialect, and I thought of Zorro, talking white. "Yassuh," he said, "you the—"

"Richard," Frankel said, "shut up."

I laid the gun back on the table, wondering how many thousand times I'd practiced that pickup-and-aim movement. "I know what happened at Lonnie Bright's that night," I said. "I always knew part of it. Now I know it all." Or at least I had a strong suspicion.

"Bullshit." Kilgallon sucked on his beer—it was a Bud Light—and put the bottle on the table.

"What happened is in the police reports," Frankel said. "But suppose you knew something different, just for the sake of argument, I mean. So what?"

"So I can make trouble for you. You, and Richie boy here;

251

and Jimmie Coletta, too. Trouble like, say, indictments, and trials, and hard time. Maybe worse."

Kilgallon leaned forward, but Frankel waved him silent. "What you know," Frankel said, "is a couple of fuckin' animals shot down some honest coppers doing their jobs, and ended up on slabs themselves. No evidence of anything else. Case closed."

"*Not* closed, though," I said. "Not by a mile. You got a transaction involving police officers and a controlled substance, and conspiracy to participate. You got a cop paralyzed, shot in the back by an unknown party. You got a homicide by an unknown party. Uh-uh. Not closed."

"There was no evidence of any cocaine," Kilgallon said. "Or . . . you know . . . heroin," he added, "or any other controlled substance."

"Careful, Richie," I said. "Your mouth'll bring you trouble every time."

"It's true, though," Frankel said. "No evidence of any drug deal. And it's also true that one bad guy—the one that shot Jimmy Coletta—got away. But there's never been a clue as to his identity."

"Fuckin' shine's dead by now, anyway," Kilgallon said. "Dopeheads don't have much of a life expectancy."

"And as for homicide by an unknown party," Frankel said, "what's that? It was the bitch put Sal Coletta down; and both her and Lonnie were shot by police officers in the line of duty, and ruled justifiable. Self-defense. So you're wrong on that."

"I'm talking about a more recent homicide," I said. "And you know what I mean."

But I couldn't tell whether Frankel knew I meant Maura Flanagan's murder or not, or whether the look in his eyes was surprise, or confusion, or a cover for something else. And I couldn't read Kilgallon, either, for a different reason.

His arrogant, sullen expression never looked anything *but* guilty to me, for everything.

So I didn't take it any farther right then, and nobody said anything for a long several seconds.

Frankel finally spoke up. "Look, you call me on the phone claiming you'll tell the world what you say you know if Richard and I don't show up here tonight. Well, here we are. Because we wonder what kinda bullshit lies you've made up about what happened at Lonnie Bright's. But it's been ten minutes and you haven't said one damn thing to make me think you can cause trouble for anyone but yourself."

"What I know is this," I said. "Sal Coletta and his partner Richie boy here happened onto a truckload of cocaine in the course of their business of protecting the public, and made a deal to sell it to Lonnie. Lonnie was as dumb as he thought he was smart. He figured he was ready for prime time and he was gonna do this deal independent of his handlers, to set himself up. Sal decided to bring his brother Jimmy in on it, which meant bringing you in, too, Jimmy's partner. Maybe Sal didn't think he and Richie boy could handle it alone; or maybe he had a burst of brotherly love; or maybe Jimmy threatened to talk otherwise. I don't know."

"You don't know *any* of this crap," Kilgallon said.

"I know the plan was to take the money," I said, "send Lonnie off on a one-way trip, and then sell the shit again to someone else." I paused, but nobody responded. "You all knew this was a secret deal for Lonnie and he was supposed to be alone, but he had his nephew there. Marlon Shades. Just a punk kid, but he had to be dealt with. So," I nodded at Frankel, "you watch from the front. Jimmy stays in the alley with Marlon to keep him busy moving the shit from one car to another, while Richie here, and Sal, go upstairs to get Lonnie's money. Well, they get the money and then Richie boy—"

253

"The name is *Richard*." Kilgallon was ready to blow. "Cut out the 'Richie boy' shit, if—"

"Oooh. Well, then, they get the money and *Richard* here pops Lonnie. One shot. Forehead, front and center. But then, surprise! Out jumps Fay Rita, Lonnie's woman. She's freaked and she opens fire on whatever moves. There's a lot of shooting then and that's when you run up to help," nodding to Frankel. "Sal goes down. You go down. Fay Rita goes down. Meanwhile, Richie boy here ducks his ass into a closet and—"

Kilgallon slammed the table forward at my belly and I grabbed the gun as the Bud Light bottle went flying. We were both on our feet and he came around faster than I thought he could move. But when he got there I sliced the barrel of the Beretta across the side of his face. It opened a gash and hurt him enough to make him stop for a second and think. But he came up with the wrong thought. He went for his gun.

While he fumbled under his leather coat I hit him again, much harder. That one put him on the floor, and by the time he'd shaken the popcorn out of his brain his coat was off and over the back of a chair behind me. The Sig-Sauer 9mm from his shoulder holster, as well as the .38 snub-nose from his ankle, were both in the coat pockets.

I sat him down in his chair, leaned close to his ear—the one with all the blood on it—and said, "If you move I'll hit you again, Richie boy, and I won't hold back this time. And then, when you wake up—*if* you wake up—you'll be wearing these." I held up the handcuffs I'd taken from his belt.

Through it all, Frankel never left his chair.

"You're smart, Frankel," I said. "If it was both of you, I might have had to shoot someone."

"I'm not armed."

"That's even smarter," I said. "Talk to me."

"You get all these lies from your client, Marlon Shades? Or is some of it from Jimmy Coletta?"

"Jimmy won't talk to me. I threatened him the same as I did you. He used born-again Christian language, but basically told me to go piss up a rope." Frankel looked like he believed me.

"Your whole story's a lie," he said. "But . . ." He paused, and I could almost see the machinery in his head try to sort things out. And then he weakened. Maybe he thought he could work a deal. "But," he repeated, "even suppose some of it was true. Say, selling the shit to Lonnie Bright. Jimmie and I wouldn't have known about anything extra Sal cooked up with this piece of shit." He nodded at Kilgallon. "About killing Lonnie, I mean; and reselling the coke."

"Shut up, Frankel," Kilgallon said. "Don't be a pussy, for chrissake. Lonnie Bright had at least four slugs in him."

"But only one killed him," I said. "Only one *could* have killed him. And that one would have been a hell of a shot if it came in the middle of a gunfight." I paused and stared at Frankel. "It's all in the autopsy reports, if anyone was ever interested in looking at them, analyzing them."

"Anyway," Frankel said, "I'm not admitting anything. There's no evidence of any drugs on the scene."

"Right," I said. "Lucky for you, I guess. Although, did you ever wonder why they disappeared? I mean, a shootout with people killed? Wouldn't it have been easier to explain things if there'd been drugs there?"

"There weren't any."

"But let's say for a minute that there *were.* Who took them?"

"Shit," Frankel said. "It would have been your client, Marlon Shades. He must have—"

"For chrissake, shut up!" Kilgallon couldn't keep his voice from rising. And apparently he couldn't keep from looking around the room, either. Toward the kitchen doors, the windows, the archway just in from the hostess station. "The guy could be wired," he added.

"So what?" I said. "It's all hypothetical, right?" I concentrated on Frankel. "Suppose there *had* been cocaine, and suppose there *had* been money up there in Lonnie's place. Someone walked away with all of it. The bags of coke, the money . . . Maybe it was you and Richie boy here. Maybe—"

"Fucker." This from Kilgallon, more a mumble than a challenge. He still seemed distracted, looking around. I was sure I knew what he was expecting—which is why I'd wanted Breaker around as back-up.

"I didn't walk away with anything," Frankel said. "They carried my ass out."

"Maybe you got your share later," I said. "Maybe Richie did too. Maybe that's how you bought your first restaurant."

Frankel gave a small laugh then. Small, but it seemed a genuine reaction to what I'd said. "The money for the first restaurant? That came from my lawyer cousin. That can be traced. Where he got it, God only knows. Maybe he scammed more than the one client he got disbarred for." That seemed genuine, too. "I didn't get shit from the Lonnie Bright deal, other than—"

"There *was* no deal, asshole," Kilgallon whined. "You—"

And that's when we heard the front door of the restaurant open . . . and then close. Shortly after that Theodosian came into the dining room, folding his raincoat and draping it over a chair as he walked.

CHAPTER

47

THEODOSIAN TOOK HIS TIME, winding his way among the tables toward us. "Sorry I'm late," he said. "The rain, the Friday night traffic, the—" He stopped a couple of yards away and slid his hands deep into the pockets of his corduroy sport coat. "Y'know, Foley, I never figured you as a killer, okay? And I still don't. But you *are* a suspect in a homicide and . . . well . . . the gun?"

Very slowly, with just the tips of my fingers, I pushed the Beretta across the table. Then I sat back, leaving the gun closer to Kilgallon than to Frankel. You have to make choices, even when you're not quite sure.

"Thanks," Theodosian said.

"I understand." I shrugged. "I mean, if I *were* a killer, how would you look if—"

"What's this guy doing here?" Frankel asked.

"I thought maybe *you* invited him," I said. "Or maybe Richie boy wanted—"

"Dammit!" Kilgallon grabbed the Beretta and stood up. "I said cut out the 'Richie boy' shit."

Frankel stood, too, which left only me sitting. Kilgallon backed up, moving away from the table, toward Theodosian.

But Theodosian stepped backward a little, too. "Take it easy, Richard," he said. "Use your head. Don't do anything foolish."

"Bullshit." Kilgallon was way beyond taking it easy. "This cocksucker's been fuckin' with me all night. But that's over."

I spread my arms wide, palms up. "Okay," I said, "what now . . . Richie boy?"

"Now," he said, "we get you out of our way." He raised the Beretta, pointed it at my face, and squeezed the trigger.

Maybe I heard a *click*. And maybe not, because Theodosian yelled something and Kilgallon spun around toward him with the gun still raised. And when he did, Theodosian shot him, once. The Beretta fell to the floor. Kilgallon seemed to stand a little taller, for just an instant, and then he went down, too.

"Him and Frankel, they were both in on it," Theodosian said. He crouched down beside Kilgallon. "Selling coke to Lonnie Bright."

By that time Frankel was on the run, headed for the kitchen doors. No sign of a limp now. "Bastard's probably got a gun!" Theodosian yelled. "I had his phone tapped. That's how I knew to come here!"

By then Frankel was pushing through the swinging doors into the kitchen, and I grabbed Kilgallon's leather coat from the chair back and went after him.

Inside the kitchen I hit the wall switch and the lights went on, but Frankel wasn't in sight. I moved forward, slipping my arms into Kilgallon's coat as I did. To my right was an exit to the outside, but a little box on the wall, with its tiny red light blinking, said going that way might bring every squad car on the North Shore screaming up. Frankel wouldn't have gone that way, and I couldn't afford to, either.

The only other door in sight was on the other side of a wide stainless-steel counter that was stacked with pots and pans, and divided the room in two. It was a wooden door, painted white like the walls, a door that might lead to a storage room . . . or maybe into the lumber yard. Running around the end of the counter seemed to take forever, but when I got there the door was unlocked.

I CLOSED THE DOOR behind me and found myself in what felt like a very large building, and smelled like wet wood and mildew and cat droppings—like an old barn. It was very dark, with the faintest of light showing here and there through cracks in the walls, mostly up near the roof, and around the edges of a set of huge, barnlike doors, off maybe fifteen feet to my right. They were wide and tall enough to drive a moving van through. They were closed, and probably had been for twenty years or more.

I heard Theodosian's voice from the kitchen behind me. "Hold on, Foley!" he yelled. "I'm calling it in. Don't take any chances. Help is on the way!"

I turned left, away from the outside doors, and moved deeper into the darkness. Whatever sounds my shoes made on the concrete floor were lost in the pounding of rain on the metal roof far above. I looked up. There were two sky-lights, but they were nothing but rectangles of gray, patched onto the inky blackness.

My eyes adjusted enough so I could tell I was headed down the length of a large building . . . the lumber shed. That had to be why the door into here had no alarm, because the shed and the other buildings must all have been inside the wired fence. This building seemed mostly emptied out and abandoned, but with wood scraps and piles of debris scattered around. Passing through, I could tell that the walls along both sides were partitioned into stalls, probably for storing different sizes and kinds of wood and building materials. Moving closer to the right side, I saw that some of the stalls were divided by horizontal shelving; some were just empty little three-sided rooms.

At the end of the building, I made out a second set of outside doors. I ran up and gave them a half-hearted shove, and they didn't budge. Facing back the way I'd come, I stood in the dark and listened, but heard only my own breathing and the incessant drumming of the rain.

I ducked behind a partition wall, got down close to the floor and poked my head around the edge. The shed had to be a good fifty yards long, by maybe twenty wide. The storage cubicles along the sides flanked an open space down the middle that was way more than wide enough to drive a truck in one end, load or unload it, and drive it out the other. I could tell now that there was a second floor, too, or really two second floors; balconies running the length of the building along both side walls, but not connected across the center. It was too dark to see, but the upper levels were probably broken up into sections, too. Safety railings ran along their outer edges, and there must have been room to walk from one storage stall to another up there. The only ladders I could see were down here at my end, primitive wooden ladders nailed to the wall and going straight up from the floor to the balcony, with hardly any pitch to them at all.

The kitchen door was on the side opposite me and lost in the darkness down at the other end, but I was sure Theodosian hadn't come through into the shed yet. And I was equally sure of the presence of Arthur Frankel. I felt him here in this big, empty woodshed with me, somewhere, even though I couldn't hear him.

And if help was on the way I couldn't hear that, either. My sense about anyone coming who'd want to help *me* was that I shouldn't hold my breath. I'd given up on Breaker Hanafan, the bastard.

So I waited, watching down the length of the building, and finally the kitchen door opened, just a little. Light came out and I instinctively pulled back. But I was far away and in deep shadow and I knew I couldn't be seen, so I looked out again. The door opened wider, but the light spilling out still didn't reach anywhere near as far down as I was.

I watched Theodosian lean out through the doorway, look both ways, then pull back again. "Frankel?" he called. "I know you're in there."

Frankel didn't answer.

"Foley? You just sit tight and stay out of trouble, okay?"

I didn't answer, either.

"Look here, Frankel. The worst—" He stopped. "Well . . . it's Arthur, right? Can I call you Arthur?" Theodosian's voice was clear over the sound of the rain, and sounded calm, almost soothing. "You were in on the Lonnie Bright deal, sure, but the worst you're facing is a conspiracy to traffic in cocaine." He paused, then stepped into the shed and closed the door at once, shutting out the light from the kitchen. "Hell, Arthur, the deal wasn't even done. What's that, then, attempt to conspire? Conspiracy to attempt? Whatever it is, the statute of limitations probably ran already. Give it up, man. Get a decent lawyer and you'll walk." He paused. "Whaddaya say, Arthur?"

There was a moment of silence, and then—to my disappointment—Frankel answered. "You said my phone was tapped." He sounded about midway between me and Theodosian, on the other side of the open space, but up on the second level. "I didn't call Richard from my phone, though. I called—"

"Not yours," Theodosian interrupted. "I said *Kilgallon's* phone. *Richard's* phone. Or if I didn't, I meant to."

"You shot Richard," Frankel called. "Why'd you do that?" At least he was asking the right questions.

"Jesus Christ, Arthur, he tried to kill Foley; then he turned on me with the gun. So he's hurtin' a little right now, but he'll survive. It's his . . . shoulder. Anyway, he's got bigger problems to face. Way more than you. He flat-out murdered Lonnie Bright."

"No one told me there'd be any killing," Frankel said. The tremor in his voice was unmistakable. "So maybe you're right. Maybe—"

"Frankel, wait!" I called. I was standing now, but still hidden behind my wall. "You don't really know if Kilgallon's alive or dead."

"Jesus, Foley, I *said* he was alive, didn't I?" Theodosian sounded disappointed in me. "Whose side are you on, anyway? Just stay put. I think Arthur's decided to use his head."

"You said help was on the way, too," I said. "But where is it? I don't hear anyone. No sirens."

"I been wonderin' that myself," he answered. "But Christ, it's not like the city. They probably got one or two squad cars in this town and a volunteer fire department."

"Frankel," I yelled, "listen to me. If this guy was on official police business, do you think he'd have come alone? And how'd he arrive at the restaurant? We'd have seen a car drive up. Where—"

"I *told* you, Foley," Theodosian cut in. "I been working with the state on special assignment, with your friend Frick-the-Prick." There was a change in the sound of his voice and I realized he'd moved farther down the shed—coming my way. "It's just Frick and me and he's taking time off, fishing or something. What was I gonna do, call in a battalion? All I knew was there was a meeting; I didn't even know you'd be here." There was a pause, and he was coming closer; I could feel it. "I didn't wanna draw outside attention, so I parked down the street and walked."

"Really," I said, knowing his answers made no sense. "If you walked, how come your pants and shoes weren't wet?"

"Are you kidding? They're soaked."

But he was lying, and I didn't say anything.

Nobody said anything. I stood there, feeling the weight of Kilgallon's guns in the pockets of his coat, then took out the

Sig-Sauer. I'd have preferred my Beretta. But making my un-loaded weapon available to whichever one most wanted me dead had seemed a good idea, at the time. Besides, what people say about the Sig proved true. It felt good in my hand; balanced, comfortable, efficient even without firing it. It was loaded, too. I'd checked that back in the kitchen.

"Frankel," I finally called out, "listen to me. Don't trust him. He's dirty. There's no phone tap. Kilgallon told him about our meeting and he was hiding in the restaurant all along."

"Forget him, Arthur," Theodosian said. "He's crazy."

"Not crazy," I said. "He and Kilgallon obviously planned to kill me—and you, too. Because we know what happened that night. Remember what Kilgallon said? 'We,' he said. '*We* get you out of *our* way.' But he lost his head and things didn't go the way Theodosian wanted them to."

"That's crazy talk, Arthur," Theodosian said. "Paranoid. The talk of a man who murdered a supreme court judge." He paused, then added, "You can either believe *him*, Arthur, or you can let me do my job. I'll arrest you and you get a lawyer and you'll do okay." But he wasn't coming any nearer to me now, and I suddenly realized he must have stopped very close to Frankel. "What about it, Arthur?" he said.

"Frankel!" I yelled. "Don't say *anything!*"

But he didn't listen to me. Maybe no one would have. "I . . . I just don't know," he said. "But answer Foley's ques-tion. Did you—"

A *chug-chugging* sound cut short his sentence; the terri-ble, frightening sound of an automatic being fired through a silencer. And the simultaneous sound of splintering wood. Then a brief silence, followed at once by more *chug-chugging*, and I looked around my wall and saw the flashes from Theodosian's automatic as, carefully and methodically, he fired up through the wooden floor . . . at where he knew Frankel must be.

The muzzle flashes, like the sound, were minimized by the silencer on his weapon. As far as I could tell from the sounds, the bullets all pierced right through the old, dry wood. He stopped once to reload, but in just seconds was firing again. And then, finally, Frankel screamed. The shooting stopped, but the screams went on, and through it all the rain pounded down on the metal roof like the hooves of a thousand horses. Then the screams died into moans, and then, finally, there was one more muffled gunshot.

And after that only the trampling rain, and some thunder I hadn't heard earlier.

I hid behind my wall and leaned my back against the wood and breathed deeply, in and out, to gain control. When I looked out again, I couldn't place Theodosian in the darkness. "Hey!" I called.

"Yeah?" I could tell then that he'd climbed up to the second level. He must have been right beside Frankel's body.

"I guess you're gonna tell me he's like Kilgallon, huh? 'He's hurtin' a little right now, but he'll survive,' right?"

"He's as dead as Kilgallon is—or as Kilgallon *will* be once he's finished bleeding to death, unless you come with me right away and we get him some help. Kilgallon tried to kill me, you saw that. Just like Frankel tried to. Sonovabitch fired at me, from above."

"Really."

"Uh-huh." There was a gunshot then, and another; these two from what I guessed was a small-caliber weapon, one without a silencer. "You didn't hear it?" Theodosian called. "He shot at me twice . . . with a cheap little .22. It's right here, in his hand." He paused, then added, "Malachy?" He got the name right this time.

"Yeah?"

"Those big doors at each end of this barn? They're locked,

with padlocks. From outside. I checked that out this afternoon."

"So much for the phone tap bullshit," I said, "and the parking and walking in the rain."

"The point is, I'll be arresting you now, and taking you in."

"But that's not the plan. The plan is to kill me."

"Only if I'm wrong, and if you *are* a desperate killer. I mean, like, if you resisted arrest I'd have to do whatever I have to do. But let me do my job, Malachy." His voice had the same calm, reassuring tone he'd used with Frankel. "You'll prove you haven't done anything wrong, and you'll be fine." I couldn't see him, but by his voice I knew he was climbing down a ladder. "Why would I shoot an unarmed man?"

I realized then that he actually thought there was a chance I'd believe him. He'd gone all the way over and was that crazy. He intended to gun me down, for sure, and if he came after me I'd have to shoot him, maybe kill him. And what then? Explain how he, the cop, was the madman; while I, the murder suspect, was sane? And that I'd shot him in self-defense? That explanation, and my outstanding résumé, would get me life without parole—and maybe a lethal injection, once Illinois got over its scruples and went back to executing people, even if about half the time they weren't guilty.

"Unarmed?" I called out. "Not to worry. Did you see that leather coat I took with me from the dining room? It was Kilgallon's coat. His gun was in the pocket."

"You're lying." He was on ground level now.

"I guess I could be. Maybe I really have *two* guns, or *three*." I didn't have to work very hard to sound desperate . . . or crazy. "Why don't you come down here and find out?"

CHAPTER

═══

48

"YOU'RE LYING." Theodosian said it a second time, but the suggestion that I had Kilgallon's gun seemed to have stopped him from moving any farther down the shed my way.

Crouched near the floor again, I leaned out from behind my wall. I couldn't spot him, but I aimed the Sig toward the upper level—where I was sure he wasn't—closed my eyes against the muzzle flash, and squeezed the trigger. Unlike his silenced weapon, the sound of mine exploded through the building. Even so, it was nearly lost in the roar of the rain crashing down on the roof. And there were long rolls of thunder now, too; and wind that shook and rattled the walls when it gusted, and threatened to lift the roof right off.

"Does that change your opinion?" I called. I was back behind my wall.

He didn't shoot back, and he didn't answer. More significantly, even though he had me trapped with no way out, he didn't turn around right then and go for help. So if I'd needed more proof—which I didn't—that he wasn't about to let me live to tell what I knew, that was it.

He might have been creeping my way through the darkness right then, for all I knew. Except I couldn't make out any movement, so maybe he was waiting me out, thinking I'd break before he did. But break for where? The big outside doors at my end were locked, for sure, and I had no reason to think those at the other end weren't. Besides, he was positioned between me and them. He was between me and the door back into the kitchen, too; and if there was some other way out, I'd never find it in the dark.

He had another advantage. He'd have seen the flash from the Sig and knew exactly where I was, and that I'd gone as far as I could go. I was in the last storage stall near the outside doors. The ladder up to the second level on my side was just a few feet away, but I'd have to step out into the open to get to it. I pulled the ski cap down over my face and took a deep breath. Then I leaned around the wall and fired once for cover, stepped out and fired twice, and went up the ladder as fast as I could.

I hadn't closed my eyes and the flashes from the Sig blinded me, so I had to feel my way to the top. I lay on the wooden floor, ten or twelve feet up, getting my breath back. I'd heard no slugs ripping into the walls around me and I hadn't been hit, so he must not have heard me over the wind and the pounding rain, or seen me climbing up. I slid sideways, stuck my head out over the edge of the floor, and looked down. I couldn't see him.

I pulled back and made my way along the floor. Inch by inch, no sound, flat on my belly. I wondered how long it would take me to get to the other end of the shed at that rate, and whether I'd find a ladder when I got there. Every few feet I eased over to the edge to look down. Finally, maybe about halfway to the other end, I was able to make him out.

He'd found a good place to wait in the dark and watch. Down below and across the open space from me, he was probably a little less than halfway down the building from where he obviously thought I still was. He stood—as still as death—behind the wall of a storage stall, a wall that had a board broken out at about eye level.

Moving more slowly than I thought I could, I eased up

into a standing position and backed away from the guardrail along the edge of the balcony. I stood in silence and stared down at him. Even if he heard me he'd have to turn around, and I could drop him before he got a shot off. He didn't move, though.

I could end it right now. I raised the Sig-Sauer and pointed it down at him. No way I could shoot him in the back. I knew that. But I didn't have to kill him. I could fire down into his legs and put him on the floor.

Uh-huh. And then what? Call for help and turn myself in? I didn't think so.

Or leave him there, maybe to bleed to death? Like he'd left Kilgallon? First, though, I'd have to go through his pockets to see if he had the unloaded Beretta, which was registered in my name. And if he didn't have it, I'd have to look around for it in this dark shed, or maybe back in the dining room. And then sneak away and hope no one saw me. And hope I'd left no prints, no strands of hair, no bits of skin or finger-nail. And then wait, and wonder how long it would take them to tie me to—

I heard something.

Or rather, I *didn't* hear something. And what I didn't hear anymore were the sheets of rain, pounding down on the roof. They were scattered drops now, pinging against the metal above my head. No thunder, either; and no screeching wind. The storm had finally blown through and gone, taking the rain with it. The night was suddenly very still, very quiet. And I didn't even know quite how long ago that had happened.

Theodosian was still frozen in place. But then—maybe because the new silence made him as uneasy as it made me, maybe because he sensed someone's eyes on him—he moved. First just a rolling of his shoulders, then a stretch of his neck. He turned and glanced behind him. I tensed, but he didn't look up—and might not have seen me in the darkness if he had.

And finally he couldn't take it anymore. "Hey!" he yelled. "Foley!"

I didn't answer. He had to be wondering whether I was still down there at the end. He made an odd movement, and I realized he was sticking his weapon into his shoulder holster. He slipped out of his sport coat and crouched to the floor, where he picked up something I couldn't see. Maybe a scrap of lumber, a two-by-four or something. He hung the jacket on it and eased it out into the open. When there was no response he started waving it around.

Nothing happened, of course, and by then, even though it was dark, he must have known something was wrong. He took a quick look around him in every direction, including up toward me. But I was in deep darkness, with Kilgallon's black coat on and my ski cap over my face, and I could tell he hadn't seen me.

He stepped out into the open, his gun back in his hand, stretched chest-high in front of him, and called again, "Foley! You sonovabitch. I'm coming after you!"

When no answer came, he made a big mistake. He should have turned around and headed back toward the kitchen door. But he didn't. Something compelled him to see if I was still hiding behind my wall. So he went that way, walking fast, and I lost him in the darkness. I went the other way, but turned sideways to keep an eye out for him, or at least in his direction.

We'd probably both have gotten to our respective ends of the building at pretty much the same time, but I hadn't yet gotten even with the door into the kitchen when my left foot went through a hole in the floor where a board must have rotted through. My ankle bent the wrong way and I groaned without meaning to, lost my balance, and fell hard against the

269

guardrail. The rail creaked and gave a little—but didn't break.

Knowing he must have heard me, I ran a few more steps as well as I could on a badly sprained ankle, no longer worried about noise. There must have been a ladder down to the floor at that end, too, but I couldn't see it and didn't have time to look around in the dark. Jamming the Sig under my belt, I climbed over the railing and dropped to the concrete below. I meant to land mostly on my right foot, but my left foot hit first, half-on and half-off what felt like a large brick, or a rock. The ankle twisted a second time, in a different wrong direction, and this time there was a definite *crack*. Pain shot up my leg and into my lower back, and I went down, hard, on my side.

I got to my knees and the pain was so sharp and so high up that for an instant I thought I'd been shot. I could hear footsteps running my way. Maybe he *had* shot at me, using the silencer. No one can run and aim at the same time, though, and by then I was up and dragging my useless foot across the open space toward the door to the kitchen. I'd have fired in his direction to slow him down as I went, but God only knew where the Sig was—because I sure didn't have it anymore.

I made it to the door and yanked it open. "Come through here," I yelled, "and you're a dead man!"

I pulled the door shut behind me, and had to close my eyes against the bright kitchen light. I still had Kilgallon's .38 snub nose in his coat pocket. It was a Smith & Wesson revolver and carried just five rounds. Theodosian might have been thinking by then that I probably didn't want to shoot him. But how could he be sure what I'd do? He'd think twice about bursting through the door after me, which gave me time to drag my broken ankle around to the other side of the stainless-steel counter.

Now what? Into the dining room through the swinging

doors? Or outside through the door with the exit sign and the burglar alarm? The pain wanted all my attention, but I had to keep my eyes on the closed door . . . and I had to think.

If I was right, the door with the alarm opened onto an area outside the fence around the lumber yard. But even so, if I went that way I still wouldn't be able to run very fast or very far. My mind raced. If the alarm brought help, would it be on my side? Or had Theodosian disabled the alarm? The whole thing was a crapshoot and, by default, I found myself backing up toward the swinging doors.

Then the door to the shed was pulled open, just a little. "Foley?" Theodosian called. When I didn't answer, he tried again. "Foley?" Then, staying hidden, he pulled the door all the way open.

Light from the kitchen spilled out across the lumber shed floor and I saw the chunk of concrete I'd landed on when I dropped from the railing. I saw something else out there on the floor, too, catching the light. The barrel of Kilgallon's Sig-Sauer.

"Foley," he called a third time, "you there?"

"Yeah I'm here. You ready to give up?"

"I'm just wondering," he said. "Do you see what I see?"

"I see an open doorway. And as soon as I see you in it, you're a dead man."

"Not likely," he said. "Not with your weapon out here on the floor."

"It's up to you. Take a chance if you like."

He pushed on the door a little and I fired out through the opening. There was a whine when the bullet ricocheted off something metallic on the other side of the lumber shed. And then it was quiet.

"Well," he finally said, "you *said* you might have two guns."

"I said maybe three. Maybe it's four now. You're a dead man if you come after me."

"You're repeating yourself," he said. "I saw you dragging that leg. I hit you. You've been shot, you're in pain, and you're repeating yourself. The fact is, you need medical attention. I'll take you in, Malachy. Everything will be fine." We were back on a first-name basis, and it was amazing how reasonable he sounded. "You're scared," he added, and that part was certainly true.

"I've been counting shots," I called back, "and you have just one round left. I'm figuring you weren't carrying more than one extra clip."

"You don't have a clue what I'm carrying." But I heard him snap open the magazine, then jam it shut again.

"Maybe," I said. I didn't even know what kind of gun he had, much less how many rounds were left

It meant something, though, that he made a sudden dash across the stream of light from the doorway, scooping up the Sig-Sauer as he passed. However many rounds he'd had left—in his gun or in his pocket—he had six more now, because I'd used four of the Sig's ten. I took the opportunity to shoot out the ceiling fixture, then the exit sign. Two rounds left in the .38.

I stood with my back to the swinging doors. "C'mon in!" I called. "I'm waiting."

CHAPTER

49

I BACKED SILENTLY through the swinging doors. Theodosian would come after me, for sure, but the dark kitchen would slow him down some.

It was still very dark in the dining room, too, but easy going compared to the lumber shed. With one eye on the kitchen doors—and using the backs of chairs for support—I hopped my way on one foot through the sea of tables to where I hoped the Beretta was, on the floor beside Kilgallon's body. It was easy to spot the only bare table in the room, but when I got there, there was no body—and no Beretta. Only smears of blood, leading in the direction of the archway. Beyond that was the front entrance.

Kilgallon could have taken my unloaded gun with him, and I had two clips for it, seven rounds each. I started after him, but felt suddenly light-headed and dizzy. I dropped to the floor—half-crouching, half-sitting—with my eyes just above the level of the tables. The pain in my ankle was way out of control, and I wasn't sure I could make it all the way to the archway without losing consciousness. So I stayed where I was, took long, deep breaths . . . and listened very hard.

I heard a sound from the kitchen—like someone bumping something. Then silence. And then another sound, more like a loud exhalation, or a sigh—but this time from another direction. Beyond the archway, near the front door.

The greater threat was from the kitchen, I decided, and not from the front doorway and a wounded Kilgallon. "Theodosian?" I called. "You out there?"

"I'm sure not going anywhere," he called back. "Not till I take you in."

"You can give that bullshit up," I said, not even trying to keep the pain and fatigue out of my voice. "You came here alone, way before the rest of us. You shot Kilgallon and didn't call for help before you came after Frankel and me. You still haven't called this in. You've gotta have a cell phone. And if you don't, you could open that exit door out there and trip the alarm."

"I must have left my phone in the car," he said, "and I've opened and closed that damn door five times. The alarm must be off." He paused. "I'm not walking out of here without you, Foley. It's my job. Let me do it. We'll get you to a hospital. After that . . . well, if you're not guilty, you'll be fine."

Damn, he could sound reasonable. "You convinced Frankel," I said, "and look what it got him."

"I told you, Frankel shot at—"

"Jesus!" I said. "You think I don't remember what I heard? Like I'm delirious, or what?" He didn't answer, so I went on. "I may be hurting and I may be shot." Let him believe that. "But you can give up trying to convince me you're clean."

"You're not thinking straight," he said.

"Could be. But I'm a better shot than you are, and if you come through those swinging doors . . . well, I don't wanna repeat myself. I could have dropped you before, in the shed, but back shooting's not my style."

"I told you," he called back, "I don't think you're a killer. I'll take you in and you'll get medical care."

"Except you don't plan to take me in," I said, "because I know everything."

"Really?" he said. "What's there to know?"

I felt less dizzy now, and it was time to go see if Kilgallon had my gun. I raised up a little. And as soon as I did, one of the swinging doors opened and Theodosian fired several shots. Glass shattered and there was the clang of a bullet against an iron table or chair. I dropped down again, firing back without looking. That left one more round in the .38.

"So much for taking me in," I said. "And y'know what? You got three choices."

"Bullshit!" At least I had his attention.

"One, call the cops and try to explain away the bodies in here. Which is impossible. Nothing adds up, and I'll tell what I know. That's choice one. Wanna hear the others?"

"Hey, I got nothing but time," he said. "You're the one needs a doctor." Plus, I thought, my voice would help him locate me if I moved.

"Two, come on in and force me to shoot you. I'm well-armed, and I'm better than you." He didn't answer. "Three, we make a deal."

"Deal? Shit. Why would I deal? If I thought I couldn't take a wounded man, I'd go out the door back here and get help."

"But you can't do that because I'd tell what I know. That Sal Coletta and Richie Kilgallon were doing a deal with Lonnie."

"So what? I've thought that for a long time. It's one of the cases Frick and I are working on."

"Right. And now Kilgallon's dead. You took care of that. Because he could have told what I'll tell, that there *was* no 'unidentified man' up there with Lonnie. Kilgallon flat-out murdered Lonnie while Sal Coletta looked on. They didn't know Fay Rita was there till she started shooting. That's when Frankel went up. But that was it. Only *after* the shooting did someone else show up. Someone who found bags of coke in the squad car and Lonnie's car. Someone who already figured Sal was rotten. His sergeant." I paused. "You. You looked around, figured there'd be money on the scene, and went upstairs and got it. And walked with the coke, too."

275

"What about Jimmy Coletta?" he said. "You think I'd shoot a fellow copper in the back for money?"

"People have done a lot worse for a lot less. But even so, that was maybe an accident. There's a call of 'shots fired.' You're very close and arrive on the scene and spot someone in the alley. It's dark. He turns and he's got a gun and . . . you shoot him. That happens. You're scared, but what's done is done. Then you see the coke, put two and two together, and . . . well, who's gonna look in the trunk of *your* car?"

"Kilgallon said there was another shooter up there. So did Frankel."

"Yeah, right. And they're both dead. Kilgallon's not the brightest cop on the beat, so you told him what to say—about seeing Lonnie with a gun and all. Then you gave him a cut of your good fortune. And Frankel? He was hurt bad and maybe never even saw you up there. He may really have thought my client ran off with the coke and the money. But he couldn't say so, of course, so he went along with Kilgallon's story."

"Take your time, pal. Talk all you want," Theodosian said. " 'Cause I got a fourth choice you didn't mention. You keep talking and keep losing blood. I just wait you out."

I wasn't losing blood, though, and time was on *my* side—as long as he wasn't shooting at me and I didn't have to move. "And Maura Flanagan?" I said. "You paid her to shut down the O.P.S. investigation. I showed her I could prove the money came from you." Not true. "That's why she had to die. Because she was ready to break."

No answer, but one of the doors opened, maybe half an inch. He was getting ready to try again.

"You think I believe it was a coincidence," I asked, "you being on the scene when they picked me up near Flanagan's house?"

"Hell, I was in the area and—"

"Won't work," I said, "and here's why. I file for reinstatement and right away I start getting threats to drop it. I barely get a subpoena issued to Jimmy Coletta to testify, and someone tries to kill me. Who? I knew the answer as soon as you let on it was *you* behind the threats from the start, I—"

He pushed the door open, firing several shots as he did. I fired back, once, and the door closed again.

"You wanna try again?" I called, and started crawling.

There was no answer . . . and I had no more bullets.

Kilgallon might be by the entrance and might have my gun, but crawling took too long. I got up and hopped toward the archway. The kitchen door opened and Theodosian got off another shot, but I raised the .38 and he ducked behind the door again.

I dropped back onto the floor, crawling, dragging my foot. He'd know exactly why I didn't shoot back. Maybe if I lay down and played dead he might—

The doors swung open and banged against the walls. "Too bad, Foley," he said, "but it's—"

"Theodosian! Hold your fire!" The shout came from in front of me, beyond the archway.

"Thank God!" Theodosian called. He'd stepped back into the kitchen. "Frick? Is that you?"

"Yeah, it's me." ·

"Thanks, partner, I—"

"Throw your weapon through the door there," Frick said, "and come out."

"What the hell you talking about?" Theodosian sounded offended. "Listen to—"

"I been listening. I've heard enough. Throw your weapon out, and come out with your hands on your head."

"But it's all bullshit."

"I hope to God it is. I'll let you explain it all, but without shooting at this asshole anymore."

277

I thought of objecting, but didn't. A few seconds passed, and then there was some noise in the kitchen and a loud buzzer sounded . . . very loud. Theodosian had gone out the door.

Several shots were fired back there. And then more shots. Too many more.

"Hold your fire!" Frick ran past me toward the kitchen. "Fucking goddamn cowboys!" he screamed "Hold your fire!"

Through it all the alarm buzzer never stopped and I couldn't stand it. I dropped the .38 and managed to hop my way across the room and through the archway. The entrance door was open and somehow I got outside. There was loud talk—but no more shooting—from the rear door of the restaurant. And across the parking lot, near the street, I saw two men—one of them very fat—load something that might have been a third man into the backseat of a car, a Jaguar.

The fat man got into the front seat, and his partner squeezed into the back and the Jag drove away with its lights off and disappeared into the dark. As it did, squad cars—Mars lights flashing, but no sirens—came from the other way and roared into the lot. And behind them a fire department trauma unit.

There was a lot of yelling and confusion, and two cops came running my way with guns drawn. I sat down a few feet from Frankel's Corvette, laced my fingers across the top of my head, and stared down at the wet asphalt. Someone sat down beside me, but I didn't dare look because a cop leaned over me, inches away, screaming in a high-pitched, hysterical voice.

"We got an officer dead out there, you bastards," he yelled. "So if one of you moves a muscle I'll be happy to blow your balls off."

Neither of us moved or made a sound, until finally the cop finished screaming and stepped back a little. Then the person beside me spoke, very softly. "Hey," he said. "I been sure worried 'bout you, big mon."

MUCH OF THE REST OF WHAT HAPPENED after Yogi spoke to me seemed to happen in a heavy fog. I didn't even answer him. My ankle pulsed with a huge, pounding ache and when I moved there was the sharper, grinding pain of bone scraping against bone. I may have blacked out for a few minutes—or gone in and out more than once.

I saw Frick as one of a hundred cops milling around, many of them busy holding back the gathering crowd. He was mad as hell and kept asking where Kilgallon was.

That got my attention. "Richie?" I asked. "Isn't he dead?" I was still on my ass on the cold, wet pavement and was starting to shake.

"Hell no," Frick said. "He took a bullet, but he was in pretty good—" He looked around. "And where the fuck's Breaker Hanafan? If that crooked sonovabitch has—"

"I'm right here, dammit."

I looked up and saw Breaker step through the crowd of police officers, then saw his Jaguar parked off to the right. There was no one in the Jag that I could see.

"I hid by my car," Breaker said. "Think I wanna get my ass shot off by one of your fucking trigger-happy cops?" Breaker always says what's on his mind . . . except when he's lying.

This time it was a little of each.

CHAPTER

==

50

I WOKE UP IN A HOSPITAL BED, listening to a woman with a clipboard in the crook of her arm tell me about the surgery they'd done to repair my ankle, and how she'd like very much to know the name of my insurance company. Luckily, Renata Carroway came in just then and said she'd take care of those questions later and chased the woman and her clipboard away. Renata told me I'd refused to answer any police questions.

"I don't remember," I said. "You mean I actually kept my mouth shut?"

"Uh-huh. The one sensible thing you've done this entire month."

"Really." I shook my head. "How'd I do last month?"

"Frick called me," she said. "He wants your statement."

RENATA CONVINCED FRICK to put off the statement for a while because of my surgery. Plus I had to cooperate first with Detective Brasher and his Maura Flanagan homicide investigation.

I explained to Brasher that my music "fake book" found at Flanagan's could have been taken from Miz Becky's Tap, and Becky verified that I always left music on top of the piano there. I'd already told him that my message on Flanagan's machine was in response to a call from her, and he'd gotten a search warrant for my place and heard her message on my machine. They obviously hadn't found the manila envelope, or the card I'd stapled to it, but I said I'd been wanting to talk to her because she was the one at O.P.S. who closed out the Lonnie Bright case so quickly, with a finding of justifiable use of deadly force by police officers.

"What business was that of yours?" he asked.

"She wouldn't talk to me before," I said, dodging his question, "but I guess she changed her mind."

We brought in Casey and he gave Brasher the exact times he'd seen me at Saint Ludella's that night, leaving no reasonable probability that I could have been at Flanagan's house at the time she was killed. Unfortunately, Brasher asked Casey whether there'd been anyone else at the rectory and he'd had to answer that Jimmy Coletta and his wife came to see me.

Brasher wasn't interested in pressing me for the contents of my conversation with Jimmy in the rectory basement. He handed that over to Frick, and crossed me off as a murder suspect.

YOGI WAS IMPROVING. He left Inverness Clinic and stayed at my place to recuperate and I got to talk to him about why he and Breaker Hanafan were so late showing up at *Le Chantier*. I didn't try to contact Breaker, but even though I'd failed to get Richie Kilgallon thrown in the slammer, one hundred thousand dollars in cash appeared at my door unannounced one day.

I guess Breaker gave credit for effort.

Meanwhile, Renata managed to get me Frick's police reports. She wouldn't say how, only that someday maybe I'd learn how helpful it could be to try to get along with people. She also found out it was true that Frick had been supposed to be taking time off when he showed up at *Le Chantier*. Some regulation regarding state coppers not accruing too many unused furlough hours. All that did, though, was give him the opportunity to work the Lonnie Bright case on his own time. He'd gotten a little fixated on it. Besides, he apparently had no family, no friends, and nothing to do but the job.

He'd been tailing Breaker from the time Breaker picked Yogi up Friday night at Inverness Clinic. The nurse had told Yogi I promised to visit him, and when I didn't show up he got worried. Then Frick came to see him on Friday and asked about me. Yogi never had much reason to trust "the fuzzies," but something—he couldn't say what—made him trust Frick. So he told Frick the truth, that Breaker had called and said he had Dr. Tyne's okay to pick Yogi up at ten o'clock that very night and take him somewhere to meet me. Frick told Yogi to go with Breaker, but not to tell him they'd talked.

So Frick was waiting at ten, and followed them. Breaker told Yogi they weren't meeting me until one-thirty, and they drove to an Italian restaurant, where Breaker ate a long, leisurely meal in a private room with some woman. A whore, probably. Meanwhile, two men—"a fat one and a mean one" Yogi said—sat with Yogi in the bar and watched TV.

Breaker and Yogi left the restaurant in the Jaguar; Fat Wilbur and Mick in a different car. Pretty soon Breaker spotted someone following him, and told Yogi they better not meet me, because he didn't know who they'd be leading to me. But time went by, and Yogi was frantic. He insisted I must be in trouble or I'd have called Breaker's cell phone to see where they were. Breaker finally gave in and drove to *Le Chantier*. They parked off to the side of the lot, and Frick pulled in right next to them.

Although he didn't say so in his report, Frick wasn't the type to let local cops screw up a case for him, so he'd brought along two state investigators he could trust. And, I thought, two guys he knew he could order around. Leaving them with Yogi and Breaker, he was headed into the restaurant when he heard two gunshots, which must have been me putting the lights out in the kitchen. He told his men not to call for help yet, and sent one of them to look for a rear entrance and keep it covered.

He went in the front door and found a man in the vestibule, wounded, but apparently stable and not losing blood. According to his report, he recognized the man as a Chicago police officer, Richard Kilgallon, and would have called for an ambulance at once, but then there was more shooting. Frick should have been in trouble for not getting help for Kilgallon right away, but maybe the brass let him slide since it appeared Kilgallon fled the scene on his own.

Anyway, Frick hid near the archway and heard the conversation between Theodosian and me, and set it out in his report nearly verbatim. He'd suspected for some time that Theodosian was involved in the Lonnie Bright incident, which was exactly why he'd asked the Chicago department to assign Theodosian to ICOP, a state-municipal joint effort to ferret out bad cops.

When Theodosian fled through the kitchen exit, Frick's man back there challenged him and Theodosian replied by opening fire. The two exchanged shots and the state guy went down. By then, though, his partner had left Breaker and Yogi and had run around back, where he emptied his .45 into Theodosian. He was still squeezing the trigger on an empty weapon when Frick got to him. That part wasn't in Frick's report, but Yogi told me he ran back there, too, and saw it.

It turned out Frick's wounded investigator was wearing a Kevlar vest and wasn't badly hurt. Theodosian was dead.

Yogi told Frick he never saw Richie Kilgallon, which was probably true. Breaker said the same thing, which was certainly not true. There was nothing in the report about anyone asking me about a fat man and another man—or much of anything else, for that matter. It seemed I was in no shape to be interrogated, and was transported to the hospital.

Theodosian may have gone out the exit door hoping to ditch the weapon with the silencer and then surrender to Frick. Or maybe he'd flipped so far he thought he could get away. Who knows? At any rate, he still had that weapon on him, in addition to his registered 9 mm. He also had my Beretta, unloaded and obviously unfired. On Frick's report, Frankel was listed as the victim of gunshot wounds inflicted by Theodosian "under suspicious circumstances." Kilgallon was listed as "wanted for questioning" in connection with at least two homicides—Lonnie Bright and Maura Flanagan.

The police considered Kilgallon as "not yet apprehended." I could have told them he never would be . . . but didn't.

EVENTUALLY I APPEARED for my statement regarding the events at *Le Chantier*. Still struggling with my crutches, I was accompanied by my attorney, a very irritable Renata Carroway. The interrogation took place in a crowded little room at Chicago's shiny new police headquarters on the south side. The officer in charge, though, was Frick, and we didn't get along that day any better than we ever had, which didn't surprise—or bother—either one of us. Also present were an assistant state's attorney from Lake County—where Highwood is—and two from Cook County, along with two investigators from the Chicago Police Department.

Renata later told me she thought the crowd made Frick more determined to make me answer some questions I didn't want to answer. I disagreed with her. Frick was just an honest cop trying to do his job—and a sonovabitch who didn't need any goddamn gallery to spur him on.

Anyway, he got right to the point. He started by giving back my Beretta. Then he asked if I'd read his report and I said yes.

"Does it accurately state what happened and what was said that night?"

"What happened and what was said during the time Theodosian was in the kitchen and I was in the dining room . . . yes."

"So tell me about before that."

I told him everything, and patiently answered his questions when he interrupted.

He broke in once and asked, "At one point I heard you tell Theodosian that it was *him*—Theodosian himself—that let on to you that he was the one behind the threats you got when you filed your petition. What did you mean by that?"

"You remember," I said, "when the three of us—you and I and Theodosian—were in Yogi's room at Inverness Clinic?" He nodded. "And I told you I picked up my mail one day and found an anonymous threat?"

"Right. A letter came in the mail and had a spider with its legs pulled off."

"Except I know I didn't say whether it 'came in the mail' or not. In fact, the letter wasn't mailed. Someone put it through my mail slot, in an envelope with no stamp, no address. And Theodosian knew that. When we talked the night Flanagan was killed, he mentioned the note someone shoved through my slot *with* my mail. He *knew* it hadn't been mailed."

"Pretty subtle thing to rely on."

"I didn't *say* it; and still he *knew* it. That's enough for me," I said. "Anyway, you asked what I meant, and that's the answer."

So Frick asked and I answered. I told him all I knew about Maura Flanagan. I told him about the green Crown Vic that kept tailing me around and I could tell by his reaction those were his men. It was clear, too, that what he heard from behind the archway at *Le Chantier* convinced him that my version of Theodosian's part in the Lonnie Bright incident was accurate—including his shooting Jimmy Coletta. First of all, Theodosian never denied any of it . . . not until he realized Frick was there. But more important was Theodosian's obvious determination to kill me, even though the proper procedure—and easier and safer by far—would have been to back off and call for assistance.

Not that Frick said all that. But it was clear from his questions.

We both knew that our beliefs wouldn't have stood up as proof beyond a reasonable doubt, and that most of what I said wasn't admissable evidence for one reason or another. But what did that matter? Four of the five bad cops were already dead. At least I hoped—for his sake—that Kilgallon was already dead. Because Breaker Hanafan, cancer patient and concerned grandfather of Stefanie Randle, was not a nice man.

Jimmy Coletta was the only one left, and I didn't talk about him. Nothing said that night at *Le Chantier* tied Jimmy to any crime, and he wasn't a bad cop—or a bad person—anymore. So why not leave him alone? Besides, hadn't I told Jimmy I'd do my best to keep him out of it?

So in the end there were a few questions I declined to answer, contrary to the advice of my attorney. Those questions included, again, what Marlon Shades said five years ago, and what Jimmy Coletta told me when we met in the rectory basement.

"You got any notes of either of those two conversations?" Frick asked.

"No."

"Tape recordings?"

I stared at him. "No one's ever asked me that before," I said, "but the answer's no." Which was true. I'd destroyed the Marlon Shades tape two days earlier.

"And you won't reveal the contents of either conversation?"

"No."

Frick didn't like that at all.

Nor did the Illinois Supreme Court, when my refusal to answer got that far in a hurry. "Compliance with this court's order five years ago," the court said, "would have prevented two recent homicides." Maybe they were right, but somehow I couldn't whomp up much of a sense of guilt over the murders of Art Frankel and Maura Flanagan.

The court, on its own motion, summarily dismissed my petition for reinstatement to the bar. "This petitioner was suspended five years ago," the court said, "because he disobeyed an order issued by this court. His present renewed contempt for the court's authority is more serious, because he not only continues to invoke a purported attorney-client privilege as to the prior conversation with his client, but also refuses to answer questions about a more recent conversation with a former police officer, a conversation not even colorably protected by any privilege. Petitioner has demonstrated that he lacks all remorse and regret for his misconduct. He persists in his contempt. The petition for reinstatement to the bar is dismissed."

They didn't give credit for persistence.

CHAPTER
51

"I HAVE TO TURN MYSELF IN TOMORROW."

"I'm aware of that," the Lady said. She poured me some brandy and we sat across from each other in her parlor. "You'll be in Cook County Jail."

"Right." I sipped some of the brandy. It didn't seem possible four weeks had passed since my interrogation by Frick. Time enough for the Supreme Court to hold me in contempt again.

The Lady swirled the brandy in her glass. "Imprisonment didn't make you tell the last time," she said. "Maybe this time they won't keep you so long."

"That's what I'm hoping." I finished my brandy and looked across at her. "You know," I said, "I haven't seen Layla around for a while."

"She's gone."

"Gone?"

"She has family in Atlanta," she said. "I managed to get her into culinary school down there."

"In Atlanta? You know people in Atlanta?"

"I know people here," she said, "who know people in Atlanta."

"Of course you do." The Lady also knew people here who might help me hold onto my private detective's license when I got out of jail again. I stood up. "I'm late. Got another good-bye to take care of."

"That charming little man, you mean? Yogi?"

"No."

"Oh," she said. "And not Jimmy Coletta, I suppose."

"No. He's called a few times, but I haven't called back. I don't need another coversation not to talk about. And he doesn't either. The lawyer Renata got for him has so far been able to fight off his having to give any statement. There's really nothing new to ask him. You can't just drag a person in and ask him did he commit a crime five years ago."

"Well good-bye then, Malachy." She stood up. "I shan't keep you."

"I thought you wanted to know where I'm going."

"I do, but—"

"To say good-bye," I said, "to Stefanie Randle."

Her eyes lit up. "Really?" she said. "I suppose she'll miss you while you're gone."

"She'll get over it. She's moving to Albany, New York."

"Oh."

"She has family there."

FIVE DAYS LATER, in the afternoon, I had visitors. Renata Carroway and Yogi. Because she was my lawyer and said Yogi was her paralegal, we got to use one of those little glassed-in rooms at County Jail.

Yogi was wearing the threadbare tweed sportcoat he'd worn to lead Stefanie through the underground pedway to Marshall Field's that night about a hundred years ago. He looked healthy. "You doin' okay?" he asked.

"Pretty good," I said.

"Not a pretty good place, this one, big mon."

"No."

"I have some news," Renata said. "Jimmy Coletta's lawyer called me yesterday. He's been on vacation for two weeks. But he'd been telling Frick all along that he's got no case against Jimmy; that if Jimmy had to appear, he could invoke the fifth amendment. Frick knows that, of course."

"But Frick still wants to put him through it, doesn't he," I said. "He knows taking the fifth will make Jimmy look guilty as hell."

"Of course."

"Frick wants to destroy Jimmy. And what good will that do? What about his wife? His children?"

"Yes, well, he *is* guilty," she said, then added, "I can voice my opinion, you know, because I'm not his lawyer. But anyway—"

"What about the foundation he's setting up to help those poor kids? It won't even get off the goddamn ground. Guys like Frick don't—"

"Hold on, big mon," Yogi said. He looked at Renata. "Best you tell him the rest, miss."

"I'm trying to," she said. "Anyway, Jimmy's lawyer called and told me Frick called him . . . to say he was withdrawing his demand that Jimmy give a statement. And to say he was closing out the Lonnie Bright case."

"Closing—" The breath went out of me and it took a while to remember how to get some back in. "Then he doesn't need my answers, either. I can get out of here."

"He *was* closing the case." Renata stared at me through her big round lenses. "When the lawyer called Jimmy to tell him, Jimmy said he'd been trying to reach you. But you wouldn't call him back."

"Right. So what?"

"Jimmy wants to give a statement. He's going to say that if there was a plan that night to kill Lonnie Bright, he knew nothing about it. But he's going to admit he was in on a deal to sell coke to Lonnie."

"What?"

"Jimmy said for a long time he thought it was enough just to tell himself he wouldn't lie about it again if he's asked. But now he says he can't keep quiet any longer. And that it's not right that you should be in jail because of him. They went in this morning to give the statement. I guess his wife went with him."

"For chrissake, doesn't he understand what will happen?"

"He knows," she said. "Thing is, the state has big statute-of-limitations problems. They may not even bring charges."

"I'm talking about what people will think. How they'll turn on him, wheelchair or not. What it'll do to his—"

"He was a cop. He knows. He told his lawyer he was leaving all that in God's hands. They say it'll be on the evening news, tonight."

"Too bad he didn't do this long time ago, hey big mon?" Yogi said.

I shook my head. "How soon do I get out, Renata?"

"I'm filing a motion first thing in the morning," she said. "But . . ."

"But what?"

"Well, I sort of informally checked with someone who informally checked, and . . . anyway, my understanding is the supreme court's really pissed off at you."

"I sort of informally knew that already," I said.

"My understanding is they'll let the motion sit until you've been in, say, thirty days," she said, "and then cut you loose."

"Thirty days? Who the hell do they—"

"Hey, thirty days," Yogi said. "Piece o' pie, big mon, for guy like you. I visit every day they let me."

"Right." I looked around the bare, dingy room, and out through the thick glass at the steel bars and the double-locked doors I'd have to pass through—just to get back into the rest of that scary, stinking toilet they called a jail. "Piece o' pie."

"None of this had to be," Renata said. "You could have just answered a few questions. In fact, you could offer to do that now. I'll contact Frick."

"No. I suppose I'm glad Jimmy decided to tell. It'll help

291

him move on with his life. But I have to live my life, too, and in my own—"

"Jesus, Mal," she slammed her hand down on the table. "If you'd learn how to give in to them, even a little, you wouldn't have to put up with shit like this."

"I know, but—" I shook my head. "I can't explain it."

"I can," Yogi said. He looked at me, and then at Renata. "What he mean, miss, he rather learn how to put up with shit like this, an' then he don't have to be givin' in, even a little."

		DATE	

23.95   3-21-02